Strong Women Book 2

Eve, the First *Liberated* Woman

Mary Jo Nickum

Saguaro Books, LLC
SB
Arizona

Saguaro Books, LLC
3212 N. Miller Rd., Ste. 127
Scottsdale, AZ 85251

ISBN: 978-0-578-69249-4
Library of Congress Cataloging Number
LCCN: 2020938388
Printed in the United States of America
First Edition

Dedication

This book is dedicated to those who are willing to imagine the lives of biblical characters far beyond what scripture tells them. What was life like in those days? Were they thinking much like we do today? What were their challenges? Did they love, fight and bleed as we do today?

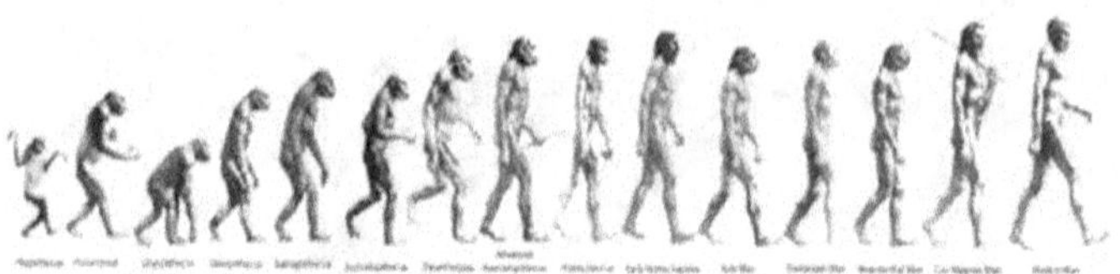

"Then God said, 'Now that the Man has become like one of us in knowing good from evil, he must not be allowed to reach out his hand and pick from the tree of life, too, and eat and live forever!' / So God expelled him from the Garden of Eden, to till the soil from which he had been taken / He banished the Man, and in front of the Valley of Eden he posted the great winged creatures and the fiery flashing sword, to guard the way to the tree of life." (Genesis 3:22-24)

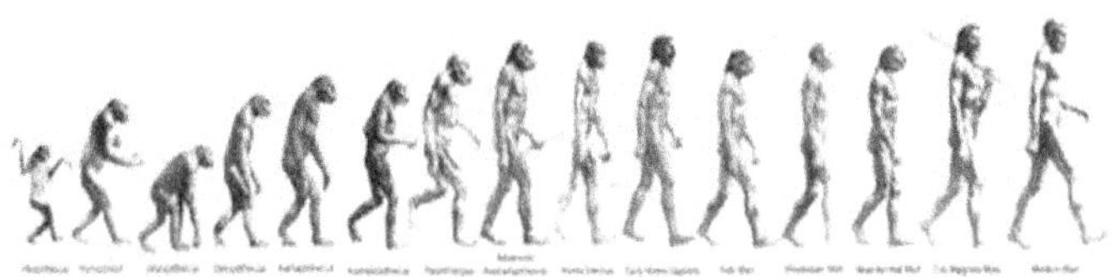

Chapter 1
Eve

Volcanos were spewing lava and ash as Eve decided to leave her homeland. Her family meant nothing to her now. *My mother hates me. She curses me daily for driving my father to other camps where available females welcome him. Why it was my fault, I'll never know.*

Eve ran from the only life she knew west to where, she did not know. She just kept running until the volcanic mountains were a distant glow behind her. She could hear a far-off roar like thunder from a distant storm; but the real storm, her mother, was far behind. Eve settled into a nearby cave for the night. Plants she recognized grew along the riverbank, which provided sustenance. Sleep came easily to her after the long run of the day. She was too tired to form a plan. *I'll leave that for tomorrow*, she thought as she drifted off to sleep.

Morning seemed to come early for Eve as the sunbeams slid into the cave opening. *Is this a day to keep running or should I develop a plan? Probably best to make a decision as to where I should go. The river seems to be getting larger so it must be heading for a larger river or a bay of some kind. There is plenty of food on this bank and caves seem to be plentiful. I think I'll follow the river for a few more suns and see what I find.* Eve was not afraid of being alone. She'd spent much of her childhood alone, exploring the mountains of her home. Though this was not similar to those mountains, she knew most of the plant life that would give her energy and keep her alive.

After a swim in the river, a morning meal of plants and dates from a nearby date palm, she continued her trek, a trek that would last several more uneventful suns. Finally, the river she had been following led to another, large river. Eve could tell it was a large river by the ridged riverbank. It was large, at least during part of the year; now, it was just an oversized stream, not much larger than the one she'd been following. Yet on the other side were lush green trees and bushes along with grasses, vines and blooming flowers of yellows, blues, pinks and white. Such a bountiful island of life she had never seen. This was going to be her home. Eve was not aware this was the Valley of Eden, not yet anyway.

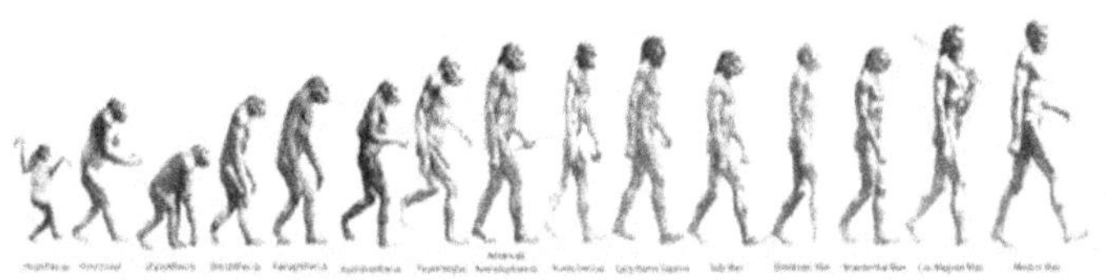

She crossed this new river on foot, just mid-calf at its deepest. The green Valley with its soft grass under foot and the bushes with berries and trees with nuts, figs and palms with dates were all a welcome sight. She had run and walked far enough to know her homeland was a distant memory. She'd seen fur covered hominids on her way here but they seemed to ignore her, or, at least, were not threatening. *So far*, she thought *this could be a place to call home, at least for now.*

She continued to walk and explore. By late afternoon, she found a cave with a wide, open mouth. She explored the inner parts of the cave, found no evidence of other animals or hominids. *This would make a good shelter. There's a hidden place in the back to sleep and plenty of fruits, berries and leaves to eat. I can use some of the leaves to weave a sleeping mat and some baskets.*

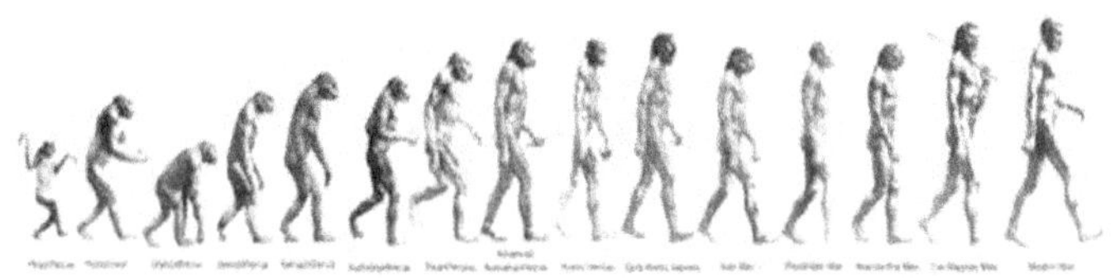

Chapter 2
Adam

Being different meant walking confidently on two legs; using one's hands and arms to carry or move objects, as well as to help propel one while walking. More importantly, it meant using one's mind to identify and solve problems.

One man, coming north to explore unknown territory, found himself in a verdant Valley[1]. Fruit and nut trees flourished as did many wild vegetables; plenty of food here. The intertwining branches provided enough cover for him under which to rest. This valley was peaceful—no marauding groups of partial humans as he had escaped in the south. He continued to explore the Valley.

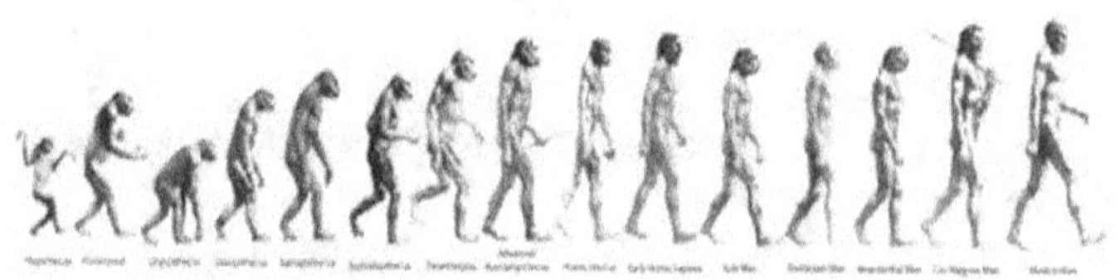

This man's name was Adam. He'd grown to adulthood in a tribe of australopithecine, where his father used his arms sometimes to help him walk and his mother, though upright most of the time, relied on her hands to help, too. Then, one day, a marauding group overtook the tribe and Adam's mother was raped by a hominid[2], clearly standing and running on two legs. The child of this rape was Adam.

Adam's parents accepted him at first. He looked like a normal australopithecine child. As he grew, however, he took on more upright characteristics. His arms were shorter, though still long enough to help, if necessary. His spine lacked the curve characteristic of quadrupeds. His head, though smaller, housed a brain capable of imagination, problem-solving, memory and the desire to explore the unknown. He became withdrawn and sulky. His mother, Elgyth, worried about his disinterest in tribal life. His father, Tamel, resorted to force.

"Adam, come here and move these rocks to make this cave larger," Tamel said.

Adam had developed a tool for spearing fish in the nearby river and was concentrating on fishing.

"Did you hear me?" Tamel roared.

Adam did not answer immediately causing Tamel to become angry. "Where are you, boy?"

"I'm coming," Adam answered, finally.

Tamel grabbed Adam's arm hard when he arrived, not noticing the fish. "I have fish for our

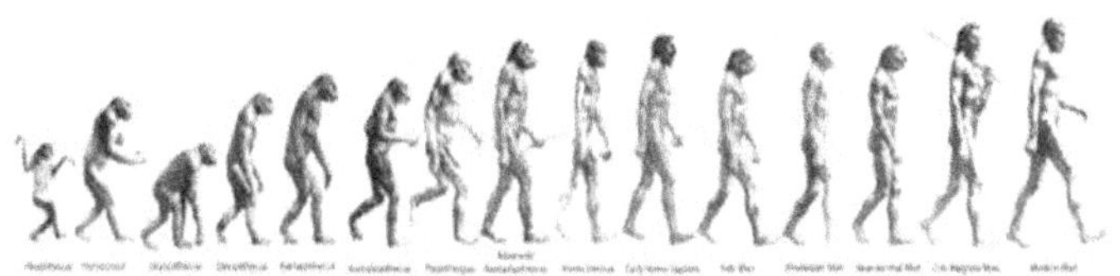

meal tonight," Adam said from the ground. He had been slung down by Tamel.

"You didn't answer me and you took too long to come when I called. Do you understand what work needs to be done? Those rocks in the cave need to be moved. Now," Tamel exploded.

At this point, Elgyth came from the cave to find out what the yelling was about. She saw Adam and the fish on the ground with Tamel standing over him in a threatening way. "I sent Adam to the river to try out his spearing idea to get fish for our meal tonight."

"You should have told me, woman. I need him to move rocks," Tamel said. Tamel kicked Adam and said "Get up and give me some help."

Adam got up and followed his father into the cave, leaving the fish. Elgyth retrieved the fish and carried them to the area near the fire pit, where she and her daughters began to prepare the meal.

"This is the largest fish I've ever seen. I didn't know they were this big in the river," Elgyth said. "Perhaps, we should invite others in the clan to join us for the meal."

"Yes," the girls said in unison. "We'll go and tell the others now."

At that point, Elgyth heard more bellowing from the cave. *Why is Tamel yelling at Adam? Doesn't he understand Adam wants to help but in his own way? He's been a good son and now he's almost a man. He'll probably be taking a mate soon and*

moving on. He'll move on sooner if Tamel keeps bellowing at him. She heard more loud, harsh words as both men came out of the cave.

"Don't talk to me that way," Tamel yelled.

"I'm leaving," Adam said. "I can't please you no matter how I try. You don't want me here. You just want me to do the hard work for you while you stand over me with a switch. I can't take it anymore."

Elgyth wanted to intervene but knew Tamel would order her away, or worse, push her to the ground. *I wish I could make Tamel understand how Adam helped with the fish for our meal. He did it without being ordered or told to help get food. Now he's been told to leave and I'll miss him so much.* She brushed tears from her eyes, knowing she must accept the rift that had come between Father and son. Tears sent Tamel into a downward spiral of anger. *It is best if Adam leaves now before things get worse.* She handed Adam a water satchel and a packet of food as he stomped past her and out of the cave.

Adam left immediately. He walked away, not bidding his family farewell. There was nothing he wished to take from home. He was on his own. He actually felt relieved. *I'm free now to see what lies beyond the caves and the river, to head north to see what is beyond the mountains on the horizon.*

He knew not which direction to take when leaving but he'd never been north so he chose to head in that direction. Adam followed the large river[3] to the delta and turned east. *I will go east until I find a*

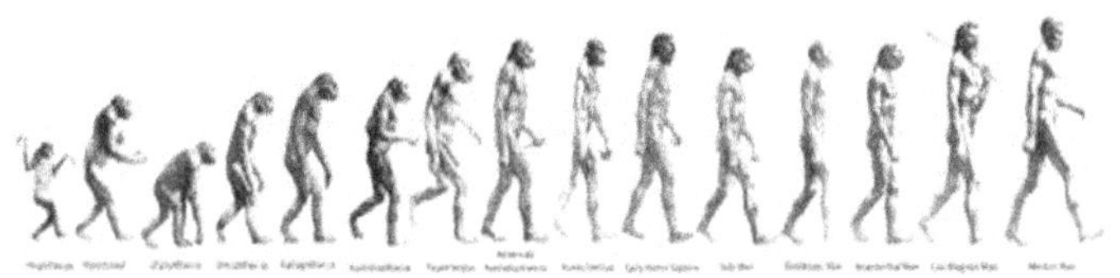

way north. This desert is hard to walk through, hot, dry and food is scarce. Strange hominids are here but don't seem to be dangerous. It was late summer and the water level in the delta was low so he could walk or wade to the far side. He filled his water satchel and moved on. He speared a fish and cooked dinner before stopping for the night, for tomorrow and on the following days; he'd be crossing a desert. Though he kept the large sea on his left in sight, he could not use the saline water for drinking. He knew he'd be dependent on oases to traverse the desert.

He walked on during part of the day, resting in the shadow of a boulder during the heat of the day. He walked on for several hours until sunset. He chose a small oasis one afternoon in which to rest, collect food and water and spend the night. He'd settled for the night when he heard loud voices. They were getting louder. He sat up and grasped his knife and fishing spear—the only weapons of defense he had. Five hair-covered hominids approached. When they saw Adam, they stopped, raised their clubs and rushed toward him. He stood, raised his pole and disarmed them, while tripping them. He picked up a club that had fallen within reach and used it to knock two of the five senseless. He hit a third hominid with a stone. The last two ran from the oasis. He slit the throats of the three who were senseless and hauled their bodies away from the oasis so any other marauding beings would see the bodies and realize there was danger in this oasis.

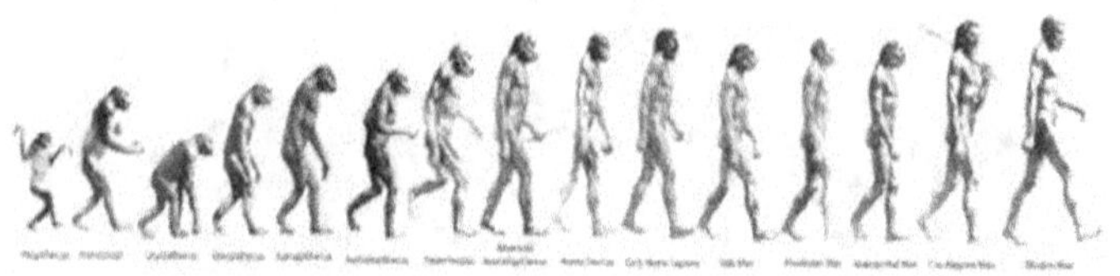

At dawn the next morning, Adam left the oasis. He walked on for nearly another moon before he turned to the east, following stars he had noticed. He'd found the stars as a child while following his father on hunting trips. As he headed east, he found more of the same—desert. He was acclimating to it but still moved from oasis to oasis. Sometimes, several days elapsed between oases.

Once, Adam chose a boulder under which to rest during mid-day. A large serpent had also claimed the space in the shadow of the boulder. Not feeling inclined to challenge the serpent, he moved on. No boulders were present so he kept pushing on, watching and hoping for an oasis, even a small one would do. It was nearly dark when he finally saw a distant palm tree, indicating an oasis. He was hobbling by this time, soles of his feet burned by the hot sand, famished because his food supply had diminished and his water satchel was empty. Adam needed this oasis more than he'd ever needed an oasis on his entire walk, so far.

Upon approaching the oasis, Adam heard voices, mostly grunts and groans. The oasis was occupied but he desperately needed to stop. He entered the oasis and found two hominids, a male and female. The oasis was a good size with a large pool and spring with several date palms. He stopped on the far side of the pool, under a date palm. The other hominids either did not see him or were so engrossed in their own activities they decided to ignore him,

which was fine with Adam. He filled his water satchel and entered the pool to relax in the cool, fresh water to ease his burning feet. He grew sleepy and pulled himself from the water and picked up some dates for the evening meal. After eating, he lay down on the warm sand and fell asleep almost immediately.

Before dawn, he awoke with a start. He felt as if he were being watched. He opened his eyes and saw both hominids staring down at him.

"What?" he said, as he sat up.

They didn't answer. They just ran as quickly as their legs and arms would allow.

Adam was now fully awake so he decided to pack up and move on. By the time he had taken to the pool again, ate a handful of dates and packed more in his food packet, loaded his spear, water satchel and food pack on his back, it was light enough to begin another day's trek. Though he'd awoken in alarm, he felt refreshed and ready for the day.

The day grew hot almost as soon as the sun rose. As he walked he came upon another oasis at which he did not stop. He passed two more that day. He was able to rest during the middle of the day and move on. Later that day, he noticed slight changes in the vegetation. In the distance, he saw a line of green, which, at first, he took as a mirage caused by the desert heat. He'd been seeing mirages along the way; of course he didn't know the name of the phenomenon, but his experiences of his homeland made him aware of their giving the traveler false hope.

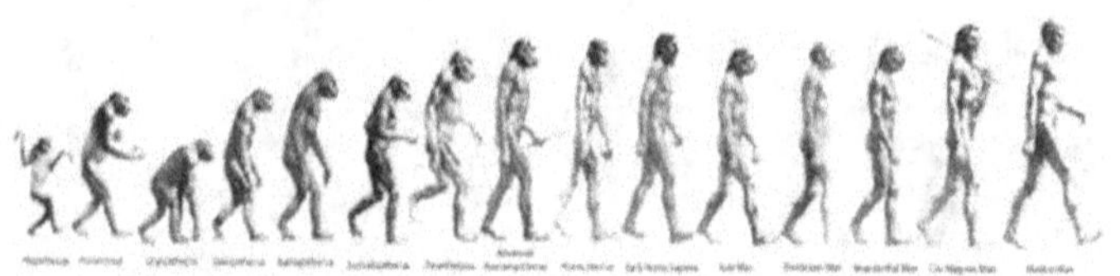

He stopped at an oasis when the sun was setting. There was a large pool of fresh, cool water and food was plentiful. He rested sitting in the pool. He thought about his journey. *I've come a long way. My home and my father are in the past. I miss my mother and sisters, though. Oh well, I've made a decision and I'm sticking with it. Life has to be better on my own. I'll keep walking to see if what I thought I saw is real. It looks even now as if the desert will end soon. What I'll find ...*

He awoke early as the sun was rising. After another brief time in the pool, he ate, loaded up his backpacks and headed toward that view of trees he'd seen last night. Now, in the cooler morning, that distant line of green on the horizon was still there. *That line was not caused by heat or my imagination from fatigue. It is real. I'm heading to a huge oasis or the end of the desert. I'll move on to see how far away it is and what it is.*

Adam walked toward the green line on the horizon for four more suns. The green line finally seemed to be closer. He wasn't walking on hot sand anymore. The ground underfoot now seemed softer, though there were small stones and tufts of grass. The grass was a welcome sight, telling Adam he'd reached the end of the desert. Another sun's walk and he'd be to the trees, he guessed. He was right, as this sun came to a close; he sat beneath palm trees on a bed of grass. *I've made it out of the desert. There*

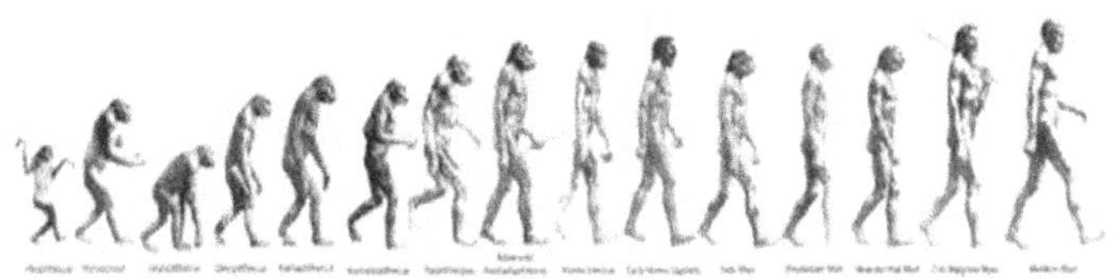

seems to be no end of this oasis, if that's what it is. I'll rest here tonight and continue on tomorrow. I'll find out how big this oasis is.

Adam continued to explore this oasis. As he moved into the tree and bush area, he found a plethora of fruits and berries, the likes of which he had never seen. He ate his fill as he walked, marveling at the floral display, the soft, cool breeze and the luxurious soft, green grass under his tired, burned feet. I think I'll stay here for now. I don't see any end to this oasis. By now, he had traveled well into the Valley, when he came upon a waterfall with a pool below it. Looking beyond, he saw a cave. There he decided to make his home.

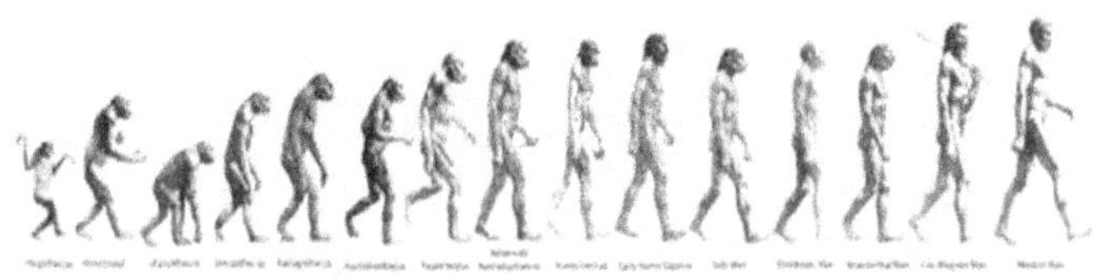

Chapter 3
Lilith

Lilith was young, perhaps 16 or 17 summers. She became self-aware as she matured. She realized her immediate need for a physical connection and charged out with an overwhelming passion. Her insatiable hunger was incomprehensible to her and it drove her to the nearest object of desire: a man—Adam, another product of the creative force of evolution. She realized her potent and dangerous passion could have only one place of containment; the earth, the Valley.

Lilith realized her beauty immediately. Her need for a male was growing by the minute. Her body twisted and ached from the need. *If I don't find a man*

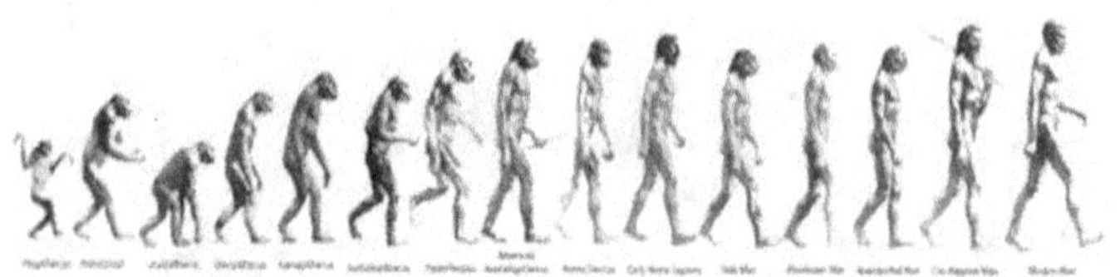

soon, I'll surely dissolve. My beautiful body will become but a river of need, flowing over a bed of soft sand. Where is the man I need?

Lilith, her need burning hot inside her, ran through the lush Valley. As the soft branches stroked her body, she felt her need rising higher. *Where, oh where, is the man I need?* Then she saw him—a tall, sleek man with shining, onyx skin. So beautiful, he would certainly fill her need. She turned to him, unleashing her most seductive moves and musical voice.

"Oh, I am searching for one like you."

"From where have you come? I've never seen you before," said Adam.

"I'm looking for one to relieve my passion."

"But I don't know you."

"Come here, lie with me and you will know me."

Lilith saw his control begin to fade as he continued to gaze at her magnificent body. She performed more seductive moves; hips swaying in a slightly slithering motion, hands beneath her breasts thrusting her nipples to him, licking her lips and humming a melodious tune. Completely captured by Lilith, Adam lay on the ground and she fell to him. Their passion exhausted for a time, they slept.

When Adam awoke, he saw Lilith lying beside him, a more beautiful woman he'd never seen. He wanted nothing but to take her as his mate. He knew her, her power over him. Seduction was a

powerful tool, making him continue to want her repeatedly. Lilith awoke, smiling shyly at him.

"What is your name?"

"Adam, and yours?

"Lilith. Now we know each other. Will we be mates?"

"Yes, I want you with me forever."

She moved to cover him as they confirmed their mating pledge.

Time passed in the Valley of Eden. The Eden Valley was covered with lush greenery, fruit and fig trees, flowering plants of all kinds, ferns and other low-growing plants. A soft layer of moss covered the ground. Life was without care or concern. Not all was harmonious between Adam and Lilith, however. Both she and Adam became aware of their physical need and attraction at the same time. Lilith believed this made her equal to Adam. She refused to lie beneath Adam and he refused to lie beneath her. To solve the impasse, Lilith decided to end her stay in Eden. Leaving Adam and the Valley of Eden, she crossed the Red Sea. Lilith met and consorted with Samael, a well-known demon. She seduced him and bore him children, known as Lilin.

Adam found life without Lilith peaceful. He roamed the Valley, appreciating all the scents from the flowering plants, the fruits from the trees, the sounds of a babbling brook and the stars in the night sky. He found this place much to his liking, never in

need of comfort or fear of marauding tribes. No one else like him was here. This was his domain. This was his home, his kingdom on earth.

Chapter 4
Eve Meets Adam

Eve sat in the opening of her cave, polishing stones and other stone tools she thought she might need for living alone in a new place. Eve only knew in her home village no one was safe, especially a woman, living alone without strong males for protection. She was, therefore, preparing to protect herself by stabbing intruders if surprised or hiding in the depths of the cave at night.

After she'd been in the Valley of Eden for some time, she relaxed never having experienced any frightening encounters. Several curious hominid types, mostly fur covered and walking with the help of their hands, passed the cave but seemed to have no

interest in the cave or what or who might occupy it. She did exercise caution when she saw these semi-hominids because they closely resembled those in her native village. She wanted no part of a life with the part animal/part human beings with which she'd been reared. Eve wanted to meet someone more like her. *There must be someone more like me. I can't be the only one. One of these days, I'll strike out around the Valley to see if I meet someone who looks and walks like me, someone who walks only on two legs and isn't fur covered.*

One day, as Eve sat in the mouth of her cave sanding a bowl using fine ochre sand and a large, thick, green leaf, a deep voice came from behind her, "Hallo."

Startled, she jumped to a standing, defensive crouch holding a sharp pointed knife-like stone object. "Stop. Who are you?"

"I did not mean to frighten you. I mean you no harm."

"Who are you?" she asked again, still pointing the knife at her intruder.

"I am Adam. I come from the south[4]."

"I don't know you nor have I seen you before."

"My cave is a day's walk from here. I decided to walk in this direction to see a new part of the Valley."

Eve relaxed somewhat, deciding there was no immediate danger. She lowered her knife and

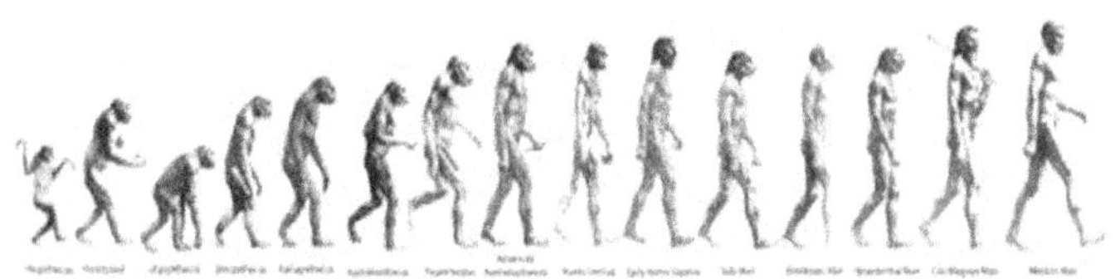

returned it to her belt. *This is a male, though his skin is almost black, much darker than mine, he seems not to be hostile and uses words I can understand. Perhaps, this is a person I've wanted to meet.* "Sit with me for a bit and tell me from where you came. Your skin is nearly black. I've never seen people like you."

"Yes, I'll sit for a while. As I said before, I came from the south. I walked for many moons before I reached this Valley. I've been here for more than two moons. I've not met anyone like you, female and lighter skinned."

"I have been in the Valley for nearly a moon and have not met anyone like me until now. What do you know of this Valley?"

"This Valley is large. I've walked in one direction for five suns and not come to the end of it. I don't really want to find the end of it. I like it here and I want to stay. It is home to me now."

"Yes, I'm happy here too but I can't help wondering how big this Valley is and what is beyond it."

"No, what's beyond it doesn't interest me. I've come a long way and I did not pass through anything nearly as good as this. Everything we need is here. Nowhere else could be better."

"I wonder if there are more like us here or maybe, out there, out of the Valley."

"Why is that important to you?

"I grew up in a village with many fur covered animal/hominids but none like me. I wondered if I

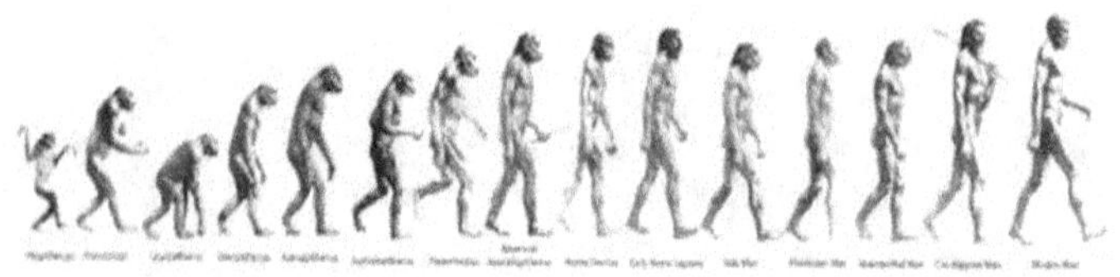

was a freak but now I've met you, I know there are others."

"Yes, there are others. My village was raided by a group of ones like me. My mother was raped by one and I am the product of that rape."

"That may have been the same for me. I've heard stories about raids in my village but my parents would not tell me specifically about them, just nodding their heads and mumbling about it being long ago."

"Where did you come from?"

"I came from the east, near mountains that belch fire and rocks. I ran away from my village because life got too difficult. My mother hated me and blamed me for all her problems. It took me more than ten suns to come here, following a small river that became a large river."

"Things will be better here. I had a disagreement with my father. That's why I left my village but I'm happy here. It is so peaceful." They sat a bit longer talking about what they found in the Valley.

Finally, Adam rose to his feet as did Eve. "I better move on. Thanks for inviting me to sit with you. Hopefully, we'll meet again."

"I'm so happy to meet you and I'd like to spend more time talking to you."

"Until we meet again."

Chapter 5
Life in the Valley

Adam spent his days relaxing, swimming in a nearby pool. The water was clear, cool and fresh. It was at the base of a watcrfall. It never seemed to overflow. Though he searched for a stream, he could never discern from where the water for the waterfall came. Adam decided to add it to his list of mysteries in the gurden. Other mysteries included the plants. The blooming flowers never seemed to wilt and die as they did elsewhere. Leaves of the trees did not change color, fall and awaken as new buds and new green leaves. No rain fell and no storms heralded a change in weather; in fact, the weather never changed. Animals were no danger. Lions and tigers

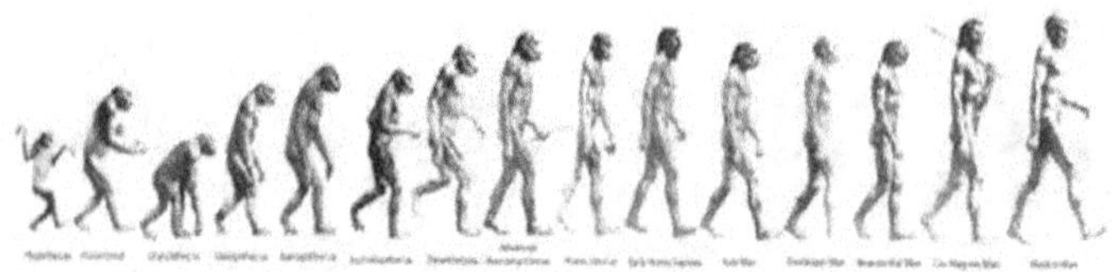

seemed friendly, unlike in his village where they were a constant threat. Herds of deer moved across the plains and through the forests, seemingly comfortable and unconcerned.

Forests were not the dark, foreboding places he'd experienced near his homeland. Here sun rays filtered through the limbs, needles and leaves making the forest a serene, welcoming place. The ground was not covered with leaves and needles as it was in the woods of his youth. Now he could spend time in the forest without the need for a weapon to protect himself. Occasionally, he saw groups of furred, human-like creatures, usually in the trees, but they seemed to ignore him or maybe didn't see him. At least, they didn't see him as a threat and he didn't see them as a danger, either. These creatures appeared to communicate with each other, groom and feed each other.

Adam found the peaceful life for which he'd longed. He was not bored, far from it. He was able to enjoy the freedom of thought. One day, sitting in the forest, birds singing while he stroked his favorite tiger, his thoughts strayed to his conversation with the beautiful Eve. She seemed willing to care for herself and was industrious. She had found a cave to her liking but still seemed to startle easily and fear the beasts and furred, 'hominid-like' creatures. Adam hoped she would lose her fear and find the serenity in this Valley he'd found. Perhaps, he could help her find that peace and, maybe, enjoy that peace together, forever. *At this point, that may be too much to hope*

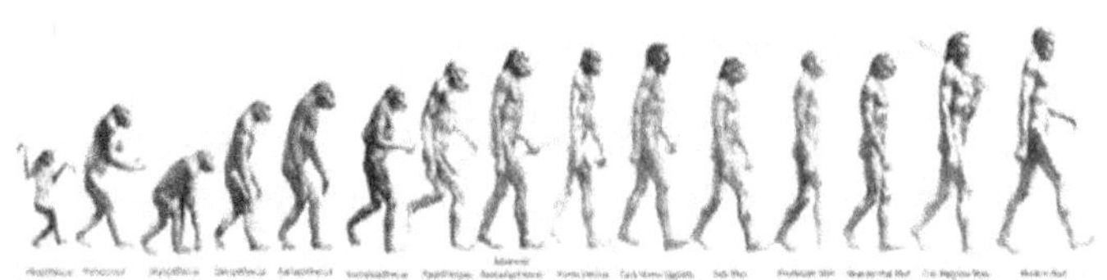

for; she did seem to be an independent woman. He needed to get to know her better to draw any conclusions.

Eve left her cave to explore the area nearby. She made sure her sharpened stone tool was tucked in her basket before venturing forth. She saw nothing to fear but she'd always carried a weapon for security and this Valley was new to her. She had not been here a moon yet, so she did not feel comfortable. She'd been wandering for nearly an hour when a big cat with a large, dark golden mane appeared before her. She knew her stone knife would be useless against such a large animal. Though the impulse to run flooded her brain, she'd learned long ago running from these large cats was useless; instead one must lie down and play dead. Her heart beating so fast and hard she thought her chest would explode; she fell to the ground in a full sweat. She curled in a fetal position and waited. She felt the lion approach. He sniffed her head and neck then with a paw; he gently rolled her on to her back. All the time she was in abject terror. Then he began to lick her face and neck. She cringed, waiting for him to open his mouth for the killing bite. It never came. She opened her eyes and the lion had positioned himself next to her, trying to warm her; he must have thought she was hurt or ill.

After several moments, Eve reached out to touch his mane. It was soft and warm. The lion made a soft, gurgling sound deep in his throat. She quickly

removed her hand. He licked her hand and, taking her hand in his mouth, pulled it toward his neck again. She thought this behavior peculiar, unlike any cat or animal she had ever experienced. *It must have been tamed*, she thought, *but how? Wild animals can't be tamed. They only know how to kill or be killed. This is the strangest beast I've ever seen.*

Finally, she decided to stand up and continue her exploration. The lion also arose from his position and nudged her with his nose. Eve patted his face and he licked her face and turned to leave. She shrugged and moved in the direction of the cave. As she walked, she remembered Adam and his talk of the peacefulness of this Valley. *I wonder if he's had a similar experience. If so, I'd like to hear about it and share my encounter with him. Oh, what am I thinking? He may never come back. Why would he? He seemed to enjoy being alone. He had a difficult time at home, too. Maybe I shared too much. Perhaps he thinks I'm not happy here and I want to leave. Oh well, it was nice to meet him. I'll just go back to my cave and think about the lion.*

When she arrived back at the cave, her jaw dropped in surprise. Adam sat in the cave mouth, petting a big, orange and black stripped cat. "Hallo, Eve," he called, as he saw her round the bend in front of the cave.

"Adam. I'm glad to see you again. You seem to have a friend."

"Yes, Eve, all animals are our friends here."

"Then, Adam, you won't think my experience this morning unusual."

"Go ahead and tell me about it anyway." He liked to hear her voice and she sounded excited.

"All right, I'll tell you how it happened. I don't want you to think me weird or silly."

"I won't."

She related the morning encounter just as it happened; trying to make sure he understood her fear. The relating of the story brought back such intense emotion she started sweating and her heart beat wildly again. When she got to the point of the lion lying down beside her, her voice lowered and she seemed visibly relaxed. Adam relaxed too. *I'm not sure how to react to this story. I can't say 'I could have told you'. That would be cruel. She seems so surprised and elated; I don't want to burst her bubble.* She finished her narration and smiled at Adam.

"What do you think of that?"

"Hmm," he said, his mind racing for an appropriate answer. "I think you've made a friend. This lion sounds like my friend, this tiger. I met him at the pond near my cave and he visits me regularly."

"Do you think the lion will come to my cave?"

"He might. He can track your sent on your trek home. Wait to see if he comes to you. He already thinks you're special. Remember, he cared for you when he thought you were down."

"Yes, I'm sure that was why he reacted the way he did. Do you think he'll react the same way to me next time, if there is a next time?"

"Yes, I think he will. All the animals are trusting and friendly. They don't seem interested in hunting and killing each other."

"That is so different outside the Valley. There animals, especially large cats, bears and snakes are an ever present danger, including our own people."

"That is true. I've never seen a snake here, though."

"I wonder why."

"Not part of this tranquil island we call the Valley of Eden, I guess."

"How did you know this place was called The Valley of Eden?"

'I heard about such a place when I was a child, from a traveling storyteller. I just remembered it now, thinking about the friendly animals. Strange how suddenly something from the past comes to mind, sometimes."

"That's interesting and reassuring. There don't seem to be any threats here. Maybe I don't need my knife, except to cut leaves for food."

"I don't think you'll encounter anything ready to hurt you."

"Would you like some tea? I found leaves that are tasty when covered with boiling water."

"Sure, that sounds interesting. I brought some fruit to share with you."

"Oh, how nice. We can relax and enjoy the afternoon."

Chapter 6
Eve and Adam Share a Cave

Eve and Adam shared several more visits to her cave. He had not yet invited her to his cave. *Perhaps, I should suggest we walk to my cave this visit. I think she's ready for a new adventure. She was so frightened by the lion, I've been hesitating to ask her but I think she's calmed down now and will be ready. She seems to enjoy my company and be open about her thoughts and ideas...a very intelligent woman,* Adam thought, as he followed a well-used path to Eve's cave.

"Hallo, Adam," Eve called when she saw him approach the cave. Her voice carried a vibe of excitement.

"Hallo, Eve," Adam returned the call in a softer, almost hesitant voice.

"Come, sit with me while I finish shredding these leaves for tea. You will have some?"

"Yes, of course. I brought some walnuts and pecans, too."

"Great, I love nuts. I found a bush with hazel nuts. I also found a banana tree, well it's not really a tree, I guess—more like a tall bush. I don't know, it's hard to explain."

"No need to explain. I know what you mean. I've seen them but not tried any yet."

"Now is your chance. We can have some with our tea. You can sample mine. If you like it, you can have a whole one from my store."

"That sounds fine but why are you storing food? There is no chance of being without here."

"Yes, I've gathered that but it's a habit left over from my village life where food was often scarce," Eve said, sounding a bit hurt.

"Food in our village could be short from time to time. I helped our mother by fishing in a nearby stream."

"That was good of you to help your family to get food."

Both sat in silence for a while, deep in their own thoughts. Each was trying to evaluate the other based on previous conversations. *He might be someone who would be a good companion. I wonder if he'd give me the freedom to explore that I need. What would he require of me? He can probably take*

care of himself so he shouldn't require much. He is beautiful and I'd like to spend more time with him ... oh, what am I thinking, I don't need a male to protect me and bring food. I can collect food and take care of myself, yet he is enjoyable to talk with and I'd like to hear more about his village in the south, Eve thought.

Adam was thinking along a different line. He felt a stirring in his loins as he looked at Eve out of the corner of his eye. *She is so beautiful. I wonder if she'd have me. She looks so touchable, with her light skin and long, silky brown hair. Her skin looks soft and creamy, I'd love to touch her but she might be put off if I tried. Better not yet, I just have to invite her to my cave. If, after that, she signals availability by allowing me to touch her then, perhaps, we can move on together. I have to stop thinking this way or my erection will spoil everything.*

In an attempt to bring them out of their reveries, Adam asked for another cup of tea. Eve came out of her reverie with a start. She had lost track of time and her tea had cooled. Obviously, Adam had continued to drink his tea and now wanted more.

"Yes, Adam, I'll get us both another cup of hot tea. Mine has cooled while I was sitting deep in thought," Eve said.

"I was thinking too. What were you thinking about?"

"Oh, nothing of importance," she lied.

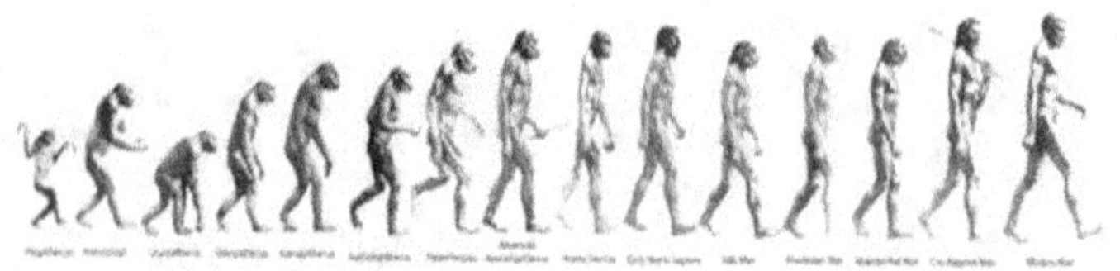

"How could you sit and think nothing of importance when you were so deep in thought you let your tea cool?" Adam probed.

"So, I lied. I was thinking about you and your previous life in the south."

"That's better. The truth is always better. I was thinking about you and that I have always come to your cave. Would you like to come to my cave?" Adam realized he was talking fast, yet he also knew if he didn't ask her to visit his cave now, he'd probably not ask today. That was the real purpose of this visit.

"Why are you asking me to see your cave, It's much like this one, isn't it?"

"Yes, but I've made some drawings on the cave walls depicting animals and plants from my village in the south."

"Now, that sounds interesting. I'd like to hear more about the south."

"Is that a 'yes'?" Adam almost begged.

"Yes, I'd like to see your cave."

"Good, we can leave as soon as we finish our tea."

"That soon? How far is it?"

"It is some distance. The cave faces a waterfall. I must cross a plain, walk through a forest and another plain to get here."

"That sounds interesting. I've not explored that far. I was near the forest when I met my lion friend."

"Has your lion friend come to see you?"

"Oh, yes, he has come a few times. He's not a regular visitor, though. I have a bird friend that comes more often. She is a small blue bird with an orange band on her throat. She sings a beautiful song as I sit to enjoy the flowers blooming on the plain. She often sits on my shoulder, sometimes on my head."

Eve and Adam finished their tea and prepared to embark on the long trek to Adam's cave. Adam said, "We'll go this way," as he pointed northwest.

"Yes, that's the way I walked when I met my lion friend."

"Maybe we'll meet him again," Adam said.

"That would be fun," Eve said.

They walked on, occasionally commenting on a gorgeous floral display or an unusual bird song. Many small animals scurried in the tall grass and a cottontail rabbit hopped along in front of them for a while before he took a detour into the tall grass. As they neared the forest, a lion became visible on the trail ahead.

"Oh, that looks like him," Eve said, "I'm sure it is," as she started to run toward the lion.

Adam followed at a brisk walk. When he arrived, Eve had buried her hands and face in the lion's mane. The lion was making soft snuffing sounds, enjoying her touch. To let her know he had arrived, he said, "Is this my competition?"

Eve tore herself away from the lion and stood stiff. "Why would you say that?" she demanded.

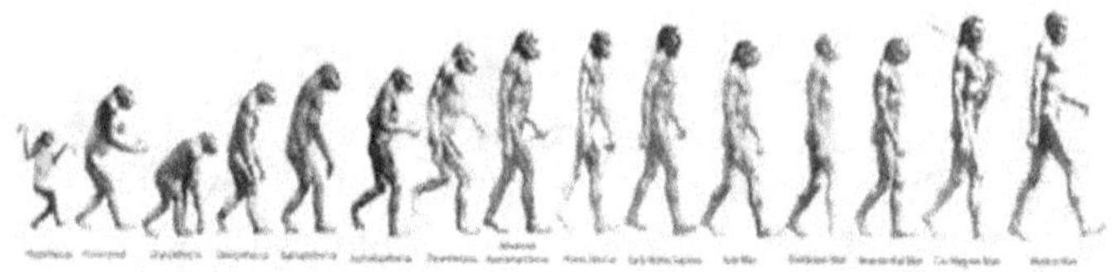

Adam knew, instantly, he'd crossed a line. "Just teasing," he said.

"You sounded as if you felt you were being ignored. I was glad to see the lion and I let him know. Is that difficult for you?"

"No, as I said, I was teasing. You looked happy to see him and I was approaching. I wanted you to hear my voice."

"I knew you were coming behind. I didn't need a warning."

"All right, can we forget about it and cool off?"

"I'll forget about it but be careful with the teasing. Come here, meet the lion."

Adam took a few steps toward the lion. The lion stretched his neck and sniffed Adam. He snuffed in a low tone and licked Adam's hand.

"I think he'll be your friend now, too," Eve said.

"It sure seems that way," Adam said. "Let's move on. If the lion wants to come, he can follow."

"All right," Eve said, as she patted the lion's head.

They moved on but the lion stayed on the edge of the forest. His pride was nearby and he chose not to leave them. Eve and Adam were unaware of the lion's pride so they were disappointed the lion didn't follow them. Eve surmised the lion had his reasons, so let the disappointment dissipate. Adam was not surprised the lion didn't follow but sensed Eve's discomfiture, so said nothing. They walked on

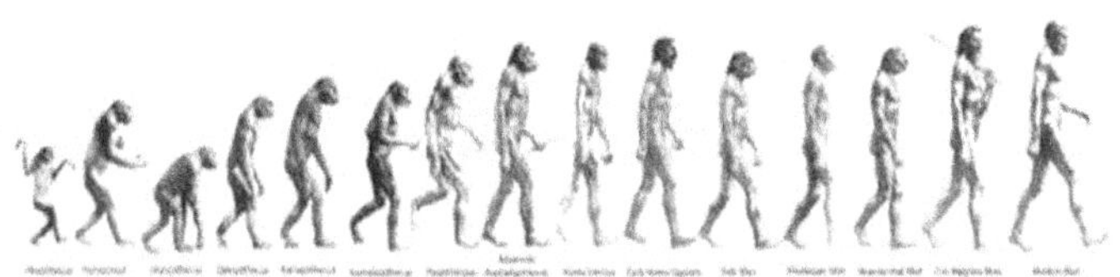

into the forest. Birds were singing and different small animals, squirrels and chipmunks, dashed up and down the trees and from limb to limb. Adam pointed out a marten crouched at the base of a limb. Eve saw a badger poke its head out of a hole and she nudged Adam. He smiled in acknowledgment. As they moved on, they saw two rolly-polly bear cubs chasing each other across their path. Adam turned and pointed to the sow bear watching her cubs a ways back from the trail.

They emerged from the forest onto another plain. Here the floral composition was different from the plain near Eve's cave. On this plain the grass was shorter and the flowers were predominantly blue, purple and red. Blue bells, purple irises and red roses abounded. There were occasional sunflowers, violets and pink daises. Eve commented on the difference between the plant life of the two plains. Adam attributed it to the rise in elevation.

"Whether you noticed it or not, we've been on a gradual climb since we left the first plain."

"Yes, I noticed a little climb but I didn't think it was enough to change things that much."

"When we get to the cave, you'll be able to look across the plain and see the treetops of the forest in the distance."

"Now that you mention it, I can feel the ground rising gradually beneath my feet."

"It will be that way the rest of the way to the cave."

They walked on to Adam's cave. His tiger friend saw or smelled him coming and trundled out to meet him. The tiger wasn't sure what to make of Eve. She smelled different but after a thorough examination, using his senses of smell, sound and taste by licking her hand, the tiger finally accepted her and they moved on toward the cave.

"We are finally here. This is my cave and over there is the waterfall I told you about. We can walk over there after resting for a while and having a drink of fresh, cool water."

"That sounds good, right now. I am thirsty and a little tired after the long walk."

The sun was getting low in the west. They decided a walk to the waterfall could wait until tomorrow. It would be dark soon and after a meal of spicy leaves, berries and nuts, they decided not much more could be done this day.

Adam had seated himself close to Eve at the fire. He dared to bring her hand to his face. To his surprise, she didn't resist. *Has she accepted me as a man?* he thought. He put his arm across the back of her shoulders. Again, she didn't resist. *This is more than I dared hope*, he thought. *Perhaps, I should wait for her to make a move*. They sat that way for a while longer. It was dark and Adam rose to get a torch to light with the flame from the dying campfire.

"I will need to spend the night. It is too dark to walk back to my cave. Do you have an extra sleeping mat? I forgot to bring mine. I just didn't think it was this far," Eve said.

"Yes, I have one from my travel from the south and I made a new one when I got here. You can have the new one and I'll use the one from my travel. It is still quite serviceable."

"Oh, Adam, you are quite thoughtful. Do you have a sleeping nook in the back of the cave?"

"Not really. I like to look at the stars and the moon. Would you like more shelter?"

"I usually don't sleep in the mouth of the cave … a holdover from my home, I guess."

"We can do whatever you prefer. It really doesn't matter to me."

"Let's sleep out here tonight the stars and the moon will be fun to explore. Do you know much about the night sky?"

"Not really. I know some things about the stars. We used them sometimes for direction in hunting but they're different this far north. I only recognize a few when I look directly south, close to the horizon."

"I came from the east so they should be the same here as they were at home but I never paid much attention to them and we didn't go out at night, too dangerous."

"That's too bad. I love the night sky almost as much as the daytime sky."

"I wonder what those stars really are. Do you think they're like here, with plants, animals and people? Or maybe they have mountains that belch fire and ground that shakes?"

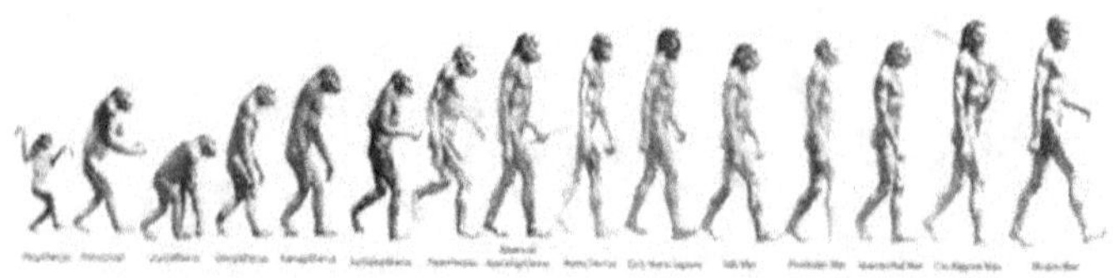

"They are probably little bright lights put there to guide us at night."

"Who put them there and how can they guide us if we don't know what they are and to what they are supposed to guide us?"

"You ask difficult questions, Eve. I don't know the answers. I've never thought of it that way. You are much more of a thinker than I am."

"Oh, I don't know. I've always got questions but I can't come up with the answers."

"Maybe someday we'll know."

"I need to get some sleep. Are you ready?"

"Yes, I'm tired and ready for sleep. Move my mat away from yours. I like space."

"All right." Adam was downhearted at that statement. *How can I get her to sleep with me? She acts as if she likes me but doesn't want to get too close. What is the secret of getting to her? It's going to take more work than the women in my village. It's just going to take time and gentle persuasion, I guess.*

The sunlight woke them both at the same time. Sitting up on the mat, Adam asked Eve "Are you ready to eat something?"

"Yes," she said. "Would you like some tea? I brought some leaves if you get the water, I'll get a fire started."

How is she going to do that? Women don't know about fire, Adam thought.

Why is he looking at me that way? It's as if I were some kind of freak, Eve thought.

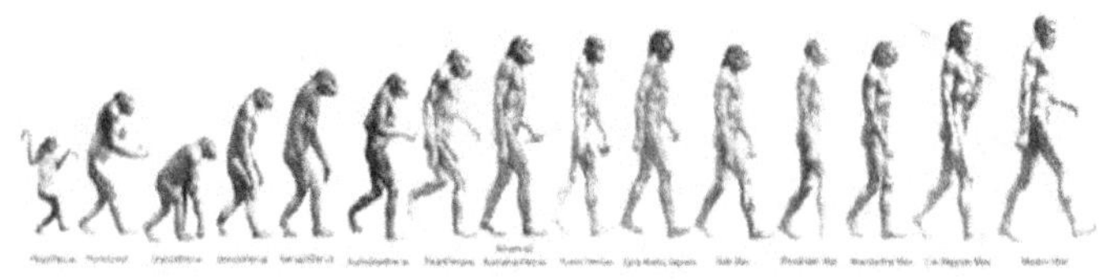

They settled down to a hot cup of tea and some berries.

"When we're finished, I want to show you my cave drawings then the waterfall," Adam said.

"Yes, that sounds great then I want to start back to my cave," Eve said.

"I'll walk back with you."

"There's no need for you to do that, Adam. I know the way." *He doesn't think I can take care of myself—that I might get lost without him. Silly man,* thought Eve.

"Are you sure?"

"Yes."

"Let's walk to the back wall of the cave to see my drawings. I better get a torch to see better."

He lit the torch from the fire and they began to move further into the cave. Adam stopped abruptly and Eve nearly bumped into him. He shone the torchlight up to the cave wall where pictures of strange animals were etched into the cave wall by something sharp.

"How did you do that?" Eve asked, in wonder.

"With a sharp stone, similar to your knife but sharper."

"What kind of animals are those?"

"Animals from my homeland. That is a camel, an elephant, a jackal, a gazelle, a hyena and that is a

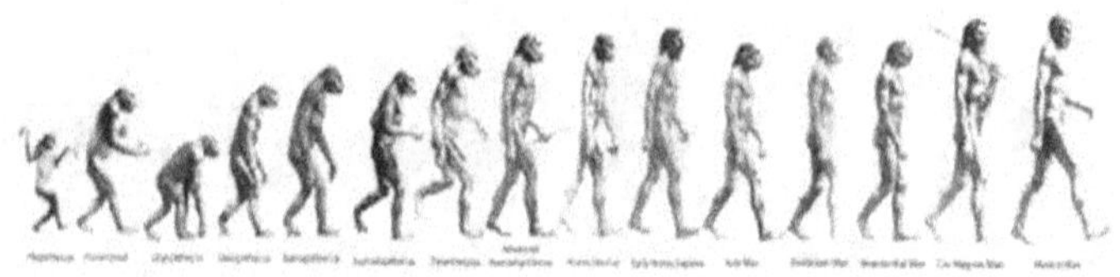

deer. Those are not all the animals but just the ones I've done so far."

"Those are good images. You'll have to tell me about each of them sometime."

"I could tell you about them now,"

"No, not now; some other time. I still want to see the waterfall."

Why is she in such a hurry ... as though she's anxious to leave? Why? Is she afraid of me? Certainly not, she can take care of herself. She seems to be trying to get away, though.

"Let's go to the waterfall then you can be off."

"I'm not trying to run away. I just miss my cave."

I'm really confused now. It's as if she read my mind. She gets more interesting as I get to know her better. She is definitely a challenge. I even have to be careful what I think.

"Are you upset with me, Adam? You don't seem to be as lighthearted as when we started out."

"Just thinking about those etchings; they made me a little homesick," Adam lied.

"I haven't seen anything that makes me homesick for my village," Eve stated and they walked on toward the waterfall in silence.

"I can hear a roar."

"That's the waterfall," Adam said.

"It's beautiful and there's a pool just below it. What keeps it from overflowing? It looks like it would fill up then what?"

"It doesn't seem to over-fill and the water for the falls seems to come from underground. There's no stream behind the falls, either."

"That's strange and interesting."

"Yes, another mystery about this Valley."

"You've gathered quite a list of mysteries about this Valley, Adam."

"Yes, and I hope to unravel them one by one."

"That may take some time."

"Time is what we have now, plenty of time to think. All of our other needs are met."

"Not all of our needs … I still need to know what is outside this Valley," said Eve

Why is that so important to her? I've seen enough of what's outside the Valley, Adam thought.

"I'd better start back to my cave. Thank you for inviting me to see your cave drawings and the waterfall. Goodbye, Adam,"

So easy for her to say 'Goodbye'. Oh well, I tried. "Goodbye, Eve. Hope to see you again." With that, Eve began her trek back to her cave.

Time passed and neither of them had visited each other. One day, outside her cave, Eve carried her stone bowl to pick some berries and nuts. She thought she saw movement behind a large bush. *What is that?* "Lion, is that you?"

"No, it's not," answered a male voice.

Eve was so surprised she dropped the bowl with a clunk. "Adam?"

"Yes, it's Adam," he said, coming around the bush.

"Adam, you could have just come up to the cave entrance instead of skulking around behind the bushes."

I did it again, another blunder. "I'm sorry if I startled you, Eve. I wanted to see you again but I wasn't sure if you wanted to see me."

"Yes, I'm glad to see you but that's not a good way to come to visit someone."

"I know. Should I go away and leave you to your activity?"

"No, Adam, I'm just going to gather some berries and nuts. Want to come along?"

"Sure." *That's better, Eve.*

"The berry and nut bushes are not far so it won't take long. Then we'll have time for tea and we can talk."

"That sounds great."

Berry and nut gathering completed, they went back to the cave, where Eve stoked the fire with leaves and animal dung she'd dried and set the stone container of water to heat.

"Adam, please look inside the cave to see if there is a wall on which you could do some etchings."

"That's a good idea. I'll take a torch and go back and look." *Wow, wonder where that came from.*

Shortly, the water was hot and Eve made the tea. She placed the berries and nuts between their seating places.

"Adam, the tea is hot. Come, join me."

"I'll be there in a minute."

Several minutes passed.

"Hurry, Adam, the tea will be cold."

"Sorry, Eve, the cave has a wall that would work, I think. I didn't bring my etching tool to try it out. I'll bring it next time and try it out on the wall."

Eve peered over her cup of tea and said, "Why would there be a next time?"

Adam was caught short again. *Now, what's that supposed to mean? I thought she was glad to see me. She criticized me for 'skulking around'.*

"I was hoping there would be another visit. I'd like us to keep seeing each other."

"Of course we will, Adam. I was just teasing you."

The afternoon passed into a lovely warm evening. The sun was setting and Eve noticed Adam wasn't rushing away. *This is my chance*, she thought. *I'll ask him to stay the night. He didn't bring a sleeping mat so I'll suggest he share mine. We'll see how he reacts. If he refuses, I'll know where I stand. If he decides to stay, perhaps there is a future for us; on my terms, of course.*

"Adam, it's growing late. Too dark for you to trek back to your cave."

"Oh, yes, but I could find my way easily enough."

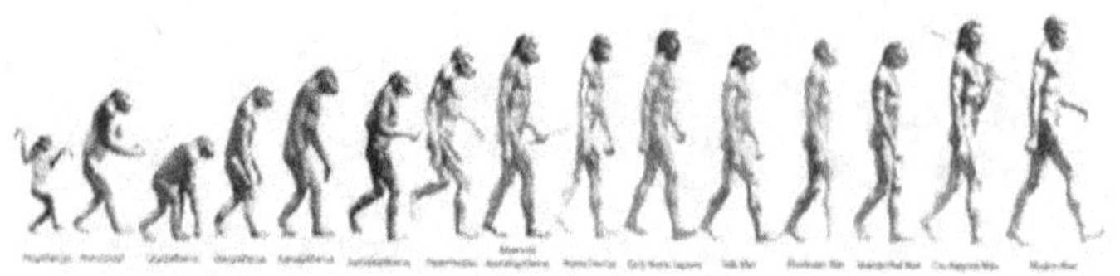

"I'm sure you could but I'm inviting you to stay the night here, with me."

Oh, my goodness. Things are changing for the better. "I didn't bring a sleeping mat. Do you have an extra?"

"No, but you could share mine."

Oh goodness, this is even better than I hoped for. "If you don't mind, I'm sure that will work."

"I usually sleep in the back of the cave, behind that notch in the rock that forms a low wall."

"Yes, I noticed that when I was back there. You can't see the stars and moon back there, though."

"I know but you don't need to see the stars and moon when you're sleeping."

Don't let this become an argument. Just give in and do it her way. "That's true, Eve. I'll share your mat in the back of the cave. I'm ready to go back there any time you are."

"I'll light the torch again, put this fire out and I'll be there as quick as I can."

Adam found the mat rolled in the corner of the niche where Eve slept. He unrolled it carefully and placed it strategically in the middle of the niche so either could get up in the middle of the night without awakening the other. All was ready when Eve arrived.

"All right, you did well, Adam. Can you see in the dark?"

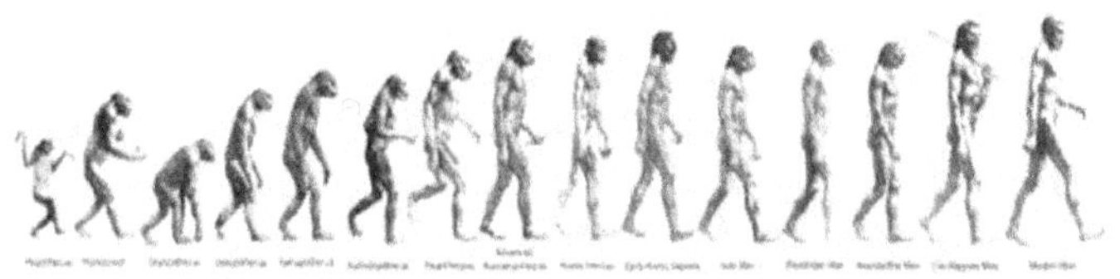

"A little. Some light shone back here from the fire and I had been back here looking at that wall so I had some idea where things were."

"I should have sent you back with the torch."

"Oh well, as you saw, not necessary."

She lay down on the mat and Adam followed. She felt his warmth close to her and she snuggled closer to him. He was on his side now, a hand roaming down her neck to her breast where he stopped, cupped her breast in his hand and felt the nipple harden. Her hand covered his and she pressed it, *a masterful welcoming gesture*, he thought. He leaned forward to take her breast into his mouth and stroke the nipple with his tongue. In response, she took his manhood in her hand and stroked it up and down as it began to leak fluid. He moved against her as she continued to stroke him faster and faster. He, in turn, reached down her abdomen, past the pubic area to find her opening, already warm and moist. He found her little swelling and stroked it as she emitted soft groans of pleasure. He could take no more, he had to enter her. She opened her legs wide; he rolled on to her there and entered that warm, moist place. His thrusts became more urgent and faster. He erupted as she thrust her hips to him and they climaxed together.

He finally rolled away from her and they both lay spent in a pool of sweat. Neither of them wanted to talk, to break the aura, the spell that had ignited feeling of attraction they'd both felt for moons. He fell asleep soon thereafter; Eve took longer as she

listened to his even breathing. *Males seem to fall asleep faster after copulating than women, I wonder why. It doesn't matter. I'll ask him in the morning, if I think of it.* She thought a bit more about their tryst then she, too, went to sleep.

Adam arose to go outside the cave to relieve himself, being careful not to wake Eve. He returned and looked down on the sleeping woman. *I want to spend my life with her. I wonder if she feels the same. I need to talk to her about it but how should I approach it or should I wait for her to bring it up. Maybe she won't and then I'll never get a chance to let her know how I feel. It doesn't matter how I feel if she doesn't feel the same. She's not shy about such matters, it seems. It just has to be brought up when she's ready. So, I'll wait to see if she brings it up this morning.*

Eve awoke while Adam stood looking down at her. "Come back to me, Adam. Why are you standing there? Have you been up long? The mat is still warm."

"I was just looking at you, realizing what a beautiful woman you are."

"I want to feel your fingers on my skin again, Adam. Let's not be in a hurry this time."

Adam joined her on the mat willingly. He took her more slowly this time, the urgency no longer as important. They kissed a long, slow joining of mouths before sliding apart and rising to begin a new day. Eve and Adam felt refreshed, comfortable with themselves and each other. The world seemed

complete, at least for now. Adam would search for a female no more; Eve was not searching for a male but she found satisfaction from Adam. These were different concepts but not identified as such by either of them.

"Adam, you could move into my cave. You said the wall would be useful for your etchings."

"Yes, but I'd have to leave the etchings I've already made."

"True, but you could still go back there from time to time."

"That's not a solution."

"Do you want to spend your life with me or the etchings? You decide."

"I want to be with you. I'll begin my etchings here but I'll have to go back to my cave to get my etching tool."

"That's better, Adam. I want you here."

Chapter 7
Disagreements Arise

Adam moved into Eve's cave and began his etching on the wall of her cave. The rock was of slightly different quality, which meant his techniques had to change somewhat. The rock seemed harder and chipped more easily, making the figure being etched appear grotesque. The work was slow and frustrating. Adam had to leave his wall and walk away before he became difficult to be with. He knew his temper might flare and Eve would be hurt and, probably, flare back. He couldn't take that.

Eve continued to try to make the cave as livable as possible. Two people in the cave felt crowded; she had not planned to live with another person and found it challenging. Though Adam was

likeable; at times, he seemed to be another person, withdrawn and distant. She did not see a pattern to his moods and behavior in the early moons of their cohabitation; however, as time passed, Eve began to connect his mood swings to his etching activity. When he walked away from the wall without a word and with a heavy scowl on his face, she knew he was not in the mood to talk. After several growling responses to her questions and the heavy stomping to exit the cave, she decided not to ask questions or try to talk to him.

Over time, this behavior tended to decrease and he put more time into his etchings and helping her gather food, carry water and collect fuel for drying. Life became orderly and they decided to take long walks to explore the Valley. They each carried a basket Eve had woven to collect fruit, nuts and leaves for food, a separate basket for dung for fuel. They found a few different plants; one, a fig tree that produced sweet, filling fruit. They picked almost a basketful to take back to the cave. On another hike they found a palm with large 'hairy' fruit on the ground beneath it. Using a stone, Adam cracked open the fruit to find white material inside with liquid that was sweet and water-like. This was, indeed, a treasure and they took as many back to the cave as they could carry. Their hikes took them to new parts of the Valley; they found their companionship almost as enjoyable as the new food they collected.

One day, on an extended hike, Eve and Adam encountered a tree with large red, delicious-looking apples hanging from the branches.

"Look at that tree," Adam exclaimed.

"The fruit is large and good enough to eat right now," Eve said.

As they moved closer to the tree, reaching for those large red apples, simultaneously, a sharp crack of lightening and a loud roll of thunder and a sudden gust of wind shook the ground and the trees close by. Eve and Adam stopped in their tracks as a voice, seemingly from nowhere and everywhere, said, **"YOU SHALL NOT EAT OF THE FRUIT OF THE TREE THAT IS IN THE MIDST OF THE GARDEN; NEITHER SHALL YOU TOUCH IT, LEST YOU DIE."**

Eve and Adam, recovering from their shock, ran back toward their cave, leaving the baskets behind. Finally, they could run no more and they dropped, breathlessly to the ground. When they could breathe comfortably again they sat up and looked at each other. "What was that?" they asked each other.

"We should never go to the center of the Valley again," Adam said.

"That was an unusual experience, scary but, yet, fascinating," Eve confirmed.

They got up slowly and retraced their steps back to the cave.

"Enough exploring for the day," Adam breathed, as he dropped to the floor of the cave.

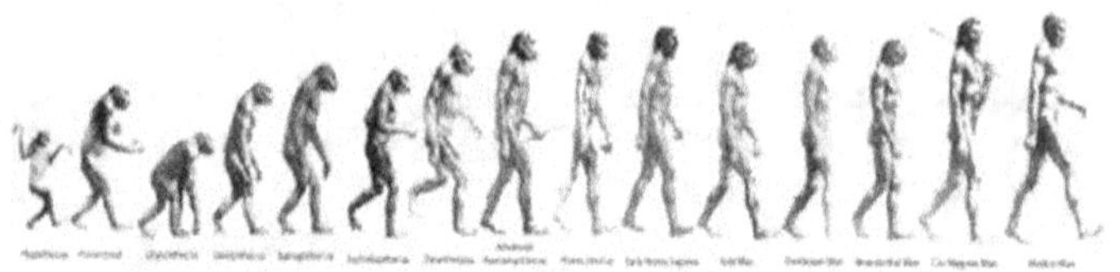

"I agree," Eve said. "I'll stay put for a while, too. I'll be more careful where I explore."

"Please do be careful, Eve. The voice, wherever it came from sounded like it had been watching us."

"I wonder what is so special about that tree?"

"I'm not sure but we better stay away from it."

I don't know, Eve thought. *I might try to go back sometime to see if that voice comes back. If so, ask it why the tree and its fruit are so special.*

As moons passed, Eve and Adam settled into a home life, of sorts. Adam continued to work on his etchings, though this cave wall was not as easy to use as was his former cave. Eve needed to weave baskets to replace the ones they'd left behind at the tree. She wove a new, larger sleeping mat for them to share and she made two new mats for sitting in the cave mouth. One day, they decided it was time to explore. They left the cave and headed south. By sun high, they noticed a river coming from the left and joining another coming from the right.

"I didn't know the river was this close," Eve said.

"Rivers, you mean. Looks like the two rivers are coming together and the ground we're walking on is wet[5]," Adam exclaimed.

"Yes and there's water between those trees up ahead. The trunks of the trees bulge near the ground[6] … a new kind of tree, too."

"Let's walk over to the river's edge. I want to see if there are any fish in this river."

They walked to the river bank and stood watching. Suddenly, a large fish jumped, splashing back into the river immediately. Then two or three jumped, splashing back into the water the same way.

"I thought there may be fish in the river. I'll come to the river and spear some fish for us. I used to do that in my homeland."

"Yes, our people did that in the mountain streams in my homeland, too."

"I want to walk along the river north to see how far it is from our cave."

"No, Adam. I think we should go back the way we came so as not to get lost."

"How could we get lost? I know my way around this Valley."

"I don't think you know your way as well as you think you do. You didn't even know this river was here." Eve's voice was getting terser by the minute.

"That's true but I want to know how far it is from our cave."

"You could find that by starting from our cave and walking west."

"But, if I walk up the river and head east, I'll find the cave."

"You don't know where to begin to turn east. You don't know how far it is."

"Give me some credit, woman. I've spent a goodly amount of my childhood in the forests of my

homeland. I know something about finding my way around." Adam was getting exasperated, too.

"Not enough, I think. I'm going back the way I came."

"Well, suit yourself. I'm going to follow the river."

They parted ways, each planning to arrive back at the cave before dark. Eve arrived back at the cave late in the afternoon. She was certain Adam would get lost. She was wrong. Adam appeared about an hour later as the sun was setting. Eve tried to disregard his arrival. She was still feeling some frustration about their parting conversation and his on-time arrival didn't help her attitude.

"I'm back, safe and sound, before dark," Adam announced.

"So I see. Think you're pretty smart, huh?" Eve retorted.

She hasn't changed. The same woman—sweet as honey one minute, sour as rotten fruit the next; no way to know when that sharp turn is taken. Better leave her alone for a while until she simmers down.

Adam started to walk out of the cave to visit his tiger that was probably nearby.

"Where are you going?" Eve asked, in an interrogating manner.

"Out to commune with tiger for a few minutes."

"I thought you'd stay here and gloat."

"I'll be back in time to do that."

"I'm sure you will."

She just can't let it go. What is her problem? This is about the worst I've seen her, thought Adam.

He's being so self-satisfied. Walking around like a clan chieftain. Ugh, thought Eve.

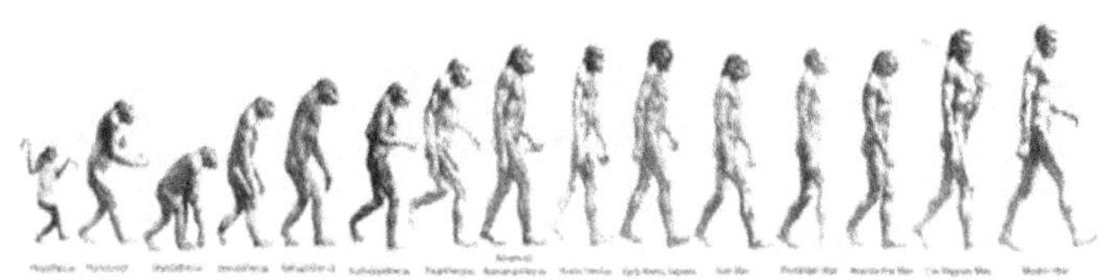

Chapter 8
Eve Grows Restless

The arguments continued about everything and nothing. Eve was becoming more difficult to live with. Adam toyed with the idea of going back to his former cave. *I'd miss her though. She is ingenious, weaving mats, knowing which leaves make the best tea, making good meals of the right kind of leaves and choosing the best fruit, nuts and berries. She is a good and willing participant in sex. She fulfills my needs and then some. I'd miss that more than all the rest put together. Leaving her is out of the question but what is the reason for her increasing moodiness? I wish I knew how to make her happy and get her to stop arguing all the time.*

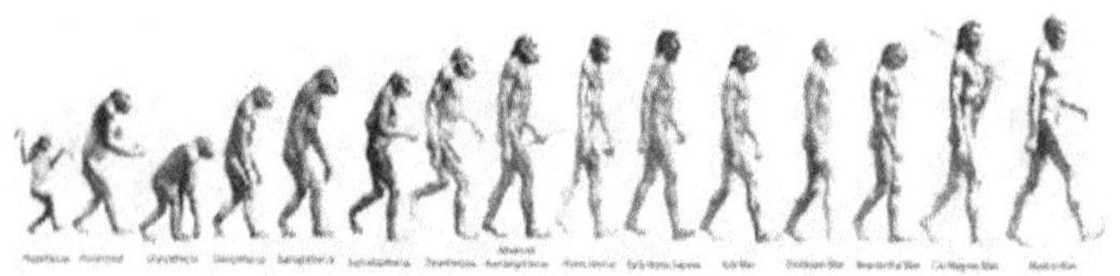

Eve, on the other hand, could understand Adam even less. *Why is he so interested in his etchings? He doesn't seem interested in exploring the Valley or what lies outside this Valley. He just wants to stay here, relax and etch. He doesn't seem to be interested in much else. He doesn't go to the river to spear fish very often. Those fish were quite tasty. He seemed to like the way I cooked them. Maybe he's just too happy. He is good at mating though. He makes me feel wanted and fulfilled every time and he doesn't force me, it's never a rape situation like those awful, crude hominids back in the village. I wonder how he'd react if I left, would he try to find me, would he wander through the Valley or would he just continue his etching and wait for my eventual return ... that's not going to happen.*

Suns passed, Adam continued to work on his etchings, paying little attention to Eve. He felt it best that way. Give her some space and she'd calm down, forget her interest in exploring. It didn't work that way in Eve's mind. She felt ignored and unhappy to the point where she was willing to leave; partly to elicit some attention from Adam and, also, to feed her inborn interest in finding what else was out there. Her mind was made up, it was now or never. One bright morning, not unlike all the other mornings in the Valley, Adam went to the wall to etch; Eve, without a word, headed out to explore.

She had been fascinated by the swamp they had visited some time ago. She headed south to find

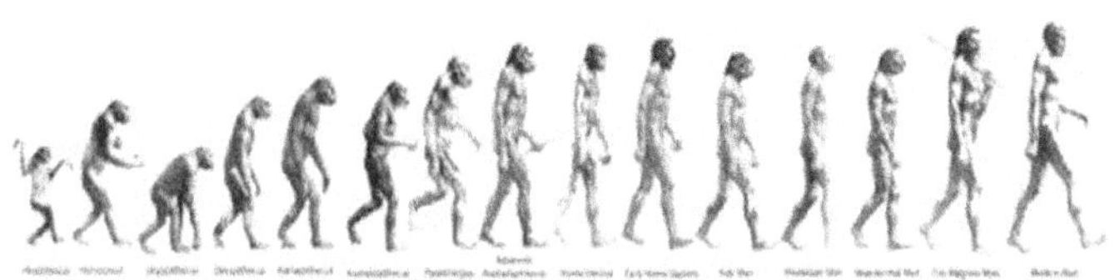

that swamp again, with the trees that had big bulges above their roots. Eve left on an expedition one day, she didn't remember the exact route they'd taken south but she knew she was going south. She walked for several hours before the vegetation began to change. The palm trees disappeared and low brush became the norm. She could not see far ahead because of the brush; in fact, she couldn't see more than a few inches ahead. Eve could not remember this much brush on their previous trip. *Perhaps, I've strayed and my direction is wrong*, she thought. *I can't change now, the brush is too thick. I can't go back because I'll lose direction to the north. Let's face it. I'm lost. What should I do? I'll try to sit and think for a few minutes.*

She decided to push forward for a while longer. Eve noticed the ground was not getting wetter, so she must not be near the swamp yet. She wanted to see that swamp so bad. *Oh, I wish Adam were here to help. No, I don't. I can solve this myself. I just need to keep going.* Then she came by a trail where the bush had been recently disturbed. *Someone else has been here recently. I'll follow this trail. Maybe it's Adam. Oh, why am I thinking about him? I don't need him. I can find my own way.* Eve walked on; it was easier now that the trail was a bit more open. Then she came to a spot where the grass was flattened where someone had been sitting. *That's where I sat. I've been walking in a circle. I need to*

walk straight ahead. There is no one out here but me. I'll not be fooled again. I will find the swamp.

Eve trudged on for what seemed to be hours. The light was changing. *The sun must be setting and I still haven't found the swamp.* She settled down on the grass as she smashed down more brush to make a mat. She opened her food and water satchels and ate a bit of the food and drank some water. She thought to save more for the morrow. She reclined on the mat made of brush. The day had been long and frustrating. *There is no need for Adam,* she kept repeating in her mind as she drifted off to sleep.

Daylight woke her and she rose with new determination to find the swamp. Eve renewed herself with a small amount of food and water then set off on her quest. Finally, nearing the end of the second day of pushing through the bushes, she could see the brush was thinning, moss covered the stones and there were more unusual tree trunks. These were not the strange tree trunks, but another kind she had not seen before. *I don't know what those trees are, but their limbs go all the way down the trunk and the branches have sharp spine-like needles instead of leaves. Adam would know. Oh, stop thinking about Adam, he wouldn't know either.*

As Eve pushed forward through the strange trees, they scraped her exposed skin. Her arms and chest were red, bleeding in a few places. Finally, past the trees, the ground was appreciably wetter. Pools of water were visible, as were the trees with the bulging

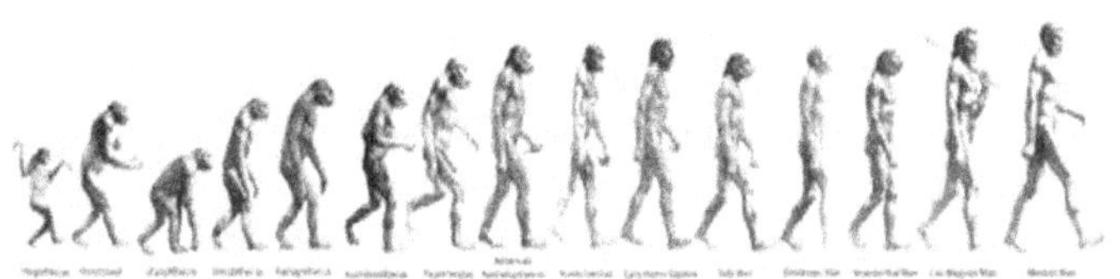

bases. *I made it. Now, I need to find a place to rest. I'll retrace my steps back to dry land for the night then explore tomorrow.* She decided to crawl back to find a sleeping place, staying below the scratchy branches as much as possible. The dry ground was covered with dead, dry needles that she had not noticed on the way into the swamp. She chose a soft place with plenty of needles on the ground. Pulling sheets of moss from nearby stones, she laid the moss sheets on top of the needles and settled. After a quick meal and drink from her satchels, Eve relaxed, feeling relieved and good about herself.

Morning came but the light was so reduced by the thick canopy of tree limbs, Eve slept later than usual. When she awoke, sat up, reached for her food and finished eating, she realized her food and water satchels were low. She'd have to replenish them soon. Not now though, exploring was first on her mind. She retraced her path by crawling beneath the branches, her back taking the brunt of the scratching, this time. That was fine; *the skin on my back is tougher,* she thought. She reached the swamp again and stood to look at it, appreciating its novelty. *This is an unusual place. Birds don't seem to sing here, they squawk. They seem to stand on long legs that look like sticks. Some are beautiful, bright pink, some are white. Those that fly are gray and they make a terrible amount of noise. I wonder if the water is drinkable. I could fill my water satchel now. I'll try it first.* She leaned down to reach a drink in her cupped

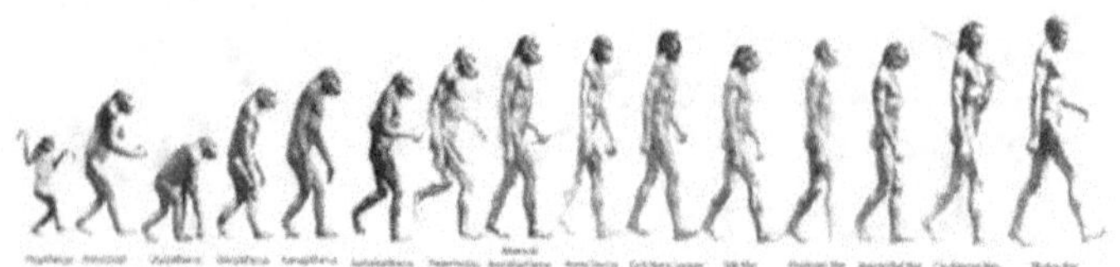

hands. "Ach," she coughed, *not nearly as good as our spring water in the Valley, but I'll have to use it.* So, she filled her water satchel and moved on, stepping from stone to stone.

A little later, she stepped on what she thought was a stone but it moved. *What kind of stone moves?* She wondered. She stayed on the stone as it moved quickly through the water. Then she noticed it had eyes and a snout some of which were just above the surface. She had ridden this animal[7] for several yards, further than she had gone into the swamp before. She saw some large fish in the water too. *Maybe I can sharpen a stick and spear a fish for dinner. That would solve my food problems.* She stepped off the moving stone as it stopped to lunch on a large fish. *Where can I find a stick out here?* Eve stepped onto a stone. This one had no eyes and extended snout and it didn't move. She stepped more carefully from stone to stone in a diagonal direction back to where she saw the trees with the needles and low branches. *This would yield a stick*, she thought. Upon arriving back to the trees, she found the sticks were brittle, though sharp. They would not work for spearing.

Undeterred, Eve snuck up behind a long-legged bird. As she grabbed the bird, she saw it had a fish in its beak. The bird squawked in surprise, dropping the fish as it turned to see its assailant. As quick as a wink, Eve grabbed the stunned fish and crossed the stones as fast as possible. The fish was coming back to its senses and flopped about, trying to get away. Eve had never killed anything before but

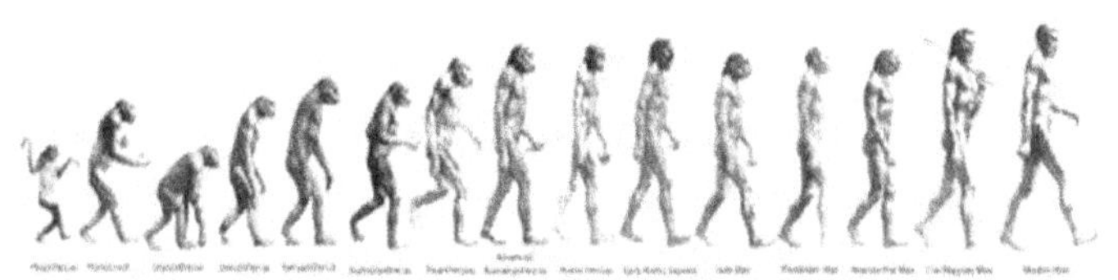

that didn't stop her from grabbing a stone and smashing the fish's head with the stone. A second later, it stopped its struggle forever. *Now I have my dinner. I will open it, scrape out the insides, just the way Adam did. Oh, stop thinking of Adam. Then I'll light a fire and cook the fish.*

Cook the fish, she did. It was succulent. A good portion of the fish was left so she wrapped it in leaves from her previous food wrappings and packed it in her satchel. Again, pulling sheets of moss from nearby stones, she made a bed on the dead needles for the night.

Meanwhile, after two days of Eve's absence, Adam was becoming alarmed. *Where could that woman be? Did she really leave for good? What would make her do that? Where did she go? I need to try to find her. I know she wanted to explore outside the Valley. Would she really try such a dangerous escapade? I'll begin by walking through the Valley calling for her.*

Adam went out of the cave to find tiger and get him to walk along for company, not being sure what he would find. As he walked further from the cave, he began to call her name,

"Eve," he called. "Oh, Eve, where are you?"

No answer came. He spent the rest of the day circling ever wider circles, calling her name. Adam could not fathom where Eve might have gone. *Tomorrow, I'll go near the apple tree. Surely she wouldn't go there. It scared her completely. If I don't*

find her there, I'll travel east. Maybe she went back to her village. No, that's unlikely because she hated her people and was frightened by some of them. I won't go that far but I will look around and call for her until I find her, if it takes a moon or more. Oh, Eve, where can you be? Adam returned to the cave for the night only to start the next day in the same manner.

The next day, Adam, with tiger, walked toward the apple tree, the only apple tree in the Valley he had seen. Adam called Eve's name as they hiked past bushes with nuts and berries and palm trees with dates, some dates on the ground. Absentmindedly, Adam reached for the food as he kept walking and calling for Eve. It was getting late as he and tiger turned back toward the cave. He always hoped, miraculously, Eve would be back at the cave when he got there. This time, however, was the same as ever. Eve was not there. *Where could she be? Oh, Eve, why did you leave. I miss you so. I don't know where else to look. I don't know what else to do but keep looking and calling for you.*

Eve had enough of the swamp and decided to move further west. She traversed what seemed to be a trail on high ground toward what she did not know. As she followed the path, actually an animal trail, the ground was smooth and soft and nuts and berries presented themselves. Food was plentiful and life was getting better again. She filled her food satchel

with berries and nuts, together with the cooked fish, meals would be good. The water, though, was still a problem. The swamp water tasted old and muddy. She knew she'd have to dump it when she came to a running water source, if she came to such a source. Eve continued to follow the trail for the rest of the day. As the sun was setting in the west, she began to look for a suitable sleeping place. Walking a little farther, she found an opening in the bushes that had been an animal bed, she supposed. She put her satchels down and proceeded to withdraw her food. Several small animals came to visit her. She shared some of her nuts with them.

As darkness came, Eve packed away her food, took as small a drink as possible from her water satchel and lay down for sleep. She was sound asleep when she was awakened by a snuffing sound. Snuff, snuff, grrr the thing sounded. *What is it? What could be out here? Just about anything,* she answered herself. She forced her eyes open. She could see nothing in the dark, no moon, no stars ... then she realized she was looking up at a large animal standing over her. Her heart and mind filled with terror. She thought first it was a hominid come to rape her. *That isn't right,* she reasoned as her mind cleared somewhat. *No, this is different.* She reached up to touch the animal, it made another snuffing sound and rose on its hind legs. It was much taller than a hominid. It lowered itself to all four legs and ambled down the trail. *I must be in its sleeping place,* she guessed. *Well, I won't be here tomorrow so it can*

have it back, she thought and, before long, fell back to sleep.

Daylight came and birds awakened, setting up a cacophony of songs, tweets, chirps and squawks. Squirrels chattered in the trees and a woodpecker knocked on a tree trunk. *That's beautiful noise compared to the swamp*, Eve thought. She arose, ate and prepared to leave. *The trail must lead somewhere, maybe to water. That would be welcome.* Eve found the trail easy on her feet but still could not see over the bushes so she had no idea where it would lead. After a break for food and another sip of ugly swamp water, Eve continued her trek.

As the sun crept further to the west, Eve heard running water, not gushing water but a slow-moving river or large creek. She picked up her pace and hurried on. *I'm coming to a river or steam. I can get water for my satchel.* Eve was nearly running now, when she tripped on a branch of a bush over the trail. "Owww," she exclaimed as she tumbled to the ground. Sitting up, she readjusted her bags. Getting up from that position with them was impossible, so she unloaded then stood and put the satchels back on her shoulders. *Now, no more running. I have to be more careful. I've never noticed anything on the trail before.* As she walked, she could see over the bushes now. There was a large river and a creek flowing into it.

She stopped at the creek, tasted the water and drank her fill. Then she dumped her water satchel, rinsed it and filled it with cool, clean, creek water.

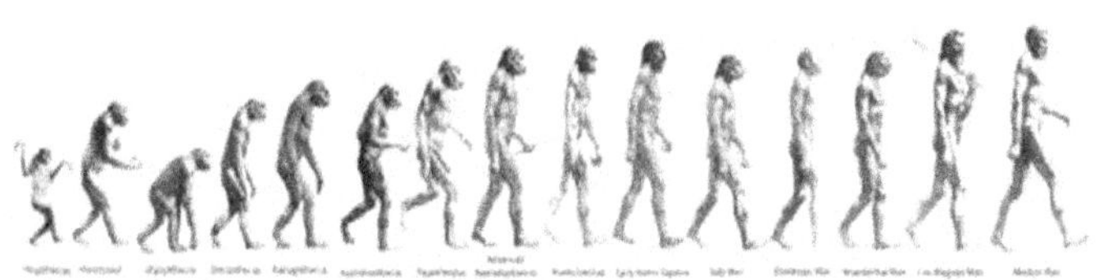

She saw the river was too high and wide to cross. The creek, though, could be crossed above the mouth where there were stones on which to jump. *I'll go north, following the river. I wonder if that's what Adam did when he found the fish to spear. Maybe I can get back to the cave that way. I wonder how he found the place to head east, back to the cave. I chided him about it but now I know how that must have hurt him. Oh, Adam, I'm so sorry. I miss you. I wish you were here right now. I've been gone so long. I want to go home. I need my cave.*

Adam continued his search with tiger by his side. He'd still received no answer to his calls. That didn't stop him from trying, though. Finding Eve became his primary concern. *Where could she be? Is she hurt? Is she sick? Oh, Eve, where are you? I miss you and I'm worried about you. Why did you leave?* Clearly, Adam was just about 'at wits end'. He didn't know what else to do. He'd looked everywhere. *Eve has been gone for six suns and still there's no sign of her. I'll walk toward the river and call for her to see if she thought of crossing the river. She's always wondered what's beyond the Valley.*

Adam did just that. He walked toward the river. It was a long walk and the sun was starting to set by the time he found a suitable sleeping place. He'd still received no answer to his calls but that didn't surprise him, he had not received an answer thus far. *I'll rest here tonight and watch across the river while the sun is in the east. If I see movement,*

I'll call out. Adam ate the meager meal he'd brought from the cave. Sleep did not come easily. His mind was filled with thoughts of Eve. Worry to the point of terror filled his mind. He felt a tear drop down his check. He had never cried before. He was consumed with worry and he knew it. *I have to find her. I can't live without her. Oh, Eve where can you be?*

Eve arose with the new day, ate a few nuts and berries and was off along the river as the sun was rising. *Oh, Adam, I have to find you. I have to find my way home. Do you miss me? Are you searching for me or are you etching? I don't care, I'm coming home to you as fast as I can. I'm tired exploring. I'll never leave again, I promise.* Eve moved swiftly along the river. The sand was soft on her feet but she stopped from time to time to soak her feet when the sand felt too warm. The sun was getting low in the west when she thought she heard a distant voice. She stopped to listen. It came again. It sounded like a male and the call sounded like "Eve". *That can't be...that can't be Adam. Oh, how I want it to be Adam.*

"Adam," she called as loud as she could. "Oh, Adam, is that you?"

I think I hear someone. His heart leapt. "Eve, is that you?" he called?

I think that's him. "Adam?" she called, "where are you?"

"Eve?" he called, "is that you?"

"Yes, it's me," Eve answered. "Adam, where are you?"

"Eve, stay where you are, I'm coming."

"Adam, please hurry."

Adam broke into a delighted run south, along the river. He had never been so excited and so relieved. She sounded well and not in pain. *Oh, Eve, this is such a great day. I've found you and I can't wait to hold you,* he thought, as he ran down the side of the river.

"I'm coming Eve. Where are you?"

"You sound closer. I'm right by the river. Keep coming." *Oh, I'll be so glad when he gets here. I can't wait to fall into his strong arms.* She sat cross-legged on the riverbank waiting and watching for him. She felt anticipation flooding her mind and chest. She strained her neck to peer up the bank. It seemed to be hours but it was less than an hour when she saw him coming around a bend in the riverbank. She jumped up and ran to him.

Adam was breathing hard as they came together, arms outstretched. They grasped each other in a desperate need to be together.

As Adam began to catch his breath, he managed to ask, "Where have you been, Eve? I was so worried."

"Oh, Adam, I wanted to explore the swamp but I was lost."

"Let's rest here for a while then I want to hear about your escapade."

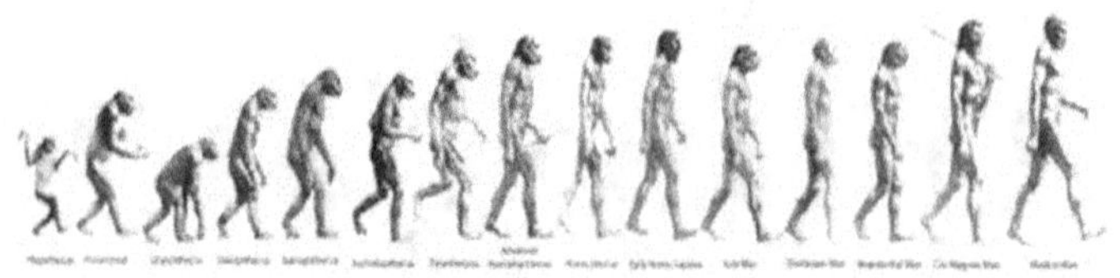

"I'll tell you all about it if you promise not to laugh or get angry."

"All right, I'll listen to your story if you'll also listen to my story of my frantic search for you."

"Did you really search for me?"

"Yes, I've searched and called for you for days."

"Oh, Adam, I'm sorry I caused you such alarm."

"I worried about you when you didn't come home day after day."

They settled down on the riverbank to watch the river together and calm their anxious nerves. This had been a more draining adventure than either could have imagined. They finally found it more comfortable to lie in the sand than sit. After a brief, energetic mating, they fell asleep in each other's arms. Life seemed to be good and complete again. Eve snuggled as close to Adam as she could. He wrapped his arms tight around her as they fell asleep, lulled by their body warmth and the sound of the flowing river.

Morning came, awakening them with the warm rays of sun peaking over the sand dunes covered with low brush. They approached the river and waded in for a quick dip in the cool water. Now, fully awake they sat cross-legged to enjoy the last of their food satchels. Eve was anxious to share the last of her cooked fish with Adam. He provided exactly the feedback for which she was hoping.

"Eve, this is the best fish I've ever eaten. How did you make it so delicious?"

"Oh, Adam, you said that the last time I cooked fish. I didn't do anything special to it, just cooked it over a fire built from bushes and leaves along the trail."

"Well, you certainly have a way with food. The fish tasted a bit salty with a fruit flavor I can't identify."

"I'm not sure; it probably came from the smoke of the bushes I used. I didn't really have a choice and I had no berries left to use on the fish as it cooked."

"That's not important. I think what is important is that you fixed it."

"Thank you, Adam. I'm so happy you like it."

From the river, they decided to go back to the cave. It was nearly a day's hike back to the cave. They agreed there would be no side trips but they would pick some berries along the way. Finally, as they neared the cave, Adam said, "I'm anxious to hear about your experience in the swamp but, maybe, it is best to wait until tomorrow, when we're both fully rested."

"Yes, there is much I want to tell you. Perhaps, you may have had some of the experiences that I had. I will enjoy your reaction to my telling."

As they arrived at the cave, it was nearly sundown and tiger and lion were waiting for them. Both animals sat in the mouth of the cave as if they

were guarding the entrance, waiting for the return of the occupants.

Eve and Adam were exhausted by the time they arrived home to the cave. After welcoming their animal friends and a quick meal and a satisfying cup of tea, they retired for the night. Talk of the adventure would have to wait until morning.

Both rose at daybreak the next morning. Eve immediately started a fire to heat the water in her stone bowl. *How much should I tell Adam? I want to find out more about that stone that moved. I wonder if he has ever seen one. How much should I tell him of why I left? How much should I let on about how much I realized I missed him? Not too much about that, lest he feels I can't live without him. That isn't true. Yes, I'd miss him but I could manage. I did before I met him and I could still,* Eve thought.

Adam went out of the cave to collect some fresh berries and nuts for the morning meal. At the same time, Adam was thinking, *She doesn't seem too eager to talk about her experience. I wonder why. Maybe it wasn't all that exciting; maybe she had problems and doesn't want to talk about it, or maybe she missed me more than she wants to admit. I wonder why she left. Should I ask her or wait for her to tell me during her explanation of her excursion. My biggest question is why she left without telling me. I need to make her understand how worried I was, how hurt I was.*

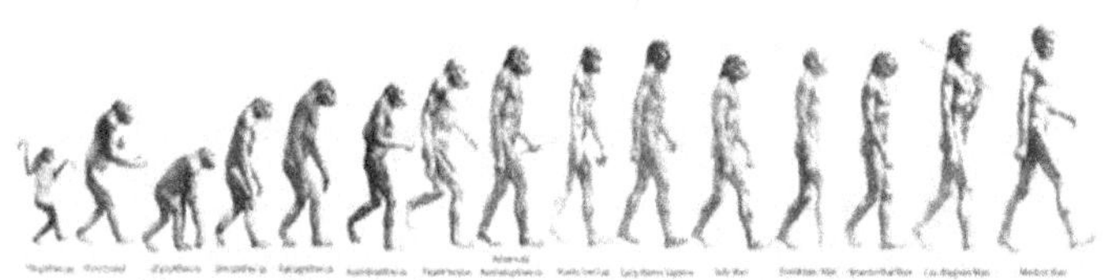

The meal was arranged and Eve served the hot tea. Conversation started about small, trivial things such as tiger and lion. Adam sensed Eve's discomfort and chose to try to steer the conversation toward Eve's exploration.

"You seem well rested and happy after your exploration. Where did you go and what did you find?" Adam asked, finally.

"I was fascinated by the swamp we had visited a while ago and I decided to retrace our trail to have a better look at the area," Eve answered, innocently.

"And what did you find?" Adam asked, trying not to sound interrogating.

"To tell you the truth, I lost the trail and saw a new part of the swamp, with dry scratchy branches all the way to the ground. The dead needles on the ground and a sheet of moss off a nearby rock made a good bed, though. I finally got to the swamp where I went out further, stepping stones. I stepped on a big one that what I thought was a large, flat-topped stone, but it moved. I rode on it quite a distance when I noticed it had eyes and a long snout. Have you ever seen something like that?"

"Yes, Eve, I have. It isn't u floating stone it's a big, dangerous water animal. It could have made you fall into the water and snapped you up in its powerful jaws. I've seen them eat people in one large snap of their jaws. That was a very dangerous ride you took."

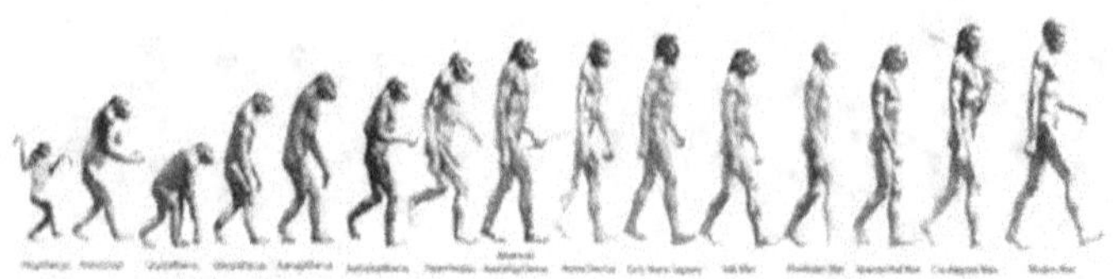

"Maybe, but it was fun. I just stepped off it and it swam away. I continued to step stones until I got back to solid ground. By the way, the water in the swamp is not very good. It tastes like mold and mud."

"That's not too surprising because the water doesn't move. It just sits there while it slowly sinks away or moves beyond, probably to a bay."

"How do you know so much about the swamp?"

"I don't know that much about that swamp. That's usually how swamps work. We had a large one a ways beyond our village. It eventually drained into a bay when the water level got high enough from rains but, otherwise, the water just sat there. There were dangerous water creatures in there too."

"Then I decided to head west to try to find the river where you fished."

"Is that where you speared the fish you cooked?"

"No, I stole that from a water bird with long, stick-like legs. I snuck up behind it, scared it, when it squawked in surprise, it dropped the fish from its beak and I caught the fish in my hands."

"You were really quick. Didn't the bird fly away?"

"Oh, yes, but it was a bit slow to take off. It was a big white bird. There were also some pink birds with long, stick legs, too.

"Then I headed west, following the afternoon sun. I followed a kind of path that wasn't very wide. I

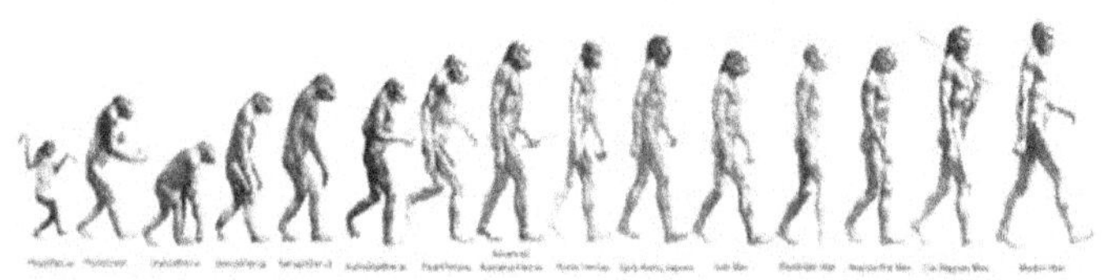

think it was an animal trail leading to the river. Then, I followed the river north."

"And finally you answered my call."

"Yes, I was glad to hear your voice."

"That's it? Nothing else happened?"

"No, why?"

"I was worried about you."

"You shouldn't have been. You know I can take care of myself."

She's back to her old self. So soon? Why does she seem so crosswise, almost hostile at times, thought Adam. "Of course you can. I still worried because I didn't know why you left or where you went."

"Well, Adam, I like being free. I don't want to have to ask your permission when I want to go exploring."

"No, you don't have to. I care about you and I don't want you to be hurt." *I better not say anymore or an argument is sure to start.*

"I know you do, Adam but I need freedom, too."

"All right, understood."

Chapter 9
Trip to the Old Cave

Several moons past while Eve wove mats and baskets, cooked fish Adam had speared at the river and she collected basketfuls of nuts and leaves for their meals and for tea. Adam continued to etch when he had time, which wasn't as often as he liked in that Eve seemed to be trying to keep him busy at other tasks. *She seems to have launched into domestic tasks with a fervor I didn't know she felt. Or, is she trying to keep me from etching? I don't know why and I don't want to ask her because it might cause another argument. She is touchy,* Adam thought.

I wonder why Adam doesn't seem interested in etching so much as he did before I left on my escapade. It's no matter, I like having him do some

things for meals. I love the fish, can't have too much of that. He doesn't talk as much as he used to. It's as if he's afraid I'll argue with him. Well, I might or I might not, depending on what he says. If he comes across as a know-it-all then, yes, I'll standup for myself as an independent woman, a woman with brains, skills and feelings. I'm liberated from the life I knew in the village and I'll not be cowed into submission now or ever, thought Eve.

"Adam, where did you find these berries? They are so juicy and sweet."

"They were a little southeast of here in the direction of my old cave."

"Have you gone back to that cave lately?"

"No, I really don't have any interest in it anymore. This is home now."

"I didn't mean anything by the question. I just thought how long it has been since we went back there. Remember what it was like the first time you invited me to your cave?"

"Yes, I do. I was intrigued by you and wanted to get to know you better."

"I was excited and thrilled to have met such a perfect being. You are like me, your skin is darker but that's all right. Your experiences differ from mine, which makes you all the more interesting."

"Yes, your experiences fascinate me too. I've never lived in the mountains. We both had a parent with unreal expectations and the only solution was to leave."

"Yes, we definitely had that in common. Let's walk back to your old cave one of these days to see what has become of it. I also want to go back to that apple tree someday."

"No, please, not that tree. Don't even think about that. If you have things in order here, perhaps we could go back to the cave in a few days."

"How about tomorrow morning? I'll pack a basket of food and another basket with the stone bowls for cooking and eating and leaves for tea. This is going to be fun."

I didn't realize she was going to be this excited about going back to my old cave. She is quite a woman. I really don't have a need to go back to the cave but, if she's interested, it will probably be fun. "Let's take tiger and lion, too" Adam said.

"Oh, yes, definitely. They'll be fun to have along."

Early the next morning, they ate a meal of nuts and berries and tea. They packed some food and water and began their trek back to his cave. They'd not been back there since their mating over twelve moons ago. They didn't know what to expect, in fact, they didn't expect anything untoward. They looked forward to a pleasant afternoon and a long, relaxing time in the pool at the bottom of the waterfall. It would be luxurious, they thought. Adam was anxious to see his etchings again. *Maybe I can add one while I'm at the cave. The stone is so much easier to work with,* he thought. *I might be able to interest Eve in it*

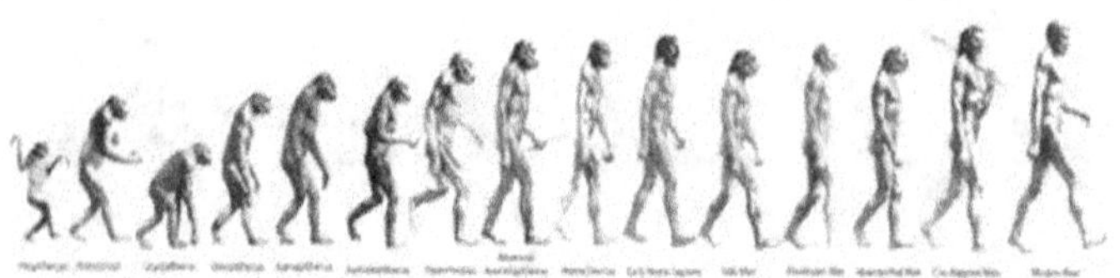

and she'd be willing to watch. On the other hand, Eve thought, *Maybe we can relax and be together and he'll forget about his etchings for a little while. I'll try to keep him occupied with other things.*

As they drew nearer to the cave, tiger and lion grew noticeably more alert. Then, as they drew closer, the animals were nervous, emitting low, guttural groans and growls. Eve and Adam looked at each other, trying to discern the meaning of the cats' behavior. They stopped walking, for they felt impending danger, too.

"I wonder what the cats are sensing," Adam said.

"I don't know. I haven't seen or heard lion act this way in a long time. The last time I saw him act this way, it meant the presence of danger," Eve replied.

"I'll take tiger and walk further toward the cave," Adam said.

"No," Eve said, "I'll take lion and we'll both go to the cave."

They walked toward the cave. Both stopped at once near the mouth of the cave. Eve advanced once more to enter the cave. Lion moved in front of Eve, not allowing her to pass. Adam moved forward with tiger. As he and tiger entered the cave, tiger emitted a tremendous roaring yowl. Several hominids came to the mouth of the cave, weapons in hand. One threw a well-aimed rock at tiger's head. It hit him, stunning him. Three other hominids attacked Adam with large

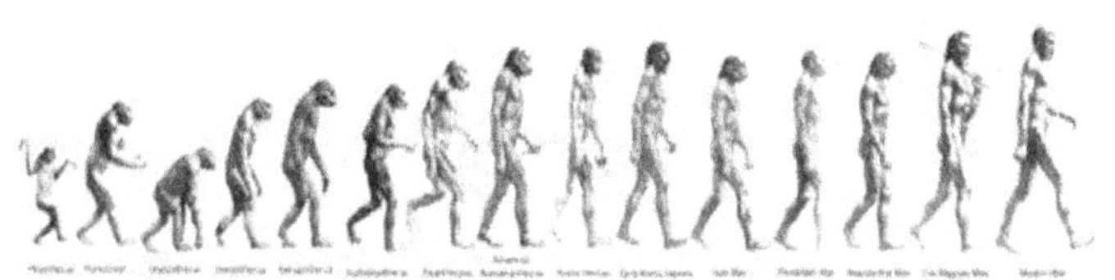

branches from trees. Eve was transfixed in horror. Adam was getting no help from tiger and, cut and bleeding from the hominid attack, unarmed, he continued to fight the three hominids. Eve finally overcame the horror of the situation and, with lion, jumped up to the cave entrance to assist Adam. She'd picked up two stones on her way to the cave mouth and used them on the hominids. Two well-aimed stones narrowed the odds and Adam quickly overcame the third hominid.

She helped Adam to the side of the cave where he could sit with his back to the cave wall and begin to recover. Tiger was beginning to regain consciousness and lion had calmed. Eve assumed there were no more hominids nearby.

"Adam, you are bruised and bleeding. I'll get some water and leaves to clean those deep scratches and scrapes."

"Is tiger all right or did they kill him?"

"No, tiger is fine. He's sitting up but a little groggy."

Eve came back with the water satchel and the leaves. Before she could begin, one of the hominids emitted a groan.

"We'd better take care of those hominid animals before they wake up," Adam said.

He rose from his sitting position, picked up a stone and hit the hominid that was beginning to stir. He went to the back of the cave where he found the etching tool he'd left behind when he moved to Eve's cave. It had a pointed tip and a razor-sharp edge used

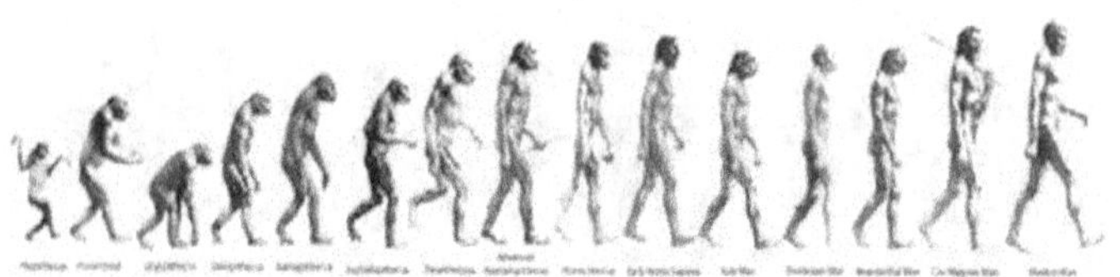

for scraping. Adam used the sharp edge to slit the throats of the hominids, killing them almost instantly. He tossed the bodies over the edge, to the side of the cave. That accomplished, he sat down to await Eve's ministrations. Eve finished the washing of the scratches and bandaging of the deepest gashes and lacerations on his arms and legs.

"What a scare. Not at all what I expected," Eve said.

"Nor I. We should have suspected something because tiger and lion were on edge."

"Yes. Should we stay longer or go back?"

"I want to stay awhile. I think the danger is over," Adam said.

"I don't. I want to go back."

"No, let's go for a swim then have some tea and something to eat."

After the leisurely time spent in the pool and the time spent eating, the sun had set and evening was upon them.

"It's too late to begin the trek back to the cave tonight. We should stay here tonight and leave tomorrow morning," Adam said.

"I know but I really don't want to sleep in this cave. More hominids might come back and cause more harm to us," Eve objected.

"I don't think they'll be back, especially if they see the dead ones outside the cave."

"I'm not sure about that. It might make them angrier and they'd attack us."

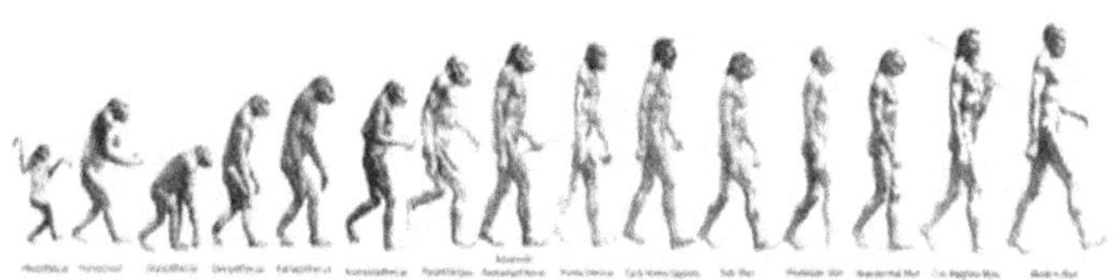

"Don't worry so much. We'll be all right. Besides, I'm here, I'll take care of you."

"Adam, I'm perfectly capable of taking care of myself. You weren't doing so well against those hominids until lion and I intervened."

"Well then, you're here so I'm not worried."

"Adam, that's not what I meant and you know it. I think we could be in danger if we stayed the night."

"What do you suggest, Eve? Do you want to walk back to the cave in the dark?"

"No, I think we could find a place to sleep down the path we used to get here."

"It's dark and if we found a shelter, we couldn't be sure it wasn't already occupied."

"Oh, Adam, you are so stubborn. Why can't you even consider alternatives?"

"There aren't any alternatives. Either we stay here as I suggested or we go running off in the dark and, possibly, run into some hominids, as you seem to be suggesting."

"I'm not suggesting that at all. I think we could find a good place to bed down along the trail we followed to get here. We didn't see any hominids on the way here and we have tiger and lion to warn us, if we listen to them."

"No, we're not going anywhere and that's an end to it."

Eve settled down to sleep, sullenly, on Adam's old mat. Adam settled to sleep on the cave

floor with a few palm leaves beneath him that he'd collected on the way back from the pool. The night passed quietly and they both slept well with lion and tiger dozing at the cave entrance.

Morning came and they both ate berries and nuts from their food satchels.

"Tea?" asked Eve.

"Yes," Adam answered.

That was the total of their conversation that morning. *She's still angry at me because I wanted to stay here last night. Why doesn't she see it didn't make sense to strike out for the cave during the night when we were both tired? I think the hominids that were here yesterday were just passing through. There's no evidence they'd been here longer. There's no point in bringing it up now, she'll just put up her defensive barrier,* Adam thought.

Adam isn't saying anything, just gloating because he was right; the hominids did not come back and attack us. The gloating makes me even angrier. Why doesn't he just come out and say "I told you so" and we could get it behind us. But he won't, he'll just not talk until I give in...not this time. I'm getting tired of his "I'm man, you woman" behavior. It might be time for me to do some more exploring. He acted as if he really missed me and cared for me for a while, now he's back to his old domineering self again. Men, I'm sick of them, Eve thought.

Another impasse had developed. They each grabbed a satchel, putting them on their shoulders and left the cave and took the trail back to their home

cave. They walked in silence for several hours. The sun had reached its zenith when Adam finally spoke.

"Eve, I'd like to stop for some food. Are you hungry and thirsty?"

"Yes, I am both hungry and thirsty." *I thought he'd never ask. I would have dropped over before I would have begged to stop. 'Woman would have appeared weak but man strong.' I wouldn't give him that consolation.*

"Did you notice the bodies of the hominids were gone this morning?" Eve asked.

"No, I meant to look and I didn't."

"I didn't go looking for them but I noticed they were not there as I looked at the corner where you threw them yesterday."

"Perhaps other hominids came and collected them during the night."

"I don't think so. We would have heard lion and tiger snuffing or growling. I think they came while we were at the pool."

"Did you know if the bodies were gone when we got back?"

"I didn't notice—the sun was going down by then and I wanted to eat."

"Well, some of them clearly came back for their dead and we didn't know it. So we were safe, just as I had predicted."

"Yes, Adam, oh great protector."

That statement set the stage for a quiet walk the rest of the way home. *Why does everything I say*

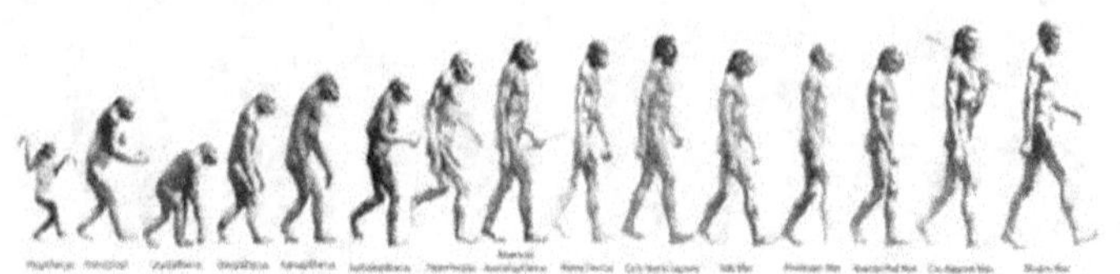

cause her to lash out? She's being unreasonable. I just can't talk to her, Adam thought.

He doesn't know when to quit being in control. Why does he have to be in control? Why can't we discuss something and come to a mutual decision without one having to give in to the other? If I don't see it his way, there's no way. It's as if my way is never good enough; my reasoning is faulty. Woman's reasoning is always faulty, Eve thought.

Chapter 10
Eve Meets Lilith at the Tree

Eve and Adam returned to their cave and resumed what they knew as a normal life. Adam seemed to have a renewed interest in his etchings. Eve resumed her household tasks of gathering food, weaving and, when the need arose, making bowls and necessary eating and cooking utensils from stone. Stone utensils lasted for a long time, mats woven with leaves tended to wear out with continued use and needed replacement on a regular basis. As she worked on these projects, her mind never ceased to wander. *The trip to the cave was a welcome diversion but I need more. I wonder what is so special about that apple tree and why that voice was so scary. Where did it come from and who spoke. Did we just*

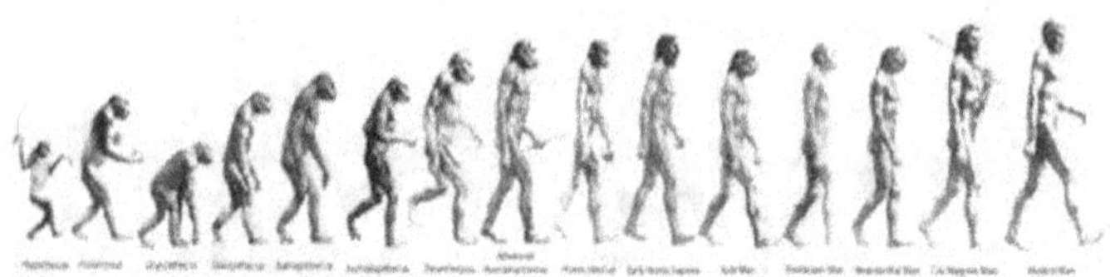

imagine it? That can't be, we both heard it. Adam was as frightened as I was. I didn't know anything could frighten Adam. He didn't question or argue with the voice either. I want to go back to the tree alone. Will I hear the voice again? I'll ask who it is and where he is. I won't be alarmed this time. I'll be ready for it.

She replaced the old mats with newly woven ones and set the old leaf mats aside to use for starting cooking fires, placed the new large stone bowl on the stone shelf and checked to make sure the food supply of nuts and berries was adequate. *I'm ready to go back to the apple tree. I won't tell Adam where I'm going. He'll try to forbid it. I'll just tell him I'll be back by evening. I want to find out more about that voice and those bright red apples. I know there has to be an answer and I'm going to find it. Why can't we eat that fruit when we can eat anything else? That doesn't make sense. I think something big wants to keep those apples for himself.*

After bidding Adam goodbye, Eve began her trek north, northeast toward where she thought she remembered the tree. *It's a big tree with bright red fruit. I know I can't miss it,* she thought. She scurried up to the top of a knoll to look around. Sure enough, in the distance, she saw a large tree but it was so far away she couldn't see if it had any red fruit. The tree seemed further away than she thought. Eve was hungry when she got to the tree, which turned out to be a big fig tree. They proved to be the best tasting

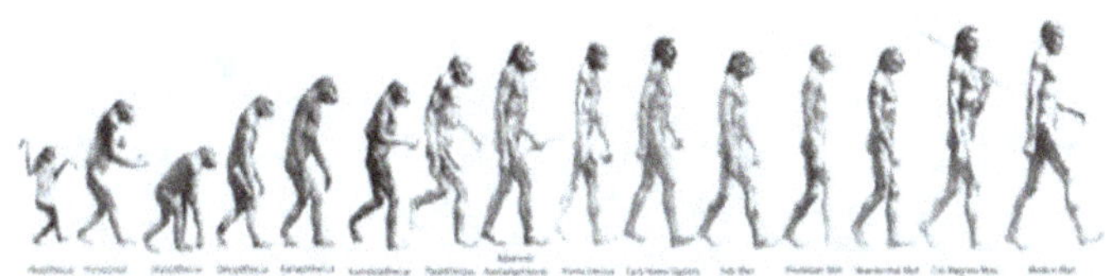

figs around, better than the smaller ones near the cave. She ate her fill and moved on in search of the apple tree, the only one in the Valley she had seen. The only other apple trees she knew of were in her village but they were smaller and somewhat sour. She couldn't understand why a beautiful tree laden with ripe, delicious looking fruit was off limits. It had to be it was being hoarded by some large hominid being.

It was late in the day when Eve finally found the tree with the large, red apples. She walked to the tree and picked two apples and put them in her basket to take back to the cave when a loud voice said **"You shall not eat of the fruit of the tree that is in the middle of the garden, nor shall you touch it, or you shall die."** Eve was not scared this time.

"Who are you?" Eve asked.

"I am the Lord, God," He said.

Eve had never heard of a lord god, so she ignored the voice and went to stand by the tree. As she looked up in the tree, she saw a golden-eyed snake. She looked away, momentarily, when she looked again, she saw a beautiful woman with the skin color similar to her own.

"Hallo," the voice called.

"Who are you and why are you sitting in the tree?" Eve said.

"My name is Lilith and I'm sitting here to show you that you can touch the tree without danger."

"That's fine. I don't need to touch the tree, I just wanted an apple. Come down so I can meet you properly."

Lilith arrived on the ground. She was lithe with a well-shaped body and flaming red hair. She sat cross-legged on the ground and invited Eve to do the same. Lilith and Eve took a minute to take stock of each other before Eve started to talk.

"I need some answers I hope you can give me."

"I'll try. What are your questions?"

"Who is this voice, lord god?"

"It's a meddlesome man who thinks he owns the tree."

"Have you met him or seen him?"

"No, just the voice."

"That's odd. He sounds really big and dangerous."

"I don't know, he hasn't bothered me. I'd forget him. I don't think he'll harm us."

"Who are you? You said your name is Lilith. Where did you come from? I've never seen you before in the Valley."

"I was here once before. I mated with your Adam. He promised to mate with me forever but I grew tired of him and I went away. Did he not tell you about me?"

"No, he certainly never mentioned you. I would have remembered."

"I had his child, too, but I killed it."

"You what? You killed it? How could you?"

"It was deformed and ugly. I just couldn't take on that. I had to get away. He sure would remember me, though; our mating was hot and wet. It went on for hours."

"That's enough. I don't want to hear anymore."

"I went on and mated with Samael. He is a king and we live in a castle. We have two sons and two daughters. I'd like for you to meet them."

"Where is this castle?"

"It is actually a fort in the desert across a sea."

"How would we get there?"

"It's actually quite simple."

"Simple, what do you mean? How long will it take? I need to tell Adam I'll be gone from the Valley. He won't want me to be gone out of the Valley. I might get lost and not able to find my way back. Besides the water scares me, I can't cross a sea."

"Hold everything. Don't bother Adam. He won't miss you and you won't be gone."

"What do you mean 'I won't be gone'? You said it was across a sea."

"Oh, Eve, slow down. First of all, I don't want to see Adam again. I don't want him to see me, ever again. Is that clear? This is just between you and me."

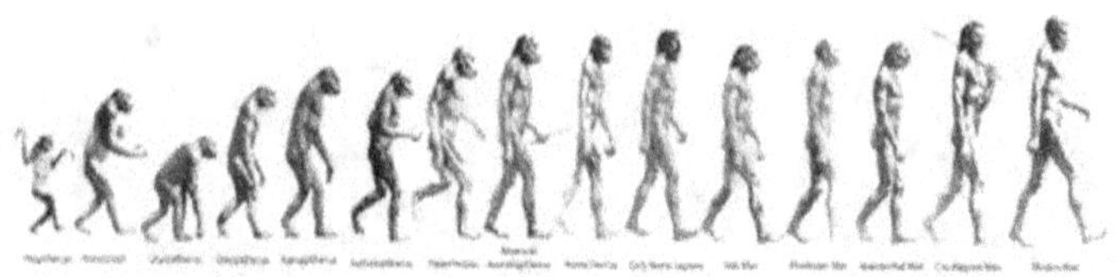

"All right, Lilith, I'll listen to you."

"This trip will be only in your mind. You will travel with me while your body stays sitting up against that apple tree."

"I don't understand how that's possible."

"Well, it is possible but you have to do exactly as I tell you. I will explain where we're going, who we're going to meet and where everything and everybody is. You will see them clear as day."

"Do I need to bring anything along?"

"No, you will be given everything you need when we arrive."

"I am excited. When do we leave?"

"Tonight, after dark.

"Why after dark?"

"You are full of questions aren't you? I am a night sorceress. That is the first of many secrets you must keep."

"All right, after dark and it is a secret."

"Wait right here while I gather some berries we need for the trip."

"No, I'll help. I know all the berries in the Valley."

"Not these. They are special."

"Another secret?"

"Yes, now relax."

Lilith moved off to find the special berries. Eve thought about following her but that would infuriate Lilith and no telling what she might do.

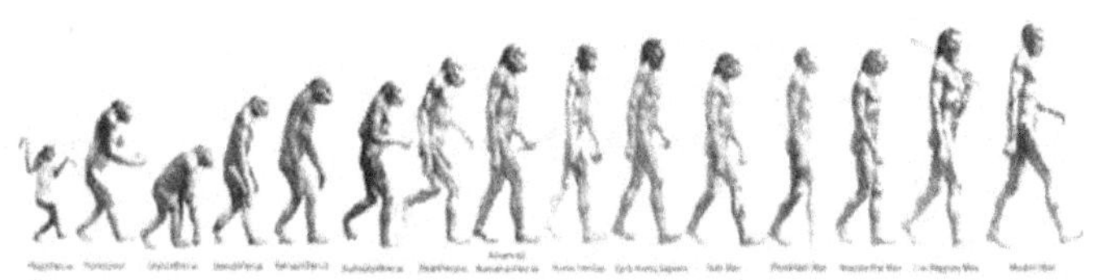

Sorceresses in Eve's village were evil and to be avoided at all costs. Lilith had several secrets, apparently, and probably would not hesitate to use them if she deemed it necessary.

Back at the cave it was early evening and Adam realized Eve had left on another exploratory venture. She had been gone since late morning. Adam hadn't given it any thought until now. *She's gone exploring again. Where to this time?* Then he remembered her statement of interest in revisiting the apple tree. *I thought she was sufficiently traumatized during our visit to the apple tree. I know I was. I don't want to go back there ever again. She may be back tonight, if not, I'll go looking for her tomorrow morning. I hope nothing has happened to her. Why does she keep disappearing? She knows I worry about her; she doesn't seem to care, though. Why? Lion is sitting here waiting patiently. I'll take him with me tomorrow if I have to look for her.*

After a time, Lilith returned clutching what must be berries in her hand.

"Come over here and sit with your back up against the tree. Get comfortable, you'll be sitting here for a while."

Eve settled under the tree. No voice came this time. *Maybe it's because I'm with Lilith. Lilith does seem to have some magic and she is a sorceress. She is evil too if she killed Adam's child but I'll take this*

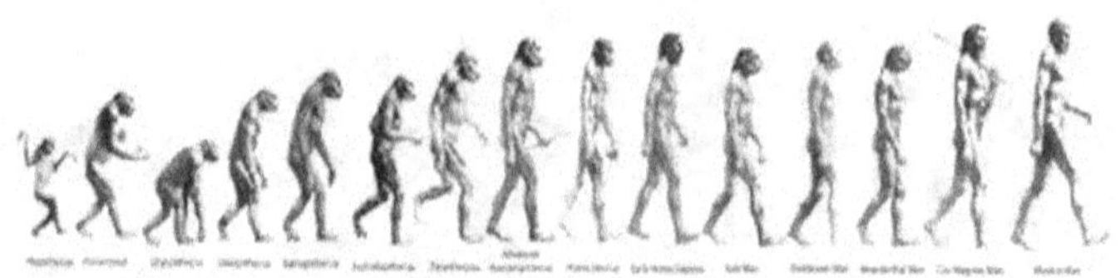

one trip with her then go back to Adam. I don't know why I trust her, I just do.

"Now, eat these berries one at a time until you start to see several colors. Then I'll tell you where we're going," Lilith said.

Eve followed Lilith's directions. The colors started after the third berry. The colors were the brightest she'd ever seen. The leaves on the trees glowed with a green she could not have described. The red apples were the brightest red she'd ever seen and they appeared larger, too.

"I see the colors. They are so bright and beautiful," Eve said.

"All right, now listen to me and I'll tell you all the details of our trip," Lilith said. She described in detail what Eve would see, who she would meet and where they would be.

Eve felt her mind expanding. She saw the shimmering sands of the desert as they approached the fort. "We don't need to stop at the gate, follow me," Lilith said.

They entered an elaborately decorated room. The draperies were a dark green and the carpet brick red. A round bed, table, chair and mirror completed the furnishings. "Now," Lilith said, "you need to dress similar to me. Here are some clothes. I'll help you into them then you'll be ready to meet the king."

The clothes were of the finest, softest material Eve had ever seen. The colors were light blue, darker blue and white. The slippers Lilith insisted she wear

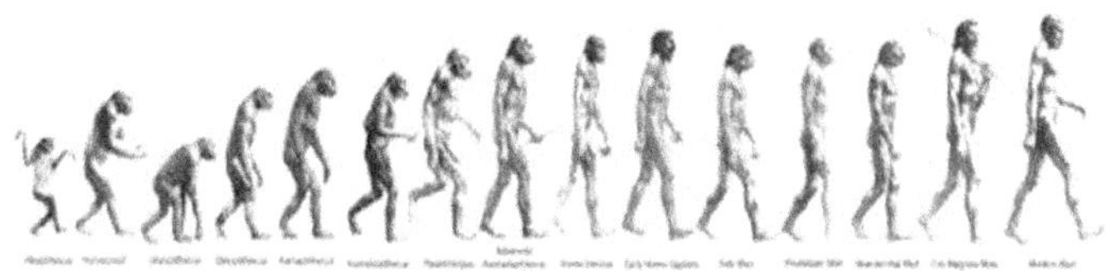

were soft, Eve felt she was almost gliding across the floor. This was becoming an exciting trip she'd never forget.

"Sit on this chair before the mirror and I'll fix your hair," Lilith said.

Eve had only seen her reflection in a pool but she was unaccustomed to the clarity of her image in the mirror, no movement or waves. Lilith continued to brush and pin her hair until it was in a style of which Eve had never dreamed.

"Now, the veil," Lilith said. "You must wear a veil covering your hair, your shoulders and your lower face. Only your eyes must be seen."

"Why must I be so covered?"

"It is our custom. If you were not dressed properly, the king could have you killed."

"Why would he go to such extreme measures?"

"Because you would be seen as brazen, an evil woman."

"Then, by all means, cover me as required by the king."

Lilith covered Eve with the white veil, carefully positioning it to cover her nose, mouth, chin and neck.

"Now you are ready to meet King Samael," Lilith announced.

They left the room and almost instantly arrived at the throne room. Eve was amazed at how quickly they moved, as if they appeared in the next

room without going through doors or walking through hallways. *Another secret,* she supposed. *This king is dressed in long sheets and he has something bright yellow on his head with sparkling stones in it. Everyone, except Lilith, is bowing in front of him. Lilith says "Lay face down on the floor." What does that mean? I'll do it though, the king might get angry.*

"Get up, let me look at you," the King said.

Eve arose without effort and faced the king.

"Hmmm," said the King. "Nice looking woman. Did you bring her for me, Lilith?"

"Indeed not, your dear highness. I brought her here to see our palace because she was aching to explore outside the Valley of Eden. She is not for you or your men; so keep your greedy hands off."

"As you request, my dear."

"I want to have a banquet in her honor tonight."

"Suite yourself. The steward will help you."

"Yes, I know, you elevated that greedy bastard to steward. Now I have to deal with him."

"Eve, we'll go meet the rest of my royal brood then you can relax in your room until the banquet."

Next, they entered a large room where several boys seemed to be fighting.

"These boys are learning the art of war, learning to kill those who come across the sea or the desert to overtake our kingdom."

"Why do you need this? Does it happen often?"

"Not too often yet. They did come across the small sea in dugout boat things. They were fierce but they couldn't scale our walls, so we were safe and they left."

"Maybe the walls will keep you safe next time."

"No, we must be ready. They may come with new ideas next time.

"Come over here. Here are my sons, Rushtl and Tutrin. They are twins, twelve summers. They are learning swordsmanship and will progress to spearing next. They will be ready to be in our army in three more summers."

"That is wonderful, I guess. Aren't you worried they'll be killed?"

"Of course, but it will be in defense of the kingdom. There is no more honorable death."

I don't understand Lilith. She's not like any of the mothers from my village who fretted about the safety of their children and mourned for their sons if something happened to them.

Lilith finished talking to her boys and their instructor and turned to Eve. "Now let's meet my daughters." As she finished speaking, we were in a room with large tapestries on the walls. These tapestries depicted hunters slaying large animals, many kinds of flowers, river scenes and people performing unbelievable feats.

"These tapestries were embroidered by girls throughout the castle and surrounding villages. They were not deemed good enough to be hung throughout

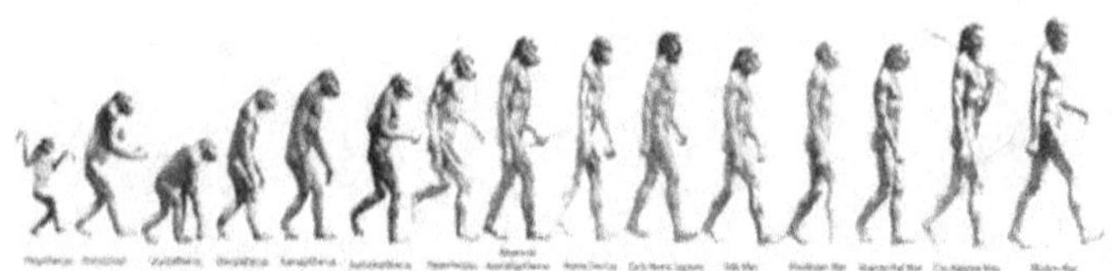

the castle so many of them are kept here for instruction purposes. Here are Mina and Bitta. Mina is nine summers and Bitta is seven summers. They are learning their stitches so as to become valuable brides for rulers who need wives to ensure good relations with neighboring kingdoms."

"You sell your daughters?" Eve asked, aghast.

"That's not it at all. Kings will come to us to insure good relations with our king. When they seem almost ready to accept the agreement, King Samael would agree that yes, I have a daughter that would make a wonderful wife for you or your son. Sometimes it's the other way around. King Samael will approach a kingdom farther away, seeking to form diplomatic relations, offering his daughter to seal an arrangement.

"It's all very complicated; nothing for you to concern yourself. It's obviously foreign to you. Now, I must talk to that fool, the steward, if we're to have a banquet tonight. You can go back to your room and rest while I attend to queenly duties."

Eve was back in her room before she realized she'd left the tapestry room. She did as she was bid and laid on the bed to enjoy the softest mattress she'd ever experienced. She really wasn't tired, just a bit overwhelmed. She did need some time to digest all she'd seen and heard. *I've never seen or heard such a culture. Not at all like my village or any of the villages around us. Boys in my village learned to hunt and fight from their fathers, not in a school.*

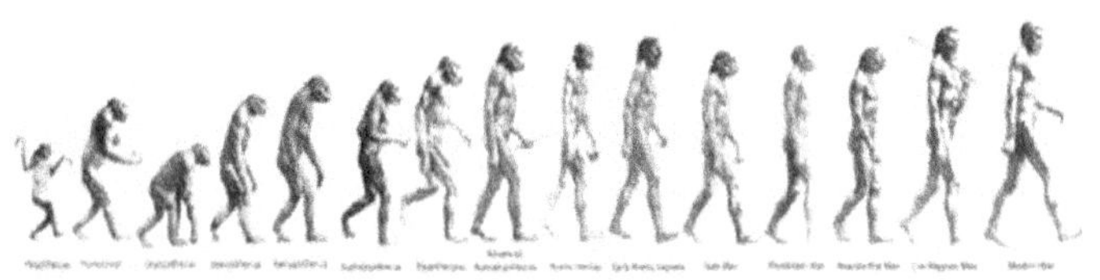

Girls usually mated within the village, sometimes outside to a man in another village but not far from home. Lilith's children look and act like their father, as if they're special and they know it. The headman's children in our village were just like the rest of us, except they had more food and had a few more rules to follow. I'd never want to live in Lilith's household, she can be frightening. With that thought, Eve drifted off to sleep.

Lilith called Eve for the banquet. They moved directly to the banquet room. Eve was given a seat at the King's table on the dais, to the left of Lilith because Lilith was on the King's right. They looked over a banquet room filled to capacity. Servers filled the cups with a red liquid, which was new to Eve. King Samael rose to speak as the room quieted quickly. We have chosen to have this banquet at Queen Lilith's request to honor our guest. "Raise your cup to welcome our guest, Eve." All the nobles stood to toast the welcome. Eve felt her face flush. While the nobles still stood, Lilith nudged Eve and whispered to her,

"Drink from your cup, now. That's how you complete the toast."

Eve was sufficiently embarrassed, her face as red as the wine. The wine was sharp but sweet. She wanted desperately to cough but she swallowed over and over until that urge passed but her eyes were watering. Either Lilith didn't notice or she decided not to comment so Eve was spared the whispered

ridiculing chide. Servants brought platters of meats including roast fowl, baked fish, slabs of spit-roasted auroch, seasoned lamb shanks, multi-colored vegetables, breads with butter from olive oil and goat milk. Eve had never seen the size of such a meal. It was more than any one person could hope to eat. Eve picked at her food, favoring the fish as this was a familiar food. She continued to drink from her wine cup and servants refilled it often during the meal. As the meal came close to finishing, King Samael introduced Lilith to give a description of their guest and to formally introduce her. Lilith rose in her regal statuesque personage to address the banquet attendees.

"Good evening all. Long live the King."

All rose with their cups held high, "Hail, Hail."

"I have brought to the banquet tonight, a most interesting and novel woman. She is from far west of the small sea. She is naive to our traditions and ceremonies, even our big events. Because of this, Eve is shy and unsure how to react to our welcoming party, even the wine is taking its toll. I met her under an apple tree in the Eden Valley and encouraged her to visit us. For her entire young life, she has had an interest in exploring. This was her chance, she couldn't resist. Please welcome, Eve.

"Come, stand by me," Lilith whispered.

When Eve stood, her head began a slow swirl. It was sickening but she managed to stand close to Lilith and smile. As the crowd stood, clapped, hooted

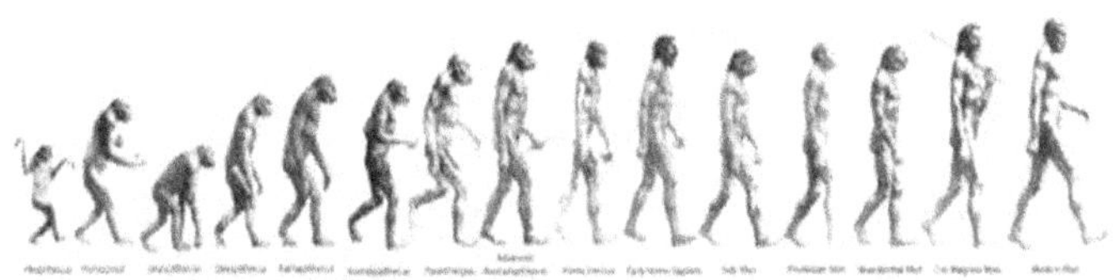

and banged their cups in a riotous clamor, Lilith could tell Eve was having trouble standing. She helped Eve stand as she waved to quiet the crowd.

"Say something," Lilith whispered in Eve's ear.

"Thank you everyone for the welcome. I am honored."

"That's enough," Lilith whispered.

"Thank you all again. Long live the King. Please join us for our last course," Lilith said.

She helped Eve return to her seat and bent to talk to Eve. "You should probably go to your room. You look unwell. I'll call two ladies to help you."

Both ladies arrived almost instantly behind her chair, assisting her to rise as they effortlessly helped her leave the dais and walk through the door behind a curtain, unobserved by the banquet attendees. The King asked Lilith about Eve and she informed him Eve had drunk too much wine too fast.

Eve arrived in her room and was immediately undressed and laid on the bed, asleep almost before she was placed and covered. When the evening closed, Lilith entered Eve's room and saw she was sleeping soundly. *That's excellent. This will be easy. I'll plant her direction back to the Valley of Eden in her mind and she will wake there. She will remember some things but not all, especially not the banquet. Now, on your way, Eve,* Lilith thought.

Eve had not reappeared in the evening hours. Adam woke and found she still had not returned.

Now, I have to look for her again. When will that woman finally understand I worry about her and I want her to stay with me? That she might go or actually went to investigate that apple tree scares me more than she knows. I thought she knew going near that tree is dangerous. The voice said it was forbidden. Why doesn't she accept that and stay away from it? If she tried to go near it or pick some apples, she could be in real trouble. I'll take lion and head in that direction, calling for her. Calling for her worked last time. We need to have another discussion about her leaving for such long adventures. They are plain worrisome.

Chapter 11
Eve is Distraught

After looking under trees and bushes and repeatedly calling her name, Adam found Eve sitting under the apple tree asleep. He tried to awaken her with no result so he hoisted her over his shoulder and lion picked up the basket in his mouth by its handle and they began their trek back to the cave. Though Adam was glad to find Eve, he could feel anger growing too. *Why does she do this? Is she trying to hurt me? What am I doing wrong that makes her leave on these trips? How can I make her understand how much I worry about her? Doesn't she care? If she doesn't care, why not? She claims she wants to be my mate for life but then she goes off like this; why?*

They arrived back to the cave by midafternoon. Eve was still asleep. Adam laid her on her sleeping mat and lion set the basket in a corner beside the cave mouth. Eve finally awoke and she promptly called Adam.

"Adam, I just woke up. How did I get home?"

"Eve, I carried you home. You were asleep under the apple tree. How did you get so close to the tree and why did you go there?"

"Adam, I'll try to explain the whole trip if you'll listen. Don't fire questions at me, if you listen to my story, your questions will be answered. Some parts of the story are my questions to you."

"Me? What in this story involves me?"

"Just wait. Let me get some water hot for tea then we'll talk."

Eve set the bowls of hot tea on the mat and they both sat cross-legged to sip the hot tea.

"Now, will you please tell me what you've been up to," Adam said.

"I will, if you promise to not be angry with me," Eve replied.

"I will try but my patience is getting thin."

"All right, they're likely to get thinner before I'm finished. Mine are already frayed. I'll begin by bringing up a name you seem to have 'forgotten'."

"And that is what?" Adam said innocently, which infuriated Eve more.

"Lilith," Eve said, watching Adam's face change from feigned innocence to pain then almost panic.

"What has she got to do with your exploration at the tree?"

"Actually, everything. She is the reason I was able to approach the tree and sit against it without the voice troubling me."

"How could she do that?"

"Lilith is a sorceress, or didn't you know? Maybe you didn't take time to get to know her before you mated with her and pledged to keep her as your mate for life."

Adam was thunderstruck. *What is she talking about? How did she meet Lilith? What was Lilith doing in the garden? Lilith was or is a sorceress?* "I don't know what you're talking about, Eve. Yes, I once met Lilith when I arrived in the Valley but she meant nothing to me."

"Oh, Adam, stop pretending. You know there was more to it than that. She described your mating with her. It certainly sounded passionate. She said she birthed your child but it was so ugly and deformed she killed it."

"Oh, Eve, that's all lies. Please believe me."

"It's hard for me to believe you now after your reaction. Why didn't you tell me about Lilith? You never mentioned her. You never told me you'd pledged to mate with another woman. You promised to mate with me for life. How many other women

113

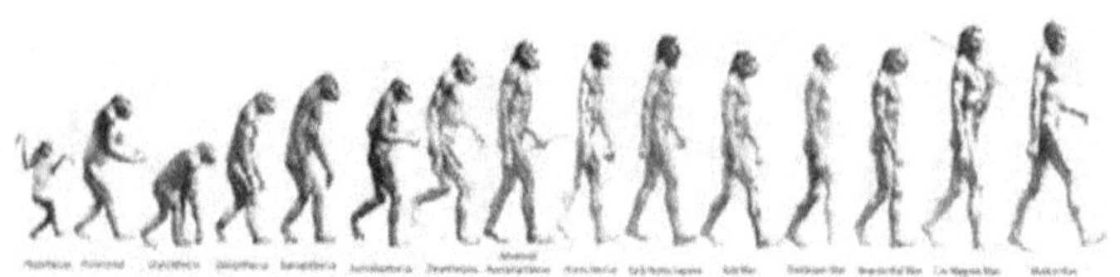

have you pledged to mate for life? I'm forced to question your pledge to me, now."

Adam could feel Eve's eyes boring into his soul. *How and where will this end? It has to end. I can't take it. If I lose Eve, it is the last of me. I need her.* "Please, Eve, give me a chance to explain. You are too distraught to listen to reason."

"Adam, I'm capable of listening, if the explanation makes sense. Right now, I'm not sure what you could say that would explain Lilith and her having your child after you pledged to mate with her for life."

"All right, I can't explain it. It's over and Lilith left."

"She definitely left. She mated with a king," Eve said, hotly.

"Is that what she told you? Don't believe her."

"I saw them, Adam. I met her children and saw their castle. It was beautiful."

"How did you visit the castle? Is it somewhere near?"

"No, Adam. It is not near, across a small sea, she said. Lilith gave me some special berries to eat and I found myself in her castle."

"That's all very strange. It sounds like she was messing with your mind."

"On the contrary, Adam. She knows how to travel without any help. It was amazing; after all, she is a sorceress."

"Don't be fooled, Eve. Sorceresses are evil and can perform horrible deeds, also tell lies and cause harm to others."

"Adam, are you still maintaining she lied about you and her? Why would she lie?"

"Yes, I am maintaining that. I beg you not to trust her."

"All right. Let's say, I believe you. Will I hear from some other woman how you mated with her and pledged to mate with her for life?"

"No, absolutely not. There is no other woman. Please believe me."

"I want to believe you, Adam, but you must understand what a shock Lilith was to me."

"Eve, yes, I'm sure Lilith shocked you. Calm down. You are my life mate and no one else can claim that right."

"We'll leave that matter for now. We don't seem to be completely solving the problem. Time will tell, I guess."

"Oh, Eve. I ask that you give me a chance to prove how much I value you."

"As I said, time will tell."

I think that means she's giving me another chance. I know there's nothing else she could find or hear. She hasn't forgiven and I know she won't forget. I had better give her more attention without smothering her. She'll take offense at too much attention.

Eve picked up the basket lion had carried back from the tree. She retrieved the big red apples and took a large bite of the apple she held. It was the sweetest, juiciest fruit she'd ever eaten. "Here, Adam, you must try this it is the best fruit I've ever tasted."

"Where did you find it?" Adam asked.

"On the way to my journey," Eve evaded.

"After you met Lilith?"

"No, before I met her," Eve lied.

"All right, I'll try it"

Adam took the apple Eve handed him and bit into it. It indeed was beyond anything he had ever eaten. They finished the apples then, feeling sleepy, they retired to their sleeping mats.

Chapter 12
Major Upheaval

The day began as any other. Adam returned to his etchings and Eve resolved to weave new sitting mats. Adam was displeased with his etching tool and opted to make another from a special stone nearby. Eve chose leaves from a stack she had collected for eventual weaving.

Eve noticed the light was fading but was surprised as it was nearing midday. *Why is the light fading so fast? I can hear a distance rumble. It sounds like thunder. I used to hear it in the village but never here. I wonder what Adam thinks it is.* Before she finished the thought, Adam came into the cave at a run and leap.

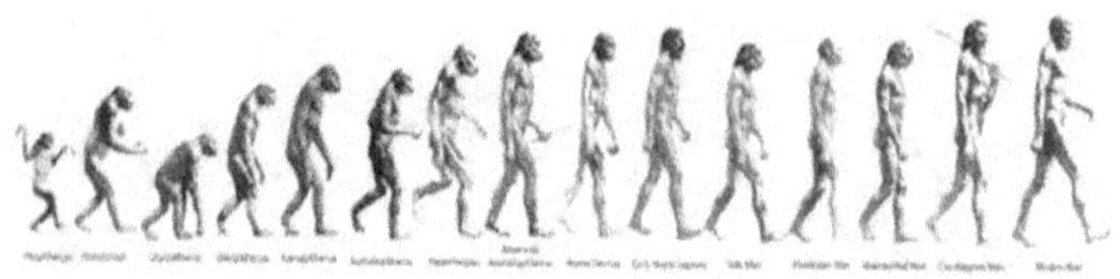

"Eve, move everything further back into the cave, quick, a dreadful storm is coming."

"What, here?"

"Yes, the clouds are darker than I've ever seen them. They look horrible, frightening."

"Why is this happening, Adam? It's never stormed here."

"No, not since I've been here either. We just have to take shelter, away from the cave mouth."

"Should we get lion and tiger and move them in with us?"

"No, there isn't time. The storm is upon us."

As he finished speaking, bright lightening flashed in front of the cave followed by a massive roll of thunder and a loud voice, which Adam heard, saying: "**BECAUSE YOU HAVE LISTENED TO THE VOICE OF YOUR WIFE AND HAVE EATEN OF THE TREE FROM WHICH I COMMANDED YOU NOT TO EAT, CURSED IS THE GROUND BECAUSE OF YOU; THROUGH TOIL YOU WILL EAT OF IT ALL THE DAYS OF YOUR LIFE.**"[8]

At the same time, Eve heard, "**I WILL SHARPLY INCREASE YOUR PAIN IN CHILDBIRTH; IN PAIN YOU WILL BRING FORTH CHILDREN. YOU WILL DESIRE YOUR HUSBAND, AND HE WILL RULE OVER YOU.**"[8]

These words struck fear in their hearts and minds. They grasped one another for strength and

understanding of this horrifying event. The rain fell in torrents; the wind blew in a terrifying, whirling, loud roar. Trees snapped, limbs hurled and bushes were stripped of their leaves. Such a storm had never been witnessed by either of them. Finally, the storm abated and calm returned. Eve and Adam peered out of the cave to see what was left of their world. Adam noted the fallen trees. Eve noted the nut and berry bushes had been stripped of leaves and fruit. Nothing remained of their food supply, only what they had in their store in the cave.

As Eve and Adam took stock of their situation, the earth started to shake as a new and terrifying noise overtook them. Eve quickly emptied their store of nuts and berries into a satchel while Adam ran to the nearby spring to fill the water satchel. The shaking and roaring grew more intense. Dust and small stones fell from the cave ceiling.

"We need to get away from the cave now," shouted Adam above the noise of falling rock and the roar of the splitting earth. He grabbed Eve's hand, pulling her out of the cave.

"No, wait," she said, "I want to bring the mats."

"No, there is no time. We need to get out of here now," shouted Adam.

"What about lion and tiger?" Eve shouted over the growing rumble.

"Don't worry about them. Come on," Adam shouted, grasping Eve's arm.

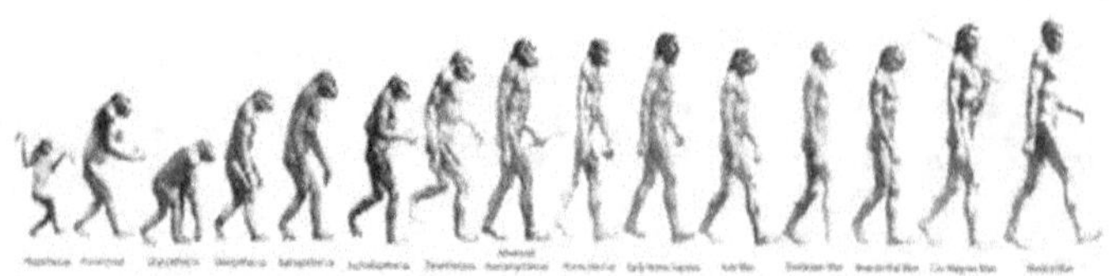

They no sooner hit the ground running than large chunks of rock fell from the cave as it began to collapse. Eve and Adam continued to run, avoiding large tree trunks, which had fallen during the storm. They were running north, the path that had fewer obstructions. As they ran, they saw more trees fall and the ground continued to shake and roll. They'd run for nearly an hour when they came upon a fissure in the earth. They stopped short.

"What happened here?" Eve shouted.

"The earth is cracked open. We need to be careful and stop running. If we fall into a crack this big while we're running, we'll never get out. It's hot. Look, it's steaming. We need to watch for these cracks. Even small ones could hurt us."

"I never realized a crack could happen. I'll be careful."

"The roar is lessened now. We should slow down. We're away from the cave and large trees. We just have to watch for cracks. Those could hurt us."

"Yes, let's walk until sunset then stop for the night, I want to stop now to eat some food and drink some water. I'm really thirsty."

"I am too. Did you bring the fire starting stones?"

"Yes, they're in the food satchel. I didn't bring any bowls, though. I didn't have time."

"You did fine. We can eat the fruit and nuts using our hands. You are safe. That's all that matters."

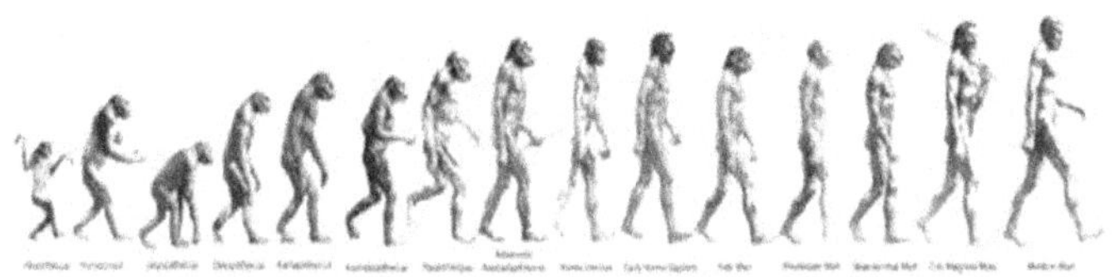

"Yes, you are safe, too. That is important to me. Did you bring your etching tool and knife?"

"Yes, I grabbed it on the way out of the cave."

"Then we have everything we need. I hope lion and tiger are safe."

"I'm sure they are. They are equipped to live on their own in the forest or in and out of the Valley. They'll be fine," Adam said, as much to assure himself as Eve.

They continued their path through the Valley, past uprooted trees, damaged bushes and plants. Nothing withstood the devastation. There was no more food in the Valley. They did not pass a single bush with berries or nuts. The devastation was total, several smaller caves had collapsed and the water from the springs stank. The water smelled of rotten eggs, unfit to drink. Of course, they were unaware of why this had happened but, far in the future, it would become known. Their descendants would unravel many secrets and laws concerning the earth.

As the sun was setting as a large, red ball on the western horizon, Eve and Adam decided to stop for the night. There was no cover and Eve had not had time to grab the sleeping mats so they looked around for soft, grassy spots on which to rest.

"This looks like a good resting place," Adam said.

"Yes," Eve said. "I am so tired. I was so frightened I feared we would die," Eve said.

"Yes, I was too. We would have been killed if we'd stayed in the cave," said Adam.

"Let's try to forget about it now so we can get a good night's sleep."

"It will be hard to forget."

"No, I meant let's not talk about it now. Let's talk about where we might be going."

"That is a big question, 'Where might we be going?'"

"Yes, that's what I'm wondering."

As they ate their meager meal, they talked of what might be waiting for them if they kept on the trail heading north.

"We'll eventually leave the Valley, I think," Adam said.

"Are we supposed to leave the Valley?"

"It seems that way. It seems as though it had something to do with eating those apples."

"I don't think so. That was just a coincidence."

"Nah, did you hear that voice? It might have been the sorceress at work."

"Lilith? I don't think so. She isn't associated with the voice. I think the voice is a very big, powerful king; a man."

"The first time we heard Him, He said I am your Lord God, remember?"

"I know but who is this Lord God? We only heard His Voice, we haven't seen Him."

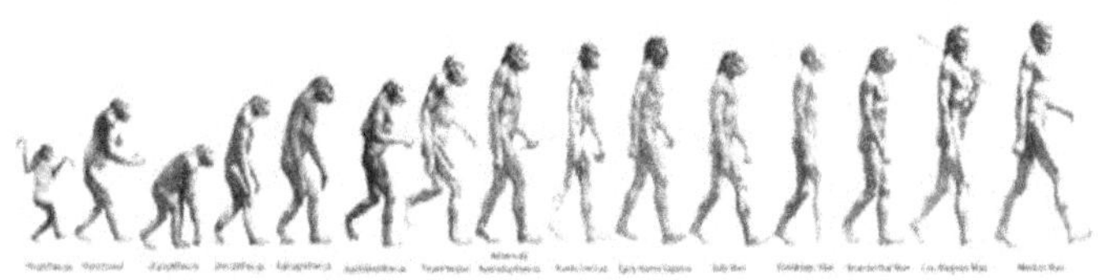

"No, if He is a big, powerful king, we may not. We are just little beings. No match for Him. If we do what He says and wants, we'll be all right."

"How do we know what He wants?"

"We have to listen to the Voice. He'll tell us and we have to obey."

"All right, we'll do as He says."

With this, they settled down for the night. Eve snuggled closer to Adam than when they'd first shared a mat. It was reassuring to be in Adam's arms. She was glad he was along on this adventure. It was sure to be a life changing experience. She felt warm and safe in his arms. *Why do I feel safe in his arms? I would be safe with or without him. I was safe when I ran from my village and left the volcanoes behind. I don't really need him; he is just someone to be with. I really don't want to tell him every time I want to explore. He says he worries about me. Why? Nothing will happen to me. I can take care of myself. He doesn't want to accept that argument.*

They hiked for three more suns, passed more fissures and a steaming pit where the earth had sunk, leaving a sinkhole larger than their cave.

"What made this hole?" Eve asked.

"I think it happened during the earthquake," Adam said.

Then, just as he finished speaking, the earth began to shake again and the low rumble began. They didn't run this time because they weren't near

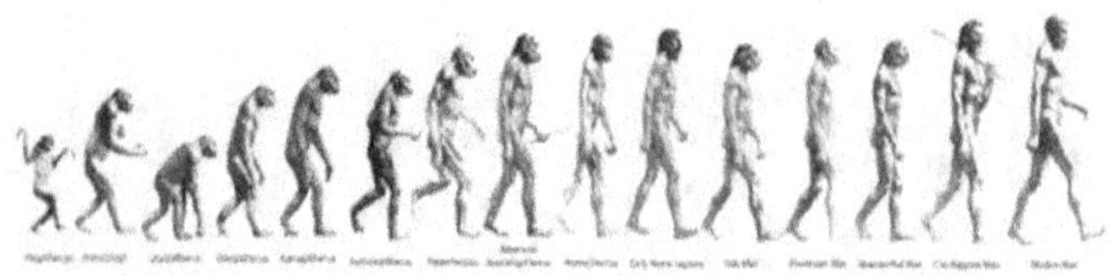

anything that would fall on them. All the trees had already fallen.

"Another earthquake," Adam said.

"Yes," Eve said, "the earth is shaking and that roar is the same."

"Not as bad and not as loud, this time," Adam said, as they stood still for several minutes.

"That's good. Now, let's keep moving north."

"We need not be in such a hurry," Adam said.

"I want to see what's beyond this catastrophe."

Looking back, Adam saw clouds of black smoke engulfing the land.

"Yes, we must keep moving. There is a large cloud of smoke behind us. The Valley is burning."

"How did a fire start?"

"It might have been a lightning strike during the thunderstorm. It was a violent storm."

"I thought so much rain would have put out a fire."

"It might have smoldered for days before coming alive again. Fires do that sometimes, you know."

"Yes, I know, like when I tried to burn bushes that were too green."

"Yes, exactly. We'll keep moving north. We're well ahead of it."

They walked a little faster for the rest of the day. The sun had set and darkness was falling fast.

"We should probably stop for the night." Eve said.

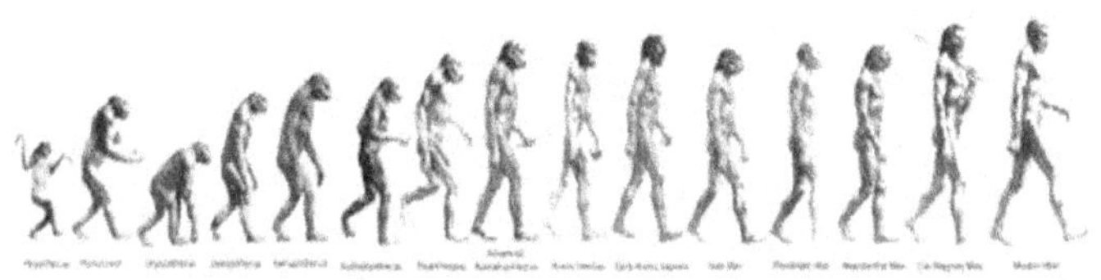

"We can stop but the fire won't," Adam said.

"True, but the ground is still wet as are the fallen trees. It hasn't had time to dry out."

"You are right, Eve. We should stop here. Listen. Do you hear water running, like a stream or small river?"

"Yes, I do. We'll have to explore that. Maybe it has fish and you could spear one or I could learn to spear one."

"I'll get up at first light and look for the stream."

Eve awoke at first light, Adam was sleeping. *I will get up and look for the stream then I'll call Adam. He's still asleep and I won't wake him. I want to be the first to see the stream.* She walked quietly away from their sleeping place. She continued walking toward the sound of running water. As she came to the top of a knoll, there it was, the water shimmered in the sunlight. She strolled down the hill to the water's edge. Eve looked into the water for several minutes, watching the fish and other animals crawling along the streambed.

"Admiring yourself while looking in the water?" a voice said behind her. It startled her, though she recognized the voice.

"Adam, you shouldn't go around startling me," Eve admonished him, with a smile.

"Did you see any fish?"

"Yes, lots of them, some of the big ones were trying to eat the smaller ones."

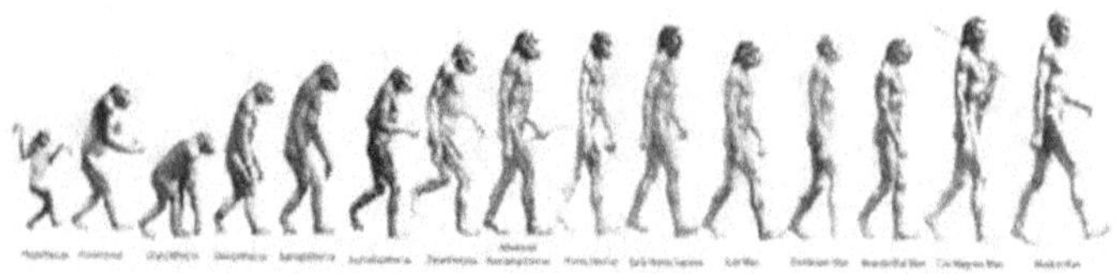

"Yes, that's how they live."

"What are the little flat things crawling on the bottom?"

"They are crabs."

"Are they good to eat?"

"Yes, but you have to catch them at night. They are too fast now and they'll head for dark places."

"I'd like to try some."

"I'll try to find a stick to whittle into a spear point then I'll get us a fish."

"I'll watch you."

"You better get a fire started. The wood is probably wet."

"The ground seems drier, as if it didn't rain so hard here."

Adam located a stick the appropriate length and set about carving the stick to a sharp point. Satisfied, he walked to the stream and peered over the edge. He watched for a larger fish to approach. He watched for long enough for Eve to start the fire and come back to watch him. Suddenly, he spied a large fish swimming in for the kill of a slightly smaller fish. As fast as lightning, he drove his spear into the fish. So strong, he actually impaled the fish to the streambed. Adam carefully moved the stick around. *I have to be careful to keep the fish on the stick; not to let it get away.* Keeping the point in the bottom mud, he flung the stick toward land in a rapid, fluid motion. The fish landed on the bank far enough away so it could not flop back into the water. He

knelt to clean the fish. Then it struck him; he'd seen this big fish eat a smaller one that wasn't so small. He opened the gut and retrieved the swallowed fish. It was still alive. He now had two fish with one spear. He couldn't wait to tell Eve.

When Adam arrived at the fire, Eve was waiting. She had salvaged a few leaves in which to wrap the fish for cooking but Adam brought two fish.

"I thought you were only going to spear one fish."

"I only speared one fish." Adam stated.

"But you have two fish. One is only slightly smaller than the big fish."

"Let's put them on the fire and I will tell you the story."

Eve wrapped both fish in the leaves, including the last of her berries in the lunch packet. Cooking them together, she knew, would take longer for them to cook. She didn't care; she wanted to hear Adam's fish story. Eve sat by Adam and looked up at him, expectantly.

"Now, I'm ready to hear your story."

"Where should I begin?" Adam teased.

"At the beginning," Eve suggested.

"All right. First there was a thunderstorm..." Adam continued to tease.

"Not there, at the stream," she laughed.

"Oh, at the stream. All right it's a long story so get comfortable,"

Adam began the story. He lengthened it but kept it moving to keep her attention, embellishing it at times. He was a practiced storyteller. During his life in his village, he had entertained many small children with his hunting stories. Obviously, Eve wanted to be entertained so he kept her waiting for the killing spear. After the story, Eve convulsed with laughter. He'd never heard her laugh that way before. It was music to his ears. *So beautiful to hear her laugh again after these trying times.*

Eve recovered quickly when she remembered the cooking fish. "Oh, I almost forgot the fish. We should be ready to eat." Checking the fish, she found it was, indeed, ready to eat. Using two sticks, she lifted it off the fire and set it on a stone to cool, slightly. Then again, using the sticks, she unwrapped the fish. *We should eat the smaller one tonight and save the larger one for future meals.*

"Adam, come over to the stone and pick out some fish."

"It smells delicious. Are we just eating the smaller one?"

"Yes, the big one will be useful for travelling north. We don't know how much food will be available. Before we move farther north, I want to climb the hill over there to see what lies ahead."

"I'll go there tomorrow morning."

"No, I want to go."

"Can't we both go? You should stay here and pack the food for travel."

"No, Adam. I want to go and I will go. You can fill the water satchel and prepare for the hike." *I shouldn't have mentioned it to him. I'll get up early, climb the hill and be back before he wakes. He wants me to do chores while he explores. I don't want to be told what to do. I'll pack the food when I get back.*

As dawn was breaking, Eve rose to climb the hill. Taking a brief break from climbing, she turned to face what was left of the Valley of Eden. In the distance, she thought she saw a large being holding a flaming sword aloft. She was sure it was in the direction of the apple tree. *The sorceress at work,* she thought and continued to climb. The sun was rising when she reached the top of the hill. She could see for miles in all directions. Eve chose not to look back; she didn't want to see the destruction of the Valley. She had climbed the hill to look north. Looking north, she saw nearby green rolling landscape becoming brown desert as far as she could see. That was the direction they would take. She hurried down the hill and back to camp.

Adam arose about the time Eve returned to camp.

"I went to the top of the hill. There is green rolling land for a distance then only desert," Eve said.

"This stream must be the end of the Valley. We must be sure the water satchels are full. Maybe we should spear another fish to take for food?" said Adam, thinking aloud.

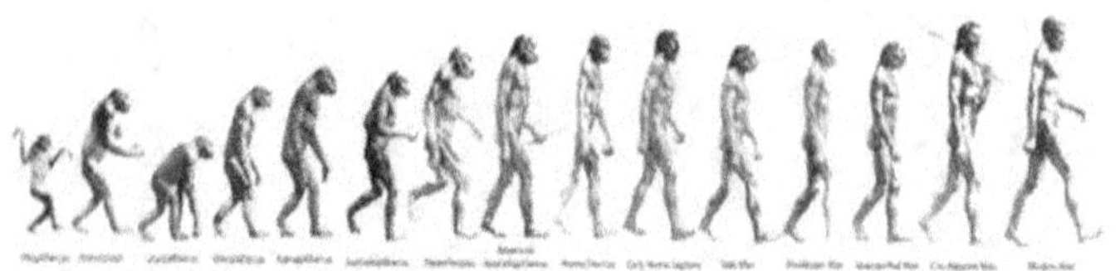

"That would probably mean we'd have to spend another night here. By the time you catch and clean the fish, I cook it and it cools for packing, we will have spent the better part of the day. Then we can start early tomorrow morning."

"That's a good suggestion, Eve. I'd like to climb the hill too, to see what's beyond. Would you like to come along?"

"No, Adam, I've already been there. See if you can find anything useful."

I want to weave some coverings for us. The desert will be intensely hot. I'll use leaves from the downed fig tree and palm tree. I can make coverings for our bodies and heads similar to the ones Mother made for Father and my brothers in the village. With these large leaves, it won't take long. Eve set to work collecting leaves as Adam made a new stick for spearing. She also prepared the branches for a cooking fire. The earth shook from time to time during the day but neither Eve nor Adam was alarmed now, because the shaking seemed better described as shivering. Both thought it was only a matter of time until the earth settled down. They did not realize that would only happen when they had completely left the Valley of Eden.

The sun was midpoint in the sky when Adam returned with a fish ready to cook. Eve had completed Adam's body and head covering and started the cooking fire. She took the fish from Adam, wrapped it in leaves and placed it on a stone

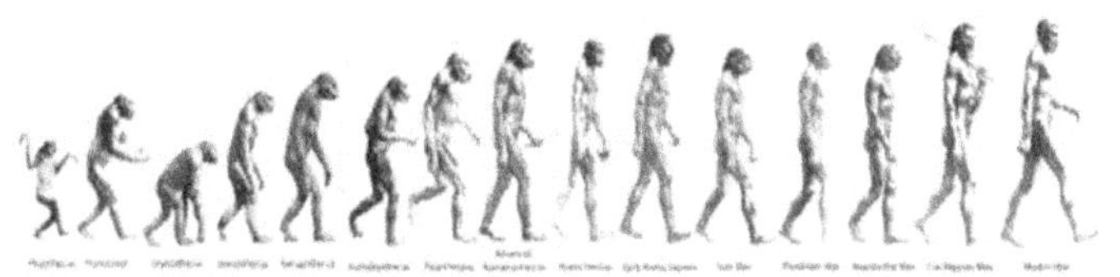

in the fire pit. She was ready to begin weaving her coverings.

"I'll climb the hill now and return before dark. We can compare what I've seen to what you saw and, maybe, develop a plan for exploring what is beyond," Adam said.

"That's a good idea, Adam. Be sure to look in all directions." Eve wondered *will Adam see the large being with the sword or was it my imagination; or, even more difficult to understand, was it meant only for me to see.*

Adam went off to explore the surrounding area and try to map a track, in his mind, of the direction they should take, noting any landmarks. He had made the trip from his village to the Valley, across mostly desert. He knew the dangers, the possibility of not having enough water or being able to find enough food. Now there would be two of them needing food, water and shelter from the sun when it reached its's zenith. *I don't think Eve realizes what we will encounter in the desert. How will she react? How can I keep her from wandering off on her own?*

Eve went back to weaving as she watched the fish cook. When she ascertained it was done, she removed the fish from the stone in the fire pit, using two strong sticks then set it on the ground on several large leaves to cool for packing. *Will Adam see the being with the flaming sword? What will he think? I didn't tell him about it because I wanted to hear what*

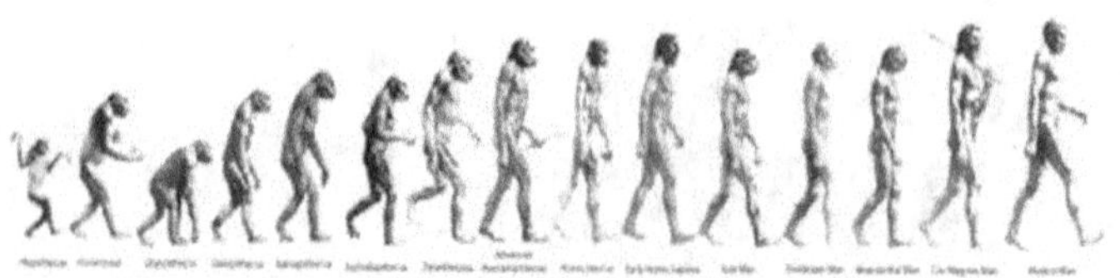

he saw and thinks. We definitely should move on; it's strange here now. We need to get as far away from this Valley as we can. I don't like it here anymore; everything that was pleasant is gone. I wonder how big the desert is. Adam knows about deserts, he can lead this exploration, with my help, of course. He doesn't know much about food preparation or packing. I'd better finish these coverings for us. We'll burn in the hot desert sun. We might meet other hominids like us. We don't want to be nude.

Adam arrived back to their camp as the sun reached the western horizon.

"You were gone much longer than I expected," Eve said in greeting.

"Yes, I saw the most interesting sight when I turned toward the Valley. It was an extremely tall being, holding a flaming sword. I had to go toward it to find out what it was. It said it was guarding the Valley so no one could enter. I turned around and tried to run away but I couldn't move. Then the thing with the sword started toward me. It said, '**Be gone from this Valley. You shall never enter it again, nor will your descendants. You are banished from here. Now go.**' I ran most of the way back to the hill. I climbed to the top and saw the green hills and desert beyond. You are right. That is the path we will take."

"Adam, what was the being? Do you think it was the work of the sorceress?"

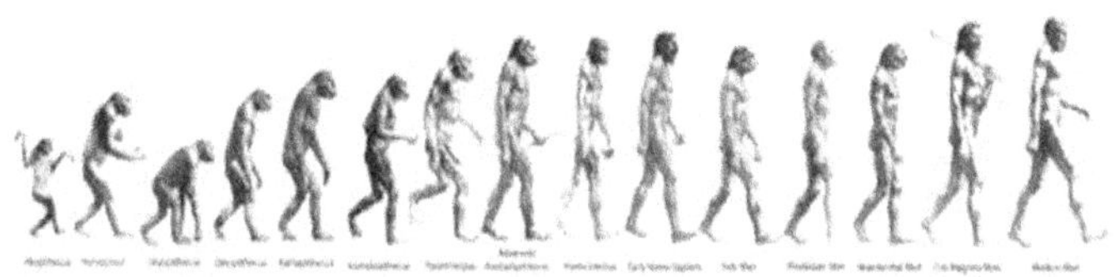

"No, this being was real, I think. I don't really know but I wouldn't go back there."

"I agree. It sounds dangerous. We need to move further north. We should leave this afternoon."

"I'd like to stay here one more night and leave at first light tomorrow morning."

"No, I think we should go now and sleep tonight in the green hills beyond the stream. The sooner we leave this cursed Valley, the better and safer for us. We are still in the Valley, albeit on the edge. If we are banished by a larger being than us, we better leave before more bad things happen."

"What more could happen? I say we stay the night." As Adam finished his retort, the ground began to shake and shiver in earnest, this time.

"No, that's another warning, let's go."

"All right, I'll fill the water satchels at the stream and we can leave."

Eve nodded in agreement and set to packing the food satchel. *That shake finally convinced him. I know we need to move on, no more delays.* When Adam returned, Eve presented him with a covering and hat made of leaves. She helped him into it and donned her own covering woven of the same material.

"This is ridiculous, Eve. We don't need coverings yet."

"Yes we do. We can't go out of the garden like this. The sun could burn us and we might meet other people like us, wearing skins and other

coverings. They might attack us, thinking we're animals."

"All right but I don't agree."

"Let's be off. We need to find a place to shelter in those hills beyond the stream. I wonder if there is a cave in the hills."

"That's certainly something we'll look for."

They crossed the stream and entered the rolling hills. Each hill seemed a little less steep than the one before. They searched for any cave-like opening in the hills. The sun was approaching the western horizon when Eve spotted a shelf-like ledge with rocks leading to it.

"Let's look at this opening. It looks like a small cave. We need to find out if it's empty."

"We'll know pretty quickly if it's empty. It is really small."

Eve and Adam approached the small indentation in the hill with caution. Eve went in the small cave and emitted a blood-cuddling scream.

"What is it?" Adam said, as he came running up to Eve.

"We can't stay here, there's a family of snakes in here—a female and dozens and dozens of little ones."

"All right. Let's move on then. It will be dark soon."

They moved over the next few hills until they found a depression in a hill. It was covered with grass but had somewhat of a covering of hillside.

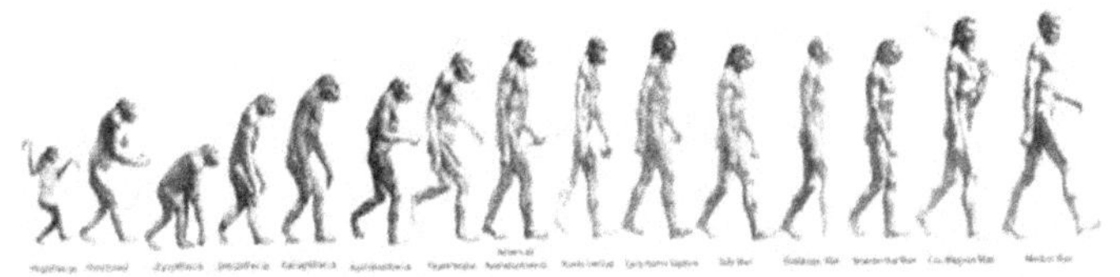

"This will have to do, Eve. It's getting too dark to go farther. We wouldn't be able to see if there were occupants in a cave now."

"I agree. Let's settle here for the night."

Eve and Adam rose with the light of dawn and ate a meager meal of cooked fish. They adjusted the coverings, put their hats on and left the camp. They needed no fire, which was fortunate for there was nothing to fuel it; no bushes or logs. They knew this day's trek would take them across the hills and onto the desert. The sun was a little past its zenith when they started to cross a sunbaked area leading to the desert.

"This looks like it used to be grass but now it's dead," Eve said.

"Yes, the desert steals the water out of the ground and the air in the summertime. That's just like it was in my village, near the desert. It will come back to life again next year in the rainy season," Adam said.

"That's so unlike my village on the mountainside. The grass stays green until the winter snows then the snow melts and the grass turns green almost immediately; and the mountainside is covered in flowers of many colors."

"That sounds beautiful but this is the desert and things work differently here."

They continued to walk north, not stepping on the stones if they could help it. The stones were hot and their feet were bare. They had only walked on

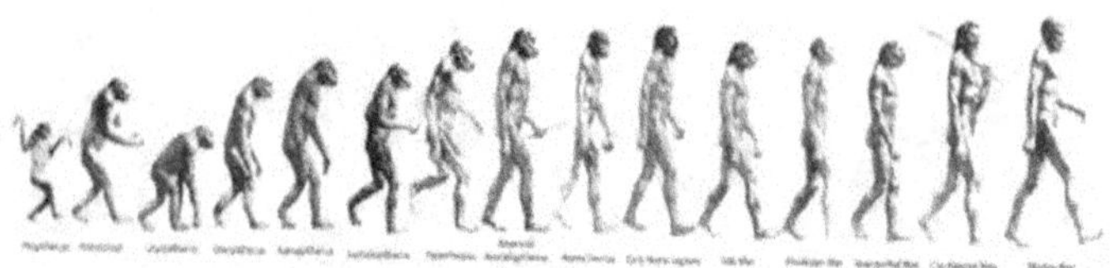

grass until now. Eve only knew how to make foot coverings from animal hides and hides were not available or needed in the Valley. *I don't think foot coverings made of leaves would be useful. I think, though, if we were near a forest, I could make foot coverings from tree bark and hold them on with leaves woven to encase the foot. There is not likely to be a forest in the desert. I don't want to tell Adam about my idea. He'll laugh at me and tell me I should have stayed in the mountains. I hate that coming from Adam. Why does he say such hurtful things? Maybe he doesn't know or maybe he doesn't care. He's a man and he knows better. Not so, I know a lot about the things I grew up with and the things needed to keep us going. I'd like to watch him cook a fish or weave a mat. He just couldn't do it. I could learn to spear a fish, though...*

"What are you thinking about, Eve?" Adam asked, interrupting her thoughts.

"Oh, nothing much. Just concentrating on not stepping on the hot stones."

"We'll be on the desert tomorrow and the sand will be hot on our feet, really hot."

"We should begin looking to find a place to rest for the night."

"Yes, we'll probably have to bed down anywhere. Just move some stones to clear a patch of ground for sleeping."

"It will be hot sleeping on the ground."

"True, but we don't have a choice."

"The sun will be setting soon. We should start setting a camping spot soon."

"Let's stop here. I need a drink of water before we start moving stones. How about you?"

Eve reached for the water satchel and drank greedily.

"Slow down," Adam said, "we have to make it last until we find an oasis. Where ever that will be."

"I am. I haven't been nipping at the water satchel like you have been all day," Eve complained. She was hot, tired and not ready to verbally parry with Adam.

"Well, what put you in such a mood?"

"I'm tired, hot and hungry. I need to rest, eat and sleep. Is that good enough?"

"Let's leave it at that," Adam said, as he started to pick up the larger stones to form a wall around their sleeping site. The wall would be three to four feet high and give them a modicum of shelter.

Eve picked up the smaller stones and threw them outside the wall Adam was building to make as smooth a sleeping area as possible. When all was finished, they sat down to eat then quickly bedded down for the night.

Eve and Adam arose in haste the next morning, finally escaping a less than comfortable sleeping arrangement. They ate, loaded their satchels on their backs and headed toward the desert. It was late morning when they reached the edge of the desert. The sand was hot beneath their feet. They

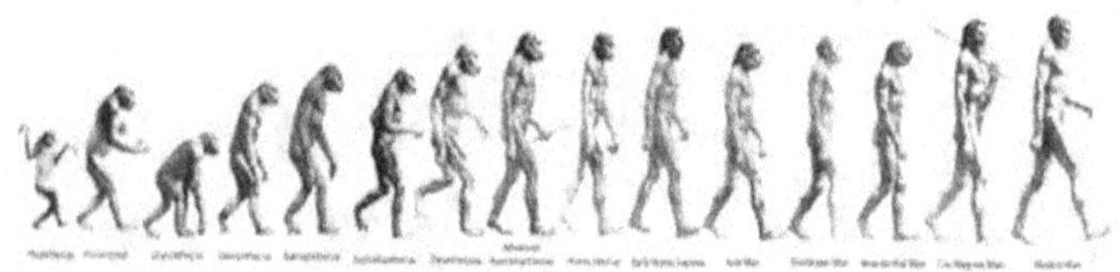

continued to walk until Adam said, "We had best find a rock or something to provide a bit of shade where we can sit out this hottest time."

"That would be welcome. Is that how you desert folk handle this heat?" Eve asked.

"Yes, I had to do that every day on my way to the Valley."

As they trudged on, Adam located a large rock shelf with a sufficient overhang. "Let's head for that rock shelf over there," he said, pointing.

"All right but if it is already occupied we can head for that large rock beyond, over there," Eve pointed, "it has a shadow too."

Adam walked to the overhanging shelf and turned around almost instantly. "Two large black snakes and a lot of desert scorpions are there. We'll check out the rock you saw."

Eve walked to the rock as Adam caught up with her. "Be careful now. You don't know what might be there," Adam warned.

"There's nothing here. I'm going to sit in the shade of this rock for a while," Eve said.

"All right, the shade won't last long but we can sit for a few minutes."

"I need a drink," Eve said.

"There isn't much left. I hope we see an oasis soon."

"I won't drink too much, just enough to moisten my mouth and throat."

"That will work. I need a little, too."

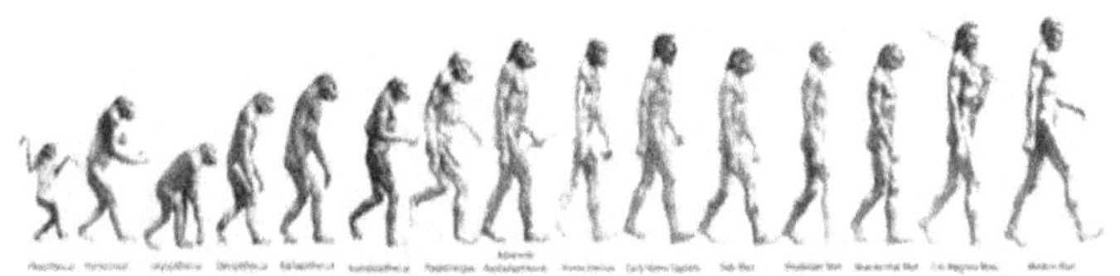

The shade had lessened almost completely when they rose to push on. "We have to keep moving to find a suitable place to lie down for the night. It has to be better than last night," Adam said.

"Yes, I agree. I thought I got the stones out of the way but it wasn't good enough."

"You did fine. There's only so much one can do. Keep an eye out for a palm tree."

"Yes, an oasis is what we need."

They walked on until the sun was getting low in the west when Eve spotted a tall tree on the northern horizon. "Over there, look, a tree," Eve said, pointing.

"That's exactly what we need, Eve."

They picked up their pace toward what they hoped was an oasis. As the sun was setting, they arrived at the tree and a small watering hole.

"It's small but it will work," Adam said.

"Yes," Eve said, "and the sand is cooler here. A good place to spend the night."

"I'll taste the water and see if it's good enough for our water satchel," Adam said.

"We'll have some of the fish then we can settle for the night."

Adam returned from the watering hole. "The water tastes good and is cool."

"I'd like to get into the water for a few minutes to cool off," Eve said.

Eve approached the pool as she removed her coverings. She stepped into the luxurious, cool water.

She waded out a little further when she completely lost her footing. Swimming closer to the edge, she still could not stand; it was as if the sand were turned to mud with no bottom. She struggled to escape the mud. Eve tried to remember exactly where she entered the pool. Then she saw the footprints leading to the water. *That must be where I entered the pool. The sand was not soft there. I can get out there. I need to tell Adam to be careful when he gets into the pool.* Eve stood and emerged from the pool, going directly to Adam with the warning.

"That's good to know, Eve. I didn't know you were having a problem."

"I was able to get my foot out of the mud. I knew about that from my village, a man got stuck in the mud and it swallowed him. Please be careful."

"I will, Eve."

"It was firm where I went in. Follow that trail."

"All right."

It was near dark when they each had a chunk of cooked fish then settled for the night on the soft, warm sand.

The sun was shining bright when they finally awoke. They rose slowly from the soft sand and prepared for another day of walking. Now they decided it was time to find a larger oasis that was not occupied. A place they could call home. Eve and Adam walked most of the way across the desert, heading north; their food supply was almost gone and the water satchel had been replenished once at

another tiny oasis. Both of them were feeling weak from the unrelenting heat and their attempt to ration the food supply.

"We can't go on like this. We'll weaken so much we won't be able to find shelter," Adam said.

"We have to keep going. There must be a place soon," Eve said.

"I've never been this hungry."

"Me too," Eve said, "just keep looking for a tree."

When they thought they could go no farther, Eve pointed a shaking finger to a distant tree. "Over there," she pointed, weakly

Chapter 13
Finding a Home

When they arrived at this oasis, it was almost too good to be true. Several palm trees and two fig trees grew here. The water in the pool was clear and cool. Best of all, there were no other occupants. Eve and Adam collapsed in the shade of a big palm tree where they finished the rest of their water and rested.

"I'm going to investigate the pool," Adam said, as he got up from his resting place.

"All right, I'll gather some figs from those smaller trees. It will be good to have something different to eat," Eve said.

"The pool is good," Adam said, sometime later.

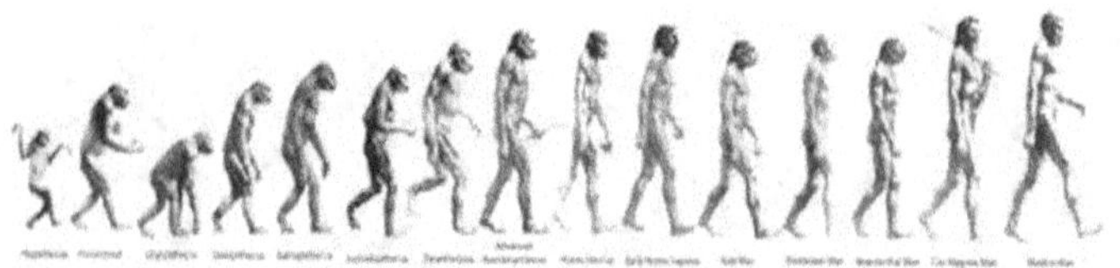

"You've been there quite a while. What did you see?" Eve asked, as she offered him some figs.

"The water is good so I filled the satchel. Then I watched the pool for a while and saw fish jump."

"Can you spear some?"

"Not tonight. I'll have to make a new pole out of a branch from the fig tree. Then spend more time watching the fish to find the best place to enter the pond. This will be harder than spearing fish in the stream. It will take me some time to get good at it."

"That's all right, take your time. We have enough food and water so we will live well here. We can have a fire for cooking because there are so many fallen palm and fig tree leaves," Eve said. *I can weave new coverings for us and mats to sleep on; some of the leaves are not brown yet. Those are best for weaving. Perhaps we can even build a shelter some time.*

Adam picked out a branch from the fig tree and set to sharpening a point at one end for spearing. As he worked he whistled, which was something Eve had never heard him do. *I didn't know he could whistle. I only heard a few men in my village do that. My mother tried to learn but was never good at it. I never tried. It seemed too hard to do but I like the sound. Maybe I can get Adam to teach me.* Eve went back to her weaving and listened to Adam's whistling. Adam stopped whistling when he walked to the pool to watch the fish. He planned to watch

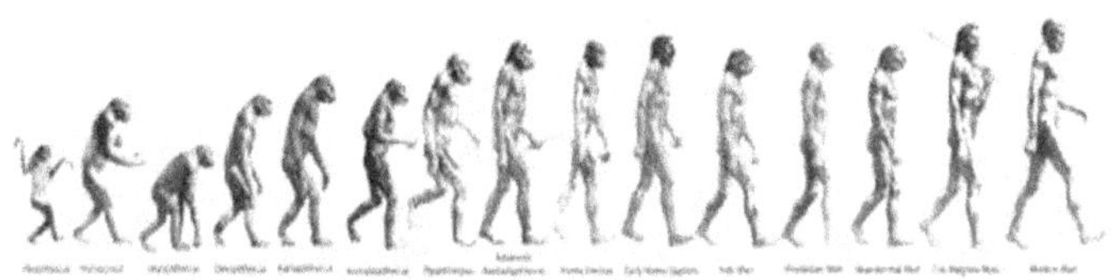

them for hours. He wanted to try to learn their movements and perhaps see one close to shore. He lay on his stomach close to the shore so he could see if they approached. He knew his standing would cast a shadow and, perhaps, spook the fish. He was right but, before he could rise to get into a spearing position, the fish was gone. *I need to see the fish after sundown but before dark when there is no shadow and they won't be able to see my movements.* With that decision made, Adam stood up and returned to Eve.

"No fish for the meal tonight," Adam said.

"Are they too hard to spear?" Eve asked.

"When it's this light, yes. I saw one close to shore but it swam away as soon as I got up and grabbed my spear. I'm going to try after sunset, before it gets dark."

"That sounds reasonable. Best if you can see the fish and they can't see you."

With that, they sat to enjoy figs and cool, fresh water. After eating, Eve laid out the fresh sleeping mats and both fell asleep almost immediately.

A moon had past and life was settled for them. Nothing had challenged their occupation of the oasis until now. Dark was approaching and they had just finished eating. Adam heard voices as he walked beyond the trees to relieve himself. He finished quickly and hurried back to camp.

"Eve," he said, "I heard voices. I think some hominids are approaching. Hurry, put things together and stand with me."

Adam grabbed his spearing stick and stone knife, their only defensive tools. They stood waiting as the voices grew nearer. A large number of people, not unlike Eve and Adam, approached. There were too many to count, men women and children, as if an entire village was on the move. The couple had not seen this many people since they'd left their home villages.

The leader strode up to Eve and Adam and said, "We will stop here tonight. My people need water and a place to rest. You must move. There is no room for you."

"This is our home we have been here more than a moon. We will not move," Adam said.

"Do not resist. Do not force us to overtake you. Move on."

"It is dark now, too late for us to move tonight. We will move to the far side of the pool and decide, tomorrow," Eve said.

"As you can see, there is a large number of us. We will need all of the space provided by this oasis," the leader said.

"We will move away but we will not leave until we decide tomorrow," Eve said.

"We will be moving on tomorrow too. Maybe you'll be forced to join us."

"We won't be joining you. We don't wish to leave this oasis. We have chosen it as our home," Eve said, pointing the stone knife at the leader.

How quickly Eve took over the defense of our home. She seems unafraid and is not willing to back down. She is a fighter and willing to stand tough. I respect that in her but she could get us in real trouble. This group out numbers us 25 to 1, Adam thought.

"We need to stay tonight and we'll leave at first light tomorrow," Adam said.

"Yes, you will," the leader said.

The wandering tribe swarmed over the oasis. The leader had been right; there was no room for Eve and Adam. The couple moved farther from the oasis but kept the trees and the pool in sight. The noise of the children playing and splashing in the pool and the general commotion of setting up camp kept Eve and Adam from settling down. They placed their sleeping mats on the warm sand and tried to sleep. The noise continued as the singing and boisterous laughter continued. *Don't those people ever sleep?* Eve wondered. *I will never sleep with all that racket. Adam has fallen asleep but I can't.* She continued to stay awake but sleep finally overcame her.

Eve was brutally awakened slightly before dawn.

"Quiet," A big, strong man whispered as he clasped his hand over her mouth.

She tried to struggle away to no avail he held her tight with what seemed superhuman strength.

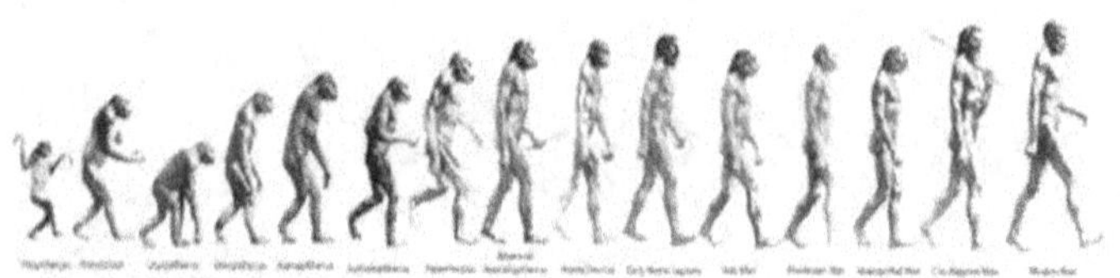

Another man held a sharp pointed knife to her throat. It pricked the skin of her throat, for she felt a trickle of blood running down her neck. "Be quiet," one man said. "We'll put you down when we get to the Headman's tent. We don't want to hurt you. The Headman likes your beautiful body. He won't want it damaged in any way."

As they reached the camp, Eve noticed the camp was packed and ready to move out. The huge man set her down on her feet and the other man with the large knife stood beside her. Both men grabbed her arms and pulled her to the Headman, as they had called him.

"Here she is. She tried to struggle so we had to prick her neck to make her quiet down, otherwise she is not hurt," the bigger man said.

"Good. Go now," the Headman said. Eve remained glued to her position, as the men backed away.

"Now, I had them bring you to me because I want you for another mate."

"What?" Eve asked. "I don't want to be your mate. I have a mate; I don't want or need another."

"It does not matter what you want. What I want is all that matters and I want you for one of my mates."

"One of your slaves, you mean, you ugly man."

"Oh, you have spirit; I like that in a woman. You'll make a good addition to my harem."

What is a harem? Eve wondered. *It must have something to do with his women. I don't like this. I'll watch for a way to get away from here.* Before she could formulate a plan, she was whisked away by two determined women dressed in colorful robes. "Come with us. You'll be living in our tent now. Joktar will call for you when he needs you."

"When he needs me?" Eve asked.

"Yes, you are in his harem. You will perform all womanly duties for his pleasure. If he is not pleased with you, it will be hard for you. He will put you out of the harem and all the other men will take turns with you," said one of the women who pushed her toward the harem sledge.

It's worse than I thought. I may have to breed with one of the other huge men in this camp. They are brutes and they are ugly. At this point, Eve was shoved onto a sledge with cushions and seven other women. A signal was sounded and the sledge moved, the entire camp was moving, she assumed and she was right. When she peeked out under the drape on the front of the sledge, she saw six yoked men leaning forward, pulling the sledge.

"Slaves are pulling the sledge. They will be whipped into a run if we need to move faster," said one of the women of the harem.

"Why do you have slaves to pull the sledge? There are beasts that can be trained to do that," Eve said. "We had them in my village."

"We don't stay in one place long enough to catch and train beasts and we don't have food for

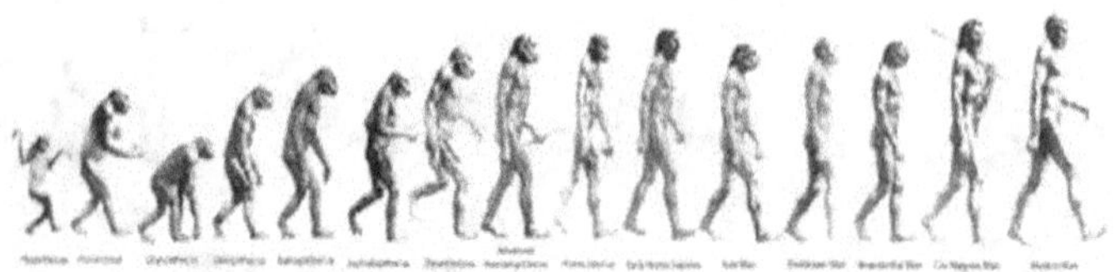

them. We barely have food for everybody in the tribe."

"Why do you move so much?"

"We move to capture food and steal supplies we cannot make for ourselves."

"Where are we heading now?"

"We will find another tribe to overcome and take what we need."

"You'll get used to this life. We, the women of the harem, have everything we need so long as we please Joktar," said another woman.

"You women amaze me. You seem so happy here. Don't you ever want to get away, to do something for yourself, with no man in control?" Eve asked.

"Why would we want to do that? Joktar gives us everything we could want. We're safe, we have enough to eat, we wear fine robes and we ride in this sledge instead of walking as do the other working members of the tribe. All we have to do is pleasure Joktar when he needs one of us. It's a good life. I can't think of a better one," the first woman said. The other women nodded their heads in agreement.

Eve shook her head in disgust and sighed. *These women only want to be kept. They don't want to have a life of their own. I don't understand them. Why not stand up to the men? Tell them we're leaving, we can support ourselves. Then go, we could raid a small clan and steal some of their food and belongings for our own use.* She decided to broach

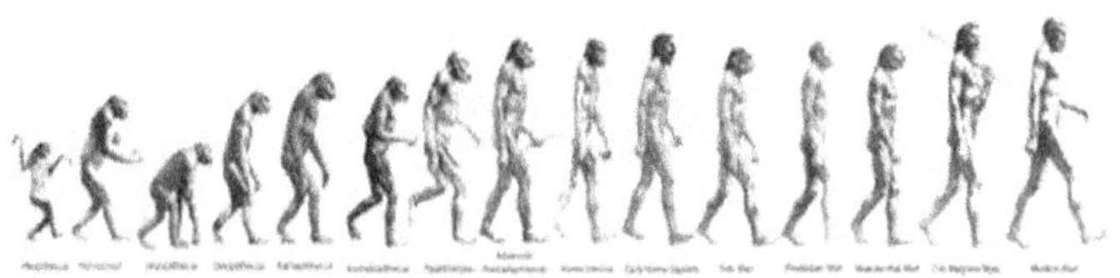

the topic with the women. When she outlined her thoughts to them, they gasped in disbelief.

"We couldn't do that," one woman said. "How would we overpower the men?"

"With knives and sharpened sticks the same as men do," Eve said.

"Men wield larger, heavier knives and larger sticks than we can hold."

"Not if you take them by surprise, in the middle of the night. Slit their throats before they can make a noise. I've seen it done by women in my village."

"That's cruel. That's not women's work; that sounds like men's work. We wouldn't want to do that, besides we'd get our robes dirty."

"So you're just willing to spend the rest of your life like this? Well, I'm not."

"What are you going to do? You can't get away. There's nowhere to go. It's just desert out there. Joktar's men will hunt you down and violate you one at a time 'till they're all finished. Joktar will have told them to have you."

This frustrated Eve even more. *Why are these women so willing to put up with this life? Why don't they think there is life outside this tribe? Probably this is the only life they know.*

"What happens to you when you get old and plump and you are no longer pleasing to look at? Will Joktar still want you?"

"No, then we will be retired and one of the men of the tribe will choose us."

"And that's your future?"

"Yes, we will still have all we need and we will be safe."

"That is not the life I choose," Eve said, ending the conversation in a huff. *I'll spend some quiet time planning my escape. I wonder if Adam is following the tribe. We must be leaving a large track even a blind man could follow and we're moving slowly so he wouldn't have to run in the heat. I hope he doesn't think I just went exploring on my own as I did in the Valley.*

Adam was following the trail left by the wandering tribe. He'd risen to find Eve and her sleeping mat gone. That and tracks of two large footed males in the sand clued Adam to her disappearance being involuntary. He followed those tracks to where the camp had been and they were swallowed by many tracks in all directions. He saw the mass of tracks heading in a northeasterly direction and followed them. *I wonder where they're going and why they took Eve. They stole her for their own needs, I bet. I'll need to rescue her but I must be careful. There are many of them and I don't know where in the group they have her. I'll follow at a safe distance until night fall then I'll sneak up to the camp and try to see her.*

The tribe stopped for the night at an oasis. One of Joktar's men came to the sledge. "Joktar wants you tonight," he said, pointing at Eve.

"He won't want me tonight. I've started my menses today. Pick another woman," Eve lied. She'd asked the women for a cloth earlier so they were not any wiser. *I have a week to make this ruse work. As soon as I find a moonlit night to run, I will. They said they would raid tomorrow and then we'd head south. I have to get away after the raid before we turn.*

Joktar's man turned to Elsta, a stunningly beautiful woman with long silky black hair and a pale complexion who said, "I'll go."

"No, not you; he had you last night. He'll want a different one tonight."

Then he pointed at Petra, a well-proportioned, black-haired beauty. "You," he said.

"All right. See you later, girls," she said breezily, as she stepped out of the sledge and followed the man on the way to Joktar's tent.

The rest of the camp, including the women in the sledge, lay on their cushions for the night.

The tribe arrived at the small encampment they planned to raid in midafternoon of the next day. There was no talking or bartering, just yelling and racing to overwhelm the campers guarding their food and belongings. The food stuffs were carried away by Joktar's men. There was nothing the small camp could do; they'd lost almost everything. Joktar's men brought some of the women and a few of the bigger men back to the camp for use as slaves. They'd be collared in the morning and put to work.

Adam continued to follow the track, wondering what the tribe was up to—no good, he reasoned. *I have to keep following until they stop for some time.* The evening was growing late as he reached the top of a knoll and saw campfires beyond. *There they are. They seem to have grown to an even larger group, they must have been raiding. They'll have to stop until they decide what to do with the new slaves they've captured. They'll probably stay the day here to get them collared and divided among the important men of the tribe. Anyway, the men and women will be busy so, if I can grab Eve tonight, they might be less likely to follow after tonight's successful raid celebration. At least that's how the hunters used to celebrate in my village.*

Adam waited for dark to approach the edge of the encampment. The camp was partying so he sat on the warm sand to wait. Then, out of nowhere, Adam was bowled over by someone who had been running at full speed. He thought it was one of the men of the tribe but as his mind cleared and he looked at the other person, he realized it was a woman clad in a light chamise. Finally, he recognized Eve. Eve was shocked, surprised and frightened. She was hurt in the collision and thought she must have run into a guard on the edge of the camp.

"Eve," he whispered, "you ran into me, Adam."

"Oh, are you really Adam?" she asked.

“Yes, Eve, I am here to get you. We can talk later. Let's go.”

As she tried to stand, she said, “I hurt my leg in the fall. I'm not sure I can walk.”

“Then I'll carry you. We have to get away.”

Adam decided to carry her on his back so he squatted so she could wrap her arms around his neck and he could hold her legs beneath her knees. He stood, adjusted his grip and her weight on his back and began to walk. It was a nearly full moon so it was light enough to see where he walked. Adam walked, carrying Eve, until the moon was near to setting. Simultaneously, they noticed a palm tree ahead.

“That looks like an oasis ahead,” Adam said.

“Yes, it does. We can stop there,” Eve said.

When they arrived, Adam set Eve on the ground and looked to survey the extent of the oasis. It was large, larger than any he'd seen so far. There were several date palms, fig and olive trees. There were two large pools of water and he could hear fish jumping and splashing.

“This will be the best place to stop and maybe stay if we think it will meet our needs in the daylight,” Adam said.

Eve agreed in a nonverbal, guttural sound, as she settled to sleep on the warm sand.

The next morning, they arose to see their new oasis. Eve's leg still pained her when she tried to stand. Adam noticed a large darkened area on her leg.

"I think that is where you collided with me in a full run last night."

Eve examined it, touching it gingerly at first then, with Adam's help, stood.

"I want to walk to the pool and soak my leg in the cool water for a little while then we can eat," Eve said.

Adam agreed then helped Eve hobble to the pool to relieve some of her leg pain. As Eve sat with her legs in the cool water, Adam brought dates and figs for the morning meal. They each looked over the massive oasis.

"This is the biggest oasis yet," Eve said.

"I think we should make this our new home," Adam said.

"Yes, it is near perfect but how will we defend it? There's just the two of us and if another tribe comes and takes it away from us, we'll be forced to move again."

"That is something that concerns me too. We'll do the best we can and hope no more marauding tribes come through."

Chapter 14
The Arrival of Cain

Eve and Adam had been settled on this massive oasis for several moons when Eve noticed her menses had stopped and she felt ill every morning. The taste of figs sickened her though dates did not. She had known of these signs at her village when the women talked to her mother. Eve knew what was happening. *I am with child. I have the same signs as the women talked about when visiting my mother. I am going to have Adam's child.* Eve was elated and sat beside Adam to give him the news.

"Adam, I have some news for you,"

"News? How could you have news when we are a long way from anyone?"

"It's not that kind of news. It's about me, about us."

"What could you possibly have to tell me about you or us that I don't already know?"

"Adam, I am with child. I'm going to have your baby."

"Oh. Oh, Eve. No, I didn't know. How soon?"

"Many moons, perhaps seven or eight moons."

"That will give us some time to prepare. What do we need to do?" Adam realized he was at a loss as to what to do to prepare. *What did they do to prepare for a birth in my village? What did my father do when my sisters were born?* He couldn't come up with any answers. He had not paid attention … babies just arrived, some lived, some did not. It didn't matter then; now, it was personal. This was his child and his mate; he didn't know what to do.

"I don't think there is much we need to do. I do think we should build a shelter. We should build it out of downed branches and palm leaves and hold them steady with mud," Eve said.

"That is a good idea, Eve. It sounds like a lot of work but I can see why you want it."

"We should build it so there is room for three inside. I will weave new sleeping mats. We could store some food inside and water in the water satchel for when I need it. No fire though; we'll keep that outside."

"You've thought of everything, Eve."

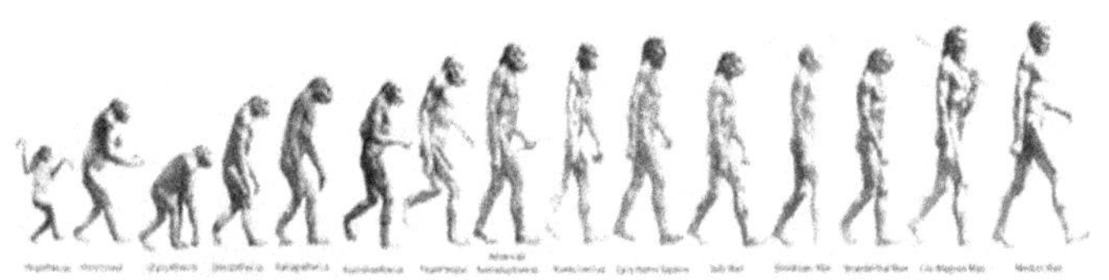

"That is similar to the way we did it in my village, except the sticks were bigger and longer. Larger huts could be built. That's what we called them, 'huts'."

"All right, let's start collecting material for the hut tomorrow."

After a morning meal and a dip in the pool, Eve and Adam set to work collecting branches, strong twigs and leaves for the building job. Eve chose a location beneath two large fig trees and a palm tree. *These trees will supply ample shade to help keep the hut cooler and the ground is flat here to provide a stable place on which to set the hut.* That decided, she pointed it out to Adam and he readily agreed.

It took several suns to acquire sufficient building materials for the hut. Eve helped as she could but tired easily and rested during the hottest part of the day. She noticed she was no longer sick in the morning, which was a relief and indicated to her that her pregnancy was moving along naturally. As time moved on, she had a little more energy but was still not up to her usual endurance level.

Adam took the building job as a challenge and worked the whole day, every day as a man possessed. He needed this work to give him purpose for his upcoming child. *I need this hut to be the best it can be to house my beautiful Eve and my child. I hope my child is a son. I will teach him everything I know...hunting, fishing, building, etching. He will be*

the best man I can make him. Nothing will be too good or too much for him. I want him to have everything I can give him.

Eve sat weaving mats for sleeping and new coverings for herself and Adam. *He is working harder than I've ever seen him work. I didn't know he was so eager to have the shelter. It may be the coming child has inspired him. I hope the child is a girl. She will be beautiful with skin as black as Adam's and like his, it will shine. I will teach her everything I know…weaving, cooking, food gathering and, yes, birthing. I won't yell at her and beat her as my mother did me. I also want to take her exploring, teach her to take care of herself and be an independent woman, not relying on a man for everything.*

Finally, the hut was completed. There was an opening for entry and openings in two walls for ventilation. The solid wall faced the prevailing westerly wind for protection from storms. The hut was high enough for both adults to stand upright. Though Eve had not been engaged in most of the building, she had mixed the water, sand and leaves to use to make the walls stronger. She helped gauge the height and width of the hut. She had woven the leaves to form a modified thatch for the roof. They entered the hut with proud faces.

"We finally have a home for our little one," Eve said.

"I have built a home for my son," Adam said.

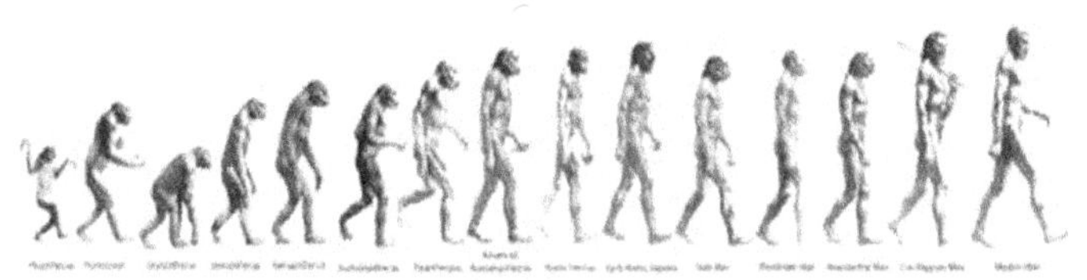

"I designed a home for my daughter," Eve countered.

Before this solemn moment could end in an argument, Eve placed Adam's hand on her enlarging belly. He felt the baby give two strong kicks and they both dissolved in laughter. Adam enclosed Eve in his arms and they sat in their hut. It was now evening so Eve went out, got the sleeping mats and they spent the rest of the night in each other's arms.

Time moved on and Eve had been pregnant for nine moons. Her time was near. She could no longer rise from a sitting position on the ground so Adam found a large stone and placed that by the fire for Eve to sit. She could feel the child had descended because the pressure from the weight of the baby made her bladder feel full nearly all the time. She had heard of this from other women in her village, too.

One night she arose to go out of the hut to relieve herself when a gush of water ran down her legs. She knew what this was. Her water had broken; the birth of her child was imminent. She peed quickly and returned to the hut.

"Adam," she said, "my water has broken. The birth will start soon."

"How soon?"

"It's hard to know. I don't feel any pain yet but I will. Lots of it."

"All right. Lie down. What should I do? I've never seen a birth before."

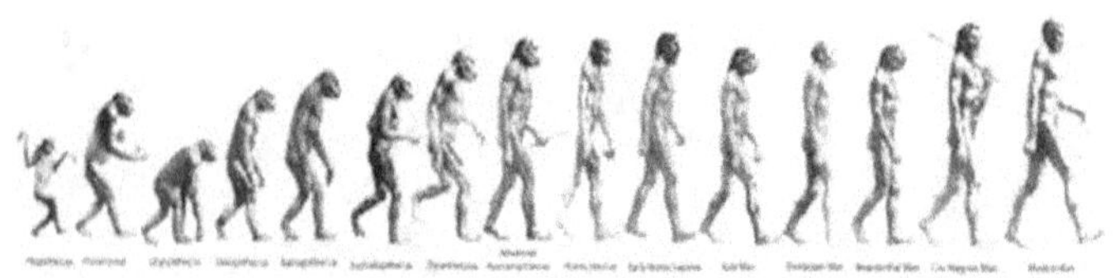

"Just follow my instructions, as the process moves on."

The sun was approaching its zenith when the labor pains began to grip Eve in earnest. She moaned as each pain rippled through her, each one a little stronger than the last. Her back hurt almost as much as her lower abdomen. The pressure in her pelvic area was intense. Finally, "Adam," she screamed.

He came running into the hut. "What can I do?" he asked, trying to stay calm. He knew she was in great pain.

"Check to see if the baby's head is showing…Ohhhhhhh, she screamed.

"Yes, it's part way out," Adam said. "Just keep pushing, I guess."

"Yes, ughhhhh."

"The head is out. Keep going."

A few more pushes and the baby was out. "It's a boy," Adam shouted.

Eve was exhausted but she told Adam, "Get some clean water to wash the baby then clip the cord next to the abdomen. The afterbirth will be expelled in a few moments. Then you can help me clean up." Fortunately, Eve had learned some things about childbirth from her mother.

Adam performed his assigned chores without question but with much ridicule from his vocal baby son. Next, Adam helped Eve to rise then clean her and provide her a clean sleeping mat. He said he

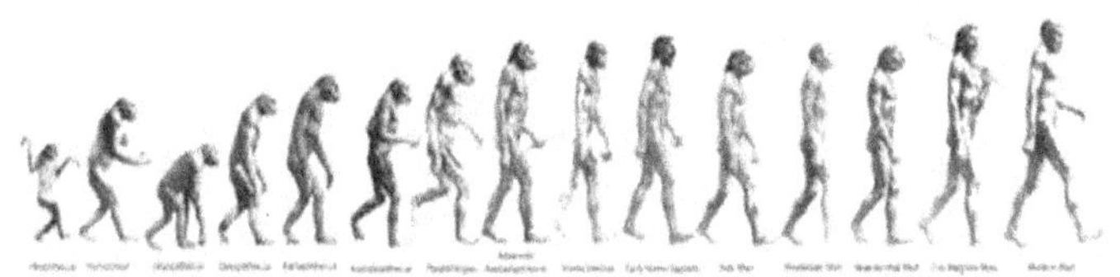

could do without until she could make him a new one.

"I'll make you one tomorrow," Eve said, as she sat down to nurse the baby.

Over the evening meal, they discussed naming the child. "Adam," Eve said, as she brought the figs to the sitting mats, "you should name your sons and I'll name our daughters."

"Have you chosen names for daughters?"

"I've thought of some but that's not important now. Have you thought of a boy's name?"

"Well, I don't know. I thought you might have a name already chosen."

"No, you pick the boys' names; I'll choose the girls, if we have any."

"All right, I was thinking 'Cain' would be a good name."

"Cain it is then. I'm fine with that. He is such a beautiful baby. His skin is black like yours and he is big. He'll be able to withstand any adversity, just like you."

"Thank you, my dear mate. You held up well through all the pain."

"I'm not thinking of the pain now I'm just concentrating on giving every advantage we can to Cain."

"Yes, I think that has to be our primary focus now. I am concerned he will be able to grow on the meagre diet we have available on this oasis."

"Are you thinking of moving again?"

163

"Not right now but we may try to get off this desert and find an area where we can grow plants and a flock of sheep or goats."

"That does sound like a good area to raise children. I'd like to explore farther north, toward those distant mountains. Not in the mountains though, I've had enough of that life. It is hard and cold through many moons."

"I'll take your advice on that. My experience is only hunting in the mountains. Our village was a distance from them."

The next morning, Eve began to weave a sleeping mat for Cain. It would not take long in that it was about the size of a sitting mat. Then she would start weaving a new mat for Adam and herself. Cain was a hungry and demanding child so her weaving time was broken by nursing times. She enjoyed those times of close contact with her son, knowing how fast children grow. As she finished the third nursing bout, her mind started to wonder. *What lies north of us, toward those distant mountains? I'd like to explore the land beyond here by myself. I cannot go now unless I take Cain with me. That would not be fair to Adam. Motherhood does slow a woman down when it comes to exploration. I'll have to wait until he's on solid food, probably at least twelve to fifteen moons. I can continue to think about it, though.*

Cain was nearly twelve moons old and had begun to walk, not far but he did get his feet under

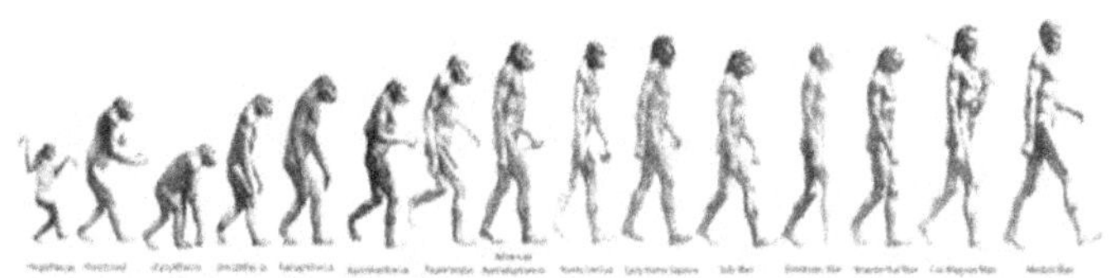

him for several steps. Adam loved to work with him in walking and all things little boys and men could enjoy together. They had races crawling across the sand that Adam almost always let Cain win. They buried each other in the sand, just the body, though, not the head and Adam explained to Cain why. As Cain continued to grow, he now had several teeth and it was time to begin feeding him mashed figs and dates. Cain found these more than acceptable. He begged for more until Eve decided he'd had enough. Then the howling started. Adam walked with him back to the hut where, with soft father to son talk, Cain finally fell asleep.

"He has become quite attached to you, Adam," Eve said.

"Yes, we're best friends. I'd like to keep it that way."

"It's as it should be."

Several suns thereafter, a small roving clan approached the oasis from the north. Adam was spearing fish for the evening meal, so she greeted the leader. "Hallo, what is your business here?" Eve asked.

"We are passing through and would like to fill our water containers at this oasis," the leader said.

"We welcome you," Eve said, "please use the pool on the left, not the one where you see the man spear fishing."

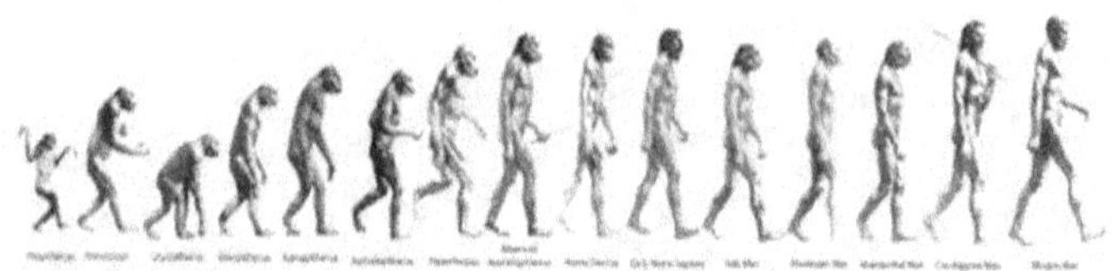

"That will be good. I will instruct my people and return." He spent a few moments to provide instruction and returned to where Eve stood.

"Did you come from the north?" Eve asked, innocently.

"Yes, far north, beyond those mountains you can see in the distance. Those mountains are several suns away and we were many suns north of them."

"We are not interested in living in the mountains but, perhaps, close to them. What kind of land is between here and the mountains?"

"It is desert then grassland until the mountains start to rise."

"That sounds most ideal. Are there any tribes there now?"

"Not that we saw but I'm sure some move through."

"Of course. I'd like to explore that area."

"You, a woman, should not explore alone."

"Why not? I've done much exploration and nothing has happened to me yet."

"You've been lucky. There are many bandits and dangerous men about."

"I've never met any I couldn't handle," Eve said, confidently, "I'll take my chances."

"I wouldn't let my mate do that."

"Well, I'm not your mate. Thank you." And Eve walked toward the hut, more determined than ever to explore the northern area before the mountains. The clan moved on.

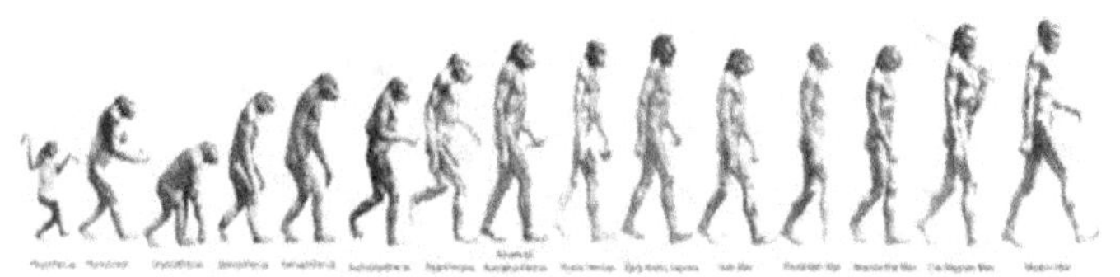

Twelve seasons later, Adam brought three good size fish for Eve to cook.

"Ma'a, Da'a taught me to swim today," Cain announced.

"He did, did he?" Eve asked, waiting for more details.

"He played like he was going to spear me and I had to swim away."

"That sounds like fun. Did you enjoy the water?"

"Oh, yes. I've been in it before with Da'a. That was our secret. I know how to swim good now."

"That's good. Now, it's not a secret anymore."

"No, Da'a said it was all right to tell you now."

"Where is your father?" Eve asked, a bit tersely.

"He went into the hut. I'll get him," Cain said, innocently.

When Adam and Cain returned, Eve was waiting for them. "Why are you teaching Cain to keep secrets from me, Adam?" Eve demanded.

"We were playing in the water when I decided to give him a swimming lesson. We agreed not to tell you until he got good at it. Then it would be a surprise for you."

"Well, it certainly was that. I don't like this 'secret' stuff. We don't keep secrets in this family"

"You've taken to exploring at least twice without telling me where you were going. Wasn't that a secret?"

"That's different. I'm going on another exploratory expedition today. I have cooked the fish so you and Cain have plenty to eat until I get back. Don't worry about me; I'll be fine."

"What's this all about, Eve?"

"Nothing for you to be concerned about, at this point. Take care of Cain and don't do anything rash." With that, Eve loaded her satchels on her shoulders and left them standing by the fire in wonder.

"Well, come on, Cain," Adam said, "I want to make some changes and repairs to the hut. You can help." Cain went bouncing after Adam full of energy and excitement to be able to help Da'a.

I think he expected me to invite him and Cain along on this trip. That would have been unconscionable because Cain is too young to travel so far on foot and Adam would have wanted to control the expedition. I didn't want that so it's better if I go alone. I'll get some ideas then maybe we can move off the desert and into a home forever and continue with our family. I want a daughter so bad, maybe two. Adam needs at least one more boy, maybe two.

After six suns of walking, Eve saw some green ahead. *I think that's grass ahead. That means*

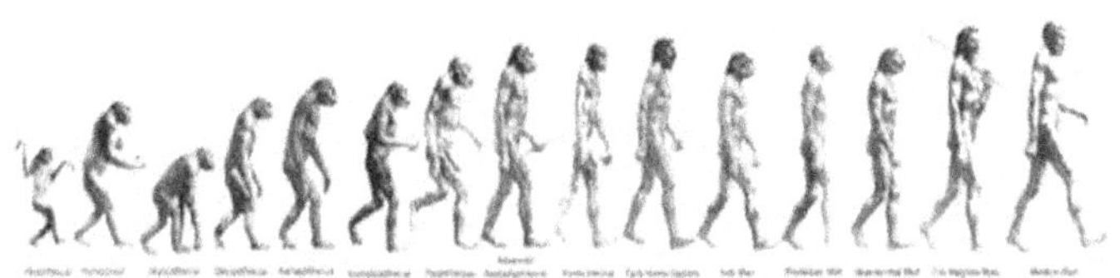

I've come to the end of the desert. The mountain is maybe less than three suns walk from here. There is plenty of water and grass here. Looks like a great place to build a hut and raise our babies. I'll walk to the mountain and see what's on the side.

Eve walked to the mountain; the grass under her feet was a welcome relief, cool and soft. As she approached the foot of the mountain, she saw several people walking upright, clad in animal skins. They did not look all that different from her, just a little shorter and a bit more ape-like. They were talking and fell quiet as they noticed her.

"Hallo," she called.

"Hallo," a man answered."

"My name is Eve," she said by way of introduction. "My mate and son and I live at an oasis on the desert and I'm looking for a new home."

"We have lived here for as long as I can remember. No one has come from the desert before. We just see passing people sometimes but none stop or raid us."

"That is good to know. We would like to move here."

"You could come and maybe join our clan."

"I'll tell my mate about this place and your offer. It will take several suns for me to return to our home camp. Then I'll try to convince him to move."

"Do you have enough food to get home?"

"I think I'll fill my water satchels at one of these springs and maybe pick some berries I see on

those bushes," Eve said, pointing at the berry bushes nearby.

"Come to my hut and my mate can give you some real food to take back."

"That would be wonderful." So, Eve trudged up the mountainside several yards to this man's hut.

"Come in. This is my mate, Hatra."

"Hallo, Hatra," Eve said. "My name is Eve."

Hatra nodded in acknowledgment.

"I will tell you everything she's told me later. She needs some of our food to take back to her oasis home," the man told his mate.

"I'll get some fresh meat, nuts and berries ready for her," Hatra said. Hatra packed the food quickly and handed the bundle to Eve.

"You are very generous," Eve said. "I appreciate your gift."

"Perhaps we will see you again," the man said.

"I think we'll be back." Eve said, as she left the hut.

Her walk back to the oasis took five suns. She tried to walk as fast as possible to get the news to Adam. Cain saw her coming first and ran to Adam yelling, "Ma'a is coming, Ma'a is coming. Adam looked up from his work on the hut.

"Eve, where have you been so long? We were beginning to worry."

"No need to worry, I told you that," Eve said, as she bent to give Cain a hug.

"Oh, Adam, I went to the end of the desert, all the way to the mountains. It is a beautiful area. I met an interesting clansman and his mate. He said we would be welcome there. They have no tribe marauders and life is peaceful there. He and some others would help us get settled. I think we should move there very soon."

"How far must we travel to get there?"

"It took me about six suns to get to the grassland beyond the desert and another three suns to get to the foot of the mountain. It will take us longer because Cain won't be able to walk so fast and the desert sand will be hard on his feet."

"I can carry him on my back but you'll have to carry more satchels."

"I can carry more than you think. I do think, though, it will take us about ten suns to make the trek."

"That is a long time. Can we carry enough food and water for that long a trip?"

"We'll have to. There were no oases on the way. We'll take packages of cooked fish and dried berries. I'll weave two more water satchels. That should be enough, if we are careful."

"Sounds like you really want to go to this place."

"Yes, I do. I think it will be a safer place to raise more children. It is cooler and the grass is so much softer and cooler on the feet."

"All right, I just completed some repairs to the hut. Must we move immediately?"

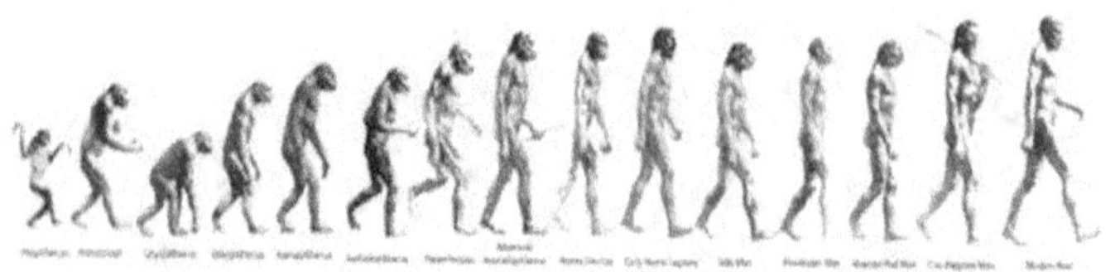

"No, I don't think we need to move right now but we should do it soon, certainly before another child arrives."

"We'll need another moon to prepare."

"That long?"

"It will take you that long to weave new satchels, coverings for the three of us and, perhaps, new sleeping mats."

"I suppose. I'll get started now."

The day arrived, almost a moon later, when Eve finish cooking the last fish and set it aside to cool before wrapping. She'd finished the new satchels and filled them with water to make sure they were watertight. The new sleeping mats were folded ready to be carried. Now the new coverings were ready to be donned. Cain was in the highest spirits of all. This was a new adventure and he was more than ready for it. Eve helped him put his new covering on. Adam loaded some of the satchels on his shoulders and Eve took the rest. Adam took all his stone tools he'd fashioned to build the hut, knowing he'd need them to build another, larger one on the new land.

They left the oasis they'd occupied for more than thirty moons; actually, they'd lost count of the moons, many moons ago. They walked and talked, stopping in whatever shade they could find for seven or eight suns. Adam carried Cain on his back after stopping for the mid-day rest. Eve took on the extra load without complaint. Cain was tiring of this unending walk, complaining and asking how much

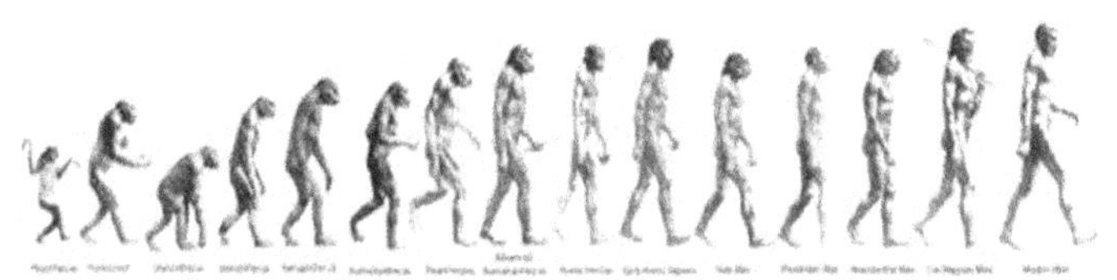

further. Then at the end of the tenth sun, the desert sand gave way to tufts of grass and the mountain was in sight through the heavy heat haze.

"We're getting close. This is the end of the desert," Eve said.

"At last," Adam said. Cain was asleep on Adam's back.

"Another sun or two and we'll be on the grassy plain at the foot of the mountain."

They walked further until they were walking on grass then they decided to stop for the night. Cain fussed, ate a little and drank some water before going back to sleep. Eve and Adam unrolled their sleeping mats after eating and went to sleep, too.

The next morning they pushed on again with renewed energy. It was cooler and the mountain breeze was a welcome respite. Eve and Adam began to watch for possible building sites. Eve wanted to get closer to the mountain. Adam thought the mountain might yield better prospects for building material, so they walked on. After two more suns, they reached the base of the mountain.

Eve pointed to the side of the mountain at the hut just visible through the trees. "That is where the clansman lives with his mate, Hatra."

"What is the clansman's name?"

"I don't know. He never told me, just his mate's name."

"We'll find out in due time. I like this area. You are right; this would be a good place to settle."

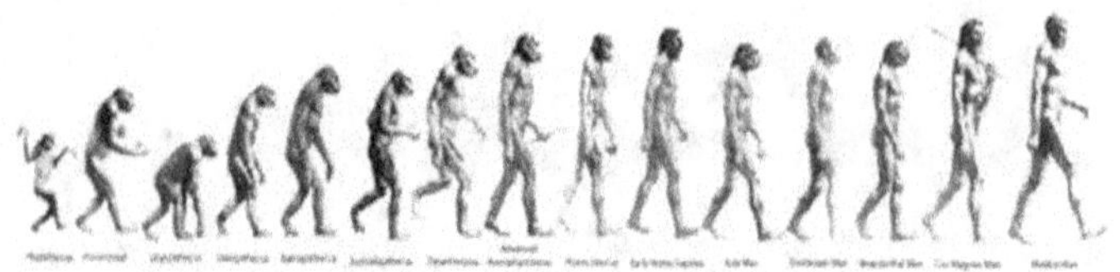

So it was decided they'd stay here and make this their new home.

Chapter 15
More Children

Another new home—this one was to be the last for most of their lives. They had survived the destruction of the Valley of Eden, life in the desert and now they could begin anew where food and water were plentiful, with neighbors who were willing to help. Eve set about finding the best location for a hut. She wanted this one to be bigger than the last, something similar to the clansman's hut. She insisted Adam and Cain trek with her to the clansman's hut to meet him and his mate. They journeyed uphill nearly to the hut, when a friendly "Hallo" rang out from their side. "You've come back," the clansman said.

"Yes," Eve said, "we're all here this time. This is my mate, Adam and my son, Cain." The clansman nodded to Adam and smiled at Cain.

"Hallo, Adam. I'm Labbo and my mate is Hatra." Adam nodded in acknowledgment. "Please come to my hut and sit for a while. Hatra may have something good to eat."

They entered the hut, were introduced to Hatra and sat by the fire pit. Hatra fell in love with Cain. Cain was shy in that he'd never met another person before. He got over the shyness quickly and began to babble about the trip from the desert. Hatra and Labbo smiled and laughed obligingly.

Then the adults began to talk about building huts, acquiring food and hunting. Cain became bored and, warmed by the fire, curled up in Eve's cross-legged lap and went to sleep. Labbo promised to assist Adam as much as Adam needed and Hatra offered to show Eve some cooking methods for meat and roasting methods for nuts. These neighbors were to become fast friends.

Labbo showed Adam where to collect the best long, dry sticks for hut building and how to make daub to seal the spaces between the sticks. This, he explained, would keep the cold winter wind out and help keep the hut warm. In addition, he said, they would hunt animals to use their meat for food and their skins for clothing and to hang on the walls, door and windows to further help to keep the hut warm.

"How cold will it get?" Adam asked.

"Colder than you have experienced," Labbo said.

"You are right; neither of us has experienced cold weather."

"You will be fine, if you take my advice."

"We certainly will," Adam said.

The construction of the hut moved along with astonishing speed. Labbo and Adam worked well together and Cain had fun procuring small items for them. Then they began placing layers of fir tree boughs as thatch for the roof. The boughs were supported by cross-beams made of young trees downed by slashing and chopping using stone knives[9], especially designed for the work by Labbo and his clan. It was at this time that Eve announced to Adam she was with child. It appeared the hut would be ready for occupancy well before the arrival of the second child.

Eve and Hatra enjoyed the time they spent together trading secrets of weaving, roasting and child rearing. Hatra introduced Eve to cooking meat. She instructed Eve about the plethora of wild vegetables, including onions, carrots and parsnips. They cooked them with the meat making a delicious stew, which the entire family talked of for days after. Cain begged Eve to make the stew every evening for their meal. Eve instructed Hatra in weaving mats and coverings from leaves. Hatra was particularly delighted to learn how to weave water-tight satchels.

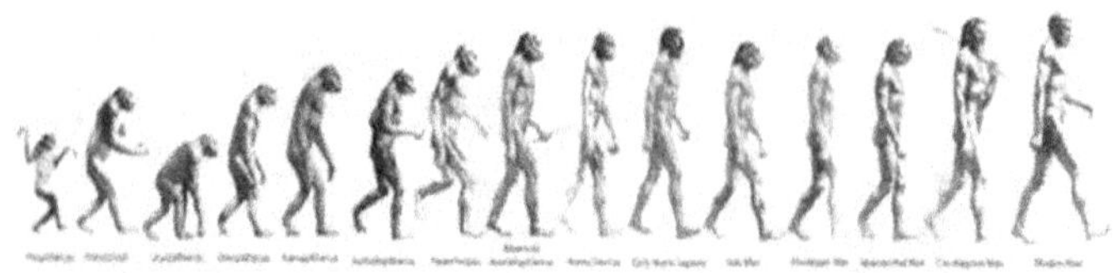

These allowed the men to carry water when working or hunting. Eve, at last, told Hatra she was with child.

"Hatra, I have something to tell you," Eve said, as she and Hatra sat to drink tea.

"I'm listening. This sounds important," Hatra said.

"Yes, it is. I am with child."

"That is wonderful news. How long?"

"I've missed my menses for two moons now."

"That means you probably have about seven moons before the birth."

"Yes, that's about how long it took before Cain's birth."

"I've had six children a few died, nine in all."

"Many children died in my village but quite a few lived … enough to keep the village expanding."

"Yes, our clan has expanded that way. We have some women who are experienced in helping at the birth time; I'm one of them. Would you want me to help?"

"Oh, yes, Hatra, that would be most welcome. Adam tried to help last time and through the pain, I had to give him instructions. It was difficult for both of us."

"It is definitely women's work. Men should not be present until the birth is complete. Labbo would not have the faintest idea what to do and that's how it should be."

"I agree with that. I look forward to this birth. I hope it's a girl."

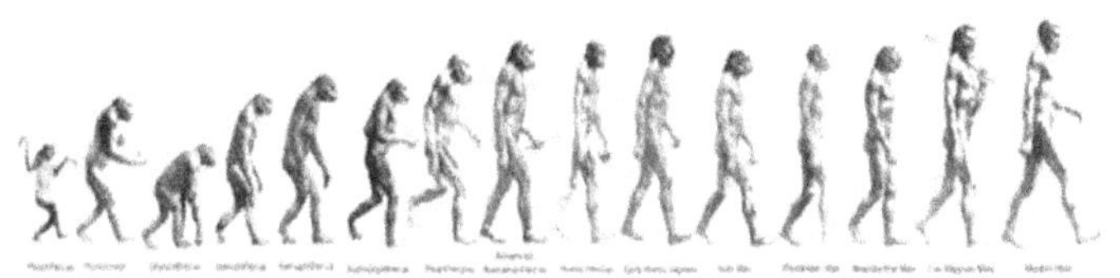

"Yes, I have two daughters. They are 'gems among the pearls' one of our northern clan members said."

"I haven't met any of your children. Are they grown?"

"No, not all, but the younger ones are gone to visit the older ones. They will return before the winter snows."

"I am looking forward to that time. I've only seen snow at a distance."

"We don't get too much, not as much as the peaks. We get much cold wind that's why we hang hides against the walls of the huts."

"Yes, I remember that's what Labbo told Adam. They will go hunting soon."

"Yes, later this moon. Then we will prepare the hides for hanging and wearing."

"And the meat for cooking?"

"Definitely, that too," Hatra said and both women dissolved into laughter.

The time passed quickly. The hunt went well; each man took at least three large animals, bear, deer and elk. Labbo instructed Adam as to skinning and cleaning the animals and the disposition of the hides. Next, Adam learned to cut the meat into usable size pieces. The meat, wrapped in leaves at Eve's insistence, was hung in the trees in bags made from animal stomachs. This procedure allowed the meat to freeze for preservation away from wild animals. Hatra instructed Eve as to the preparation of hides for

hanging. That process was simpler than the preparation of making coverings for everyone. Hatra also showed Eve how to make foot coverings for the winter.

"Take bark from the tree. You have much bark from the building of your hut. Cut the bark slightly longer than your foot. Then using one of these bone needles, 'stitch' the hide to the bark. For added warmth and softness, cut a strip of hide and place it fur side up on the bark where your foot will be. Stitch everything into place and you will be able to walk outside without freezing your feet," Hatra instructed.

"Adam will be so glad to hear of this and Cain will have fun in them too," Eve said.

"When my two youngest children get home, they can take Cain sledding. They slide down the snow-covered mountainside on bark sleds."

"I'm sure Cain will enjoy that. He's never had children his age to play with. It will be good for him."

So Eve thought. She was right; Cain had never had other children his age as playmates. This, their first outing, nearly started a war between Eve, Adam and Cain and the friends. Cain was introduced to Letta and Lobert. Cain overcame his shyness when they decided to race and Lobert beat Cain by a substantial distance. Cain argued with Lobert, accusing Letta of having moved the end marker. Such screaming and fist fighting as the parents had not

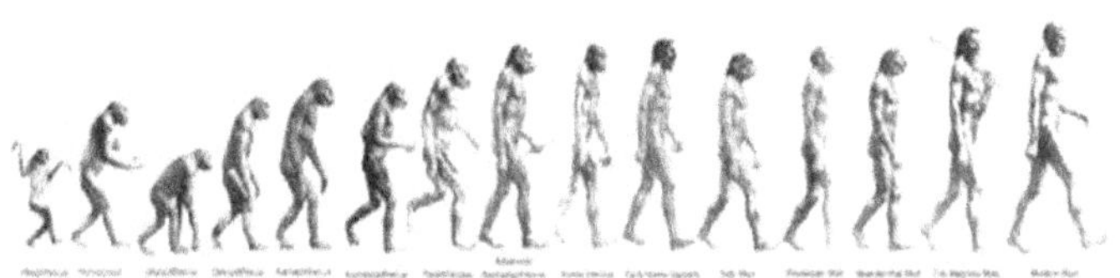

seen in a long time; Eve and Adam, never had seen. No one was seriously hurt—cuts, bruises and torn coverings. Letta and Lobert were sent immediately to their hut and Cain was ushered to his hut by Eve and Adam. All the children were admonished and told to apologize. Letta and Lobert were ready to apologize. Cain was sent to their hut to apologize because the parents had agreed Cain started the fuss. Cain refused to apologize. Adam took him to Labbo's hut but Cain would not apologize. It was several moons before the children played together again. Cain never sought Letta and Lobert to play, they came to him but he often refused to join them. Cain made it uncomfortable for the adults, as well.

The tenseness between the adults finally softened when Eve went into labor for their second child. True to her promise, Hatra assisted at the birth, which went easier and faster than the first. Another boy—Adam named him Abel. Abel was lighter skinned as his mother and favored her features from the start. Abel grew quickly, both families enjoying his antics, except Cain. Cain was jealous of the attention paid to Abel. He resorted to his own antics, which involved hitting Lobert and tripping Letta then laughing as she fell on the hard-packed floor. The only way to solve the problem was for Eve to visit with Abel while Adam stayed home with Cain. Neither parent liked this arrangement. Cain needed discipline but Adam was at a loss. Eve suggested giving Cain additional chores. Adam tried this but it just seemed to increase Cain's feeling of resentment.

In a father-son talk with Cain—Adam heard Cain say Abel was the cause of his problems. All was well before Abel came. Adam thought now he knew what Cain's problem was. He knew he needed to discuss this with Eve.

"Eve, I had a talk with Cain today. I think I know what his problem is," Adam said.

"Well, what is his problem?" Eve asked.

"Abel."

"What? How could Abel be his problem?"

"Abel is in the way. He gets everybody's attention."

"That's not true, Adam. Did you tell him that?"

"Of course, I did but Cain says Abel has to go to make things right again."

"That's not going to happen, Adam. It can't happen," Eve said, her voice rising.

"No, of course it can't and I told him that. Then Cain said 'It's never going to be right again, ever and I'm going to leave as soon as I can'."

"Idle threats won't work."

"Yes, I told him that too. I don't know where to go from here."

"I'll try to talk to him and see what kind of answers I get from him," Eve said, finally.

"Be my guest. If you can get to him, so much the better," Adam said.

Giving time for Cain to cool down, Eve sat by the fire with Cain two suns later for the talk she had

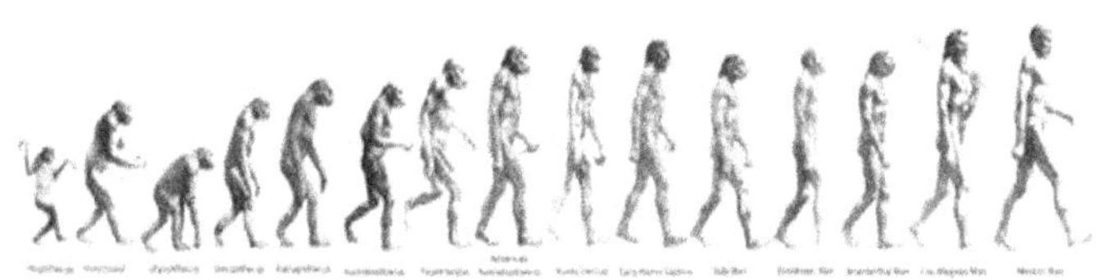

not looked forward to having with Cain. She broached the subject of his discontent and got exactly the same answers as Adam had received. Cain was still adamant about Abel being the problem minus his threat to leave. He could not or would not understand why they just couldn't give Abel back to from wherever he came. Eve tried to explain that Abel did not come from anywhere. She and Da'a had made him just as they had made Cain. Cain could not come up with an argument for that and he gave up and went outside to Adam.

In the evening as they settled for the night, Adam asked Eve, "So how did your talk with Cain go earlier today?"

"He didn't tell you?" Eve asked.

At the shake of Adam's head as a negative, Eve continued.

"I told him we couldn't send Abel back because we made him, same as Cain. He didn't have an argument for that. He got disinterested and left to find you."

"I wondered why he came out looking abashed."

"I think he met his match, at least for now."

Moons past and Abel grew to play outside with Adam and Cain. It worked well as long as Adam played with them but just the two invariably ended with Abel coming to Eve in tears. Cain had hit him with a stick, Cain had thrown dirt in his face, Cain had pushed him down, it was always something Cain

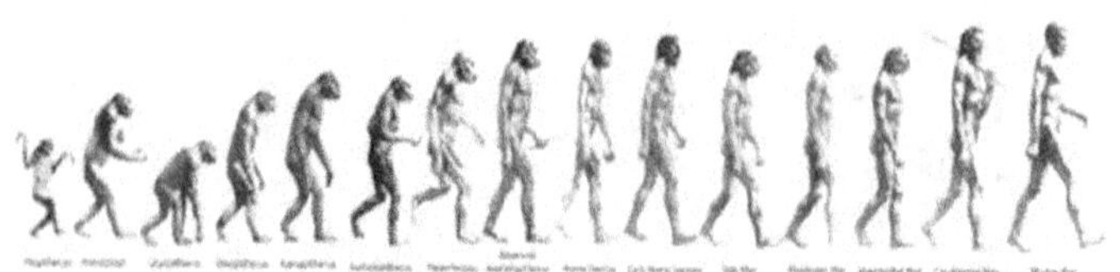

had done to him. Cain was five summers and Abel was two. Eve was with child again and not willing to listen to the constant issues with the boys. Her nerves frayed easily and she was sick most of the time. Life in the hut became a challenge for Adam as he tried to take on most of the chores, outdoors and inside, keep the boys calm and get a little rest himself. Hatra brought a kettle of stew to the hut every week for them all to enjoy without Adam having to cook something. Eve ate very little and Adam tried to cut pieces of meat for her to eat that were small and easy to swallow. They did not come back up if she ate small amounts over a longer period of time.

Eve's time for delivery came and Hatra took over the hut, expelling Adam, Cain and Abel to join Labbo in his hut. There they enjoyed the time together with little or no competition between Cain and Abel. Letta and Lobert were not home. Adam sent Cain down to the hut after several hours to find out if there was any word. He came back saying they were almost done. Not long afterward, Hatra came to their hut, announcing that Eve had a girl. Adam and the boys rushed to their hut and found Eve on their woven mat, sleeping. She awoke when they arrived and smiled.

"We have a girl and I named her Iyanna. She is beautiful," Eve said.

"A beautiful name for a beautiful baby girl," Adam said, as he lifted Iyanna in his arms. She had

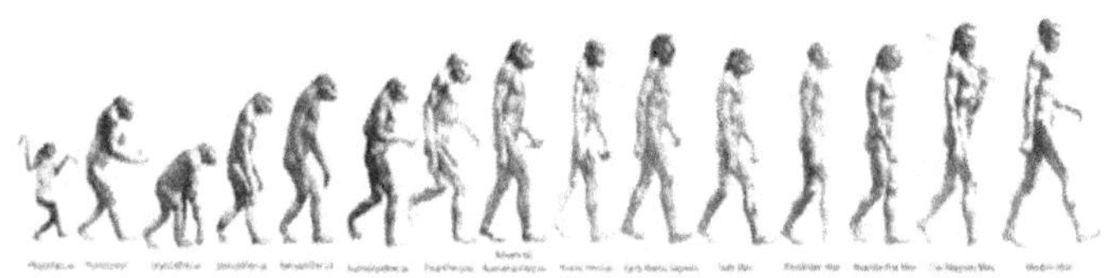

his ebony skin color and features similar to her mother.

The parents were happy, the boys were not.

"Why is everybody so happy about a girl?" Cain asked.

"Yeah, we don't want a girl," Abel chimed in. This was something on which the brothers could agree. Eve and Adam recognized they were going to have another challenge adding Iyanna to their family.

Time moved on and Iyanna grew to wanting to go everywhere her brothers went. Predictably, that did not go well with Cain and Abel. At this time, Cain and Abel were old enough to learn to hunt. This was not an activity for girls and women, Eve tried to make Iyanna understand. Iyanna would have none of it and badgered Adam to teach her some of the same skills. She threw stones at targets, accidentally hitting Cain once, which started a hard to control brawl. Eve consoled Cain and Iyanna. Eve realized her need to provide Iyanna with some household responsibilities while Adam sternly tried to make Iyanna understand she was too young to handle the tools for the hunt.

The next winter Eve birthed another girl, this one was named Yesima[10]. She was a healthy child with skin color and features of her mother. By this time, her brothers had given up fussing over the arrival of a sibling and went on with becoming men. Iyanna was excited to have a sister and announced she would teach her everything she needed to know.

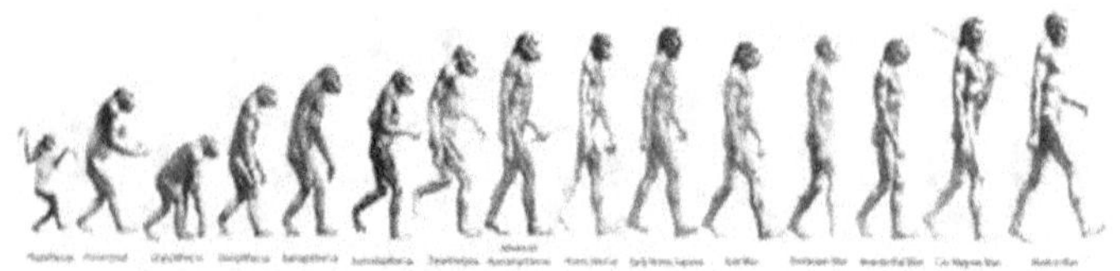

Eve laughingly chided Iyanna, "You're making me feel left out and unnecessary."

"No, you are necessary. You make Da'a happy," Iyanna answered with insight that made both parents smile and wink at each other.

Eighteen moons following Yesima's birth came Seth. He was a smaller version of Abel. Seth did not nurse with the vigor the other children had and Eve took that as a sign Seth would need extra care. She was right. Seth had some respiratory problems his first two years. After that, as he grew, he grew out of the problems as his lungs matured.

That same year, Cain brought home his first deer. He had become accomplished with a sling. After that, several months later, Abel brought home a brace of rabbits. The boys were maturing quickly.

Chapter 16
Cain vs. Abel

Abel was at least as capable with the sling as Cain, yet it seemed to Cain he never got the wholehearted praise from his parents that Abel did. Cain just thought Abel was their favorite son. He was never able to discern why, nor did he try. They hunted well together and one day he'd saved Abel's life. *I don't know why I saved him, should've let him drown; then I'd been rid of him. It just didn't seem right, though. Saving him was the right thing to do, I guess,* Cain thought as he looked back on that summer's day when they were trying their sling skill on ducks. *We were on the shore aiming for ducks floating on the pond. I shot and missed. Abel whirled his sling over his head and lost his balance and*

plopped into the pond. It wasn't that deep but Abel had never taken to swimming. He always resisted when Da'a or I tried to teach him. This time, he splashed and hollered in a panic, going farther out with all his thrashing. It didn't look as if he had control; in fact he kept going under. I dived in and swam out to him. Then he panicked more, afraid I was going to dunk and hold him under, a boyish prank. "No," I said "I'll pull you to shore. Don't fight me; just grab your arms around my neck." I knew I could swim that far with him holding onto me. We got back to shore and he let go, coughing and gaging. After he recovered, we went back to the hut, agreeing not to tell anyone, especially our sisters.

Cain and Abel took on most of the responsibility for many of the outdoor chores. Cain was interested in attempting to transplant wild onions, carrots and parsnips in an area of the grassland outside their hut. He wanted to grow them to be as big as Labbo's garden. Cain conversed with Labbo to determine the best plants to dig up and how to prepare the soil with a stone hoe-like tool. The garden planted, he tended it with extra water and weed removal.

Abel took interest in the small herd of goats and sheep gifted to Adam by Labbo shortly after they settled. Abel took the herd to new pasture in the fields beyond the hut. He always brought them home to the pen at night. One evening two of the goats got away from the herd, unnoticed by Abel, and headed straight to Cain's garden. They had ripped out a

couple of plants and were chewing them contentedly when Cain came storming out of the hut.

"Abel, your beasts are eating my garden," Cain screamed.

Abel came running, "I'm sorry, I didn't see them," Abel apologized.

"I can't keep a garden if those blasted furry beasts are going to eat it all," Cain continued to scream.

"I said I was sorry, Cain. They didn't eat the whole garden, just two plants."

"Now, I have to build a fence around it so your blasted animals can't get into it," the one-sided shouting match continued; one-sided because Abel refused to raise his voice.

"I'll help you build it," Abel offered.

"I don't need your help. Just stay out of my way."

Iyanna and Yesima learned from Eve and Hatra the technicalities of being a good and proper stone-age mate. The clan they'd joined required men to be able to build their huts, herd their animals and hunt to provide meat and skins for their families. The women were required to have babies, nurse and teach them, cook meals for their families, process hides for clothing and weave sleeping and sitting mats. All of the clan women learned to weave grass and leaf mats to place under skins for sitting and sleeping. Eve showed Hatra and on through the clan it went. Now, almost everyone had a bit of insulation under their

sitting and sleeping hides—one more layer between them and the hard-packed earthen floor.

Seth tried to follow Cain and Abel but he was much too young so Adam kept a strong hand out to him and they could be seen ambling about as Adam kept a view, though distant, of his growing family and animal herd. *Cain's garden is somewhat of an anomaly*, Adam thought. He didn't understand exactly what Cain was doing but Cain was under Labbo's tutelage so he was willing to leave it at that.

Autumn came and it was time to hunt in earnest. Cain and Able spent a day collecting stones for their slings. Each had a bag made of deer stomach to hold the stones. They were ready for the hunt. Adam, Cain and Abel joined Labbo and several other clansmen for the hunt. Of course, Eve was left to console Seth because he was not old enough to go on the hunt. She had to explain to Seth his older brothers had been left behind also when they were his age. He could go too when he was as big as they are and as good with a sling.

"Maybe next year?" Seth asked through tears.

"We'll see," Eve said, in the standard motherly reply.

Another sob and Seth was back to watching his sisters comb each other's hair with a bone comb. There were plenty of Ouches and You're hurting mes to provide entertainment for a long while. Iyanna's hair was long and silky black; Yesima's was long,

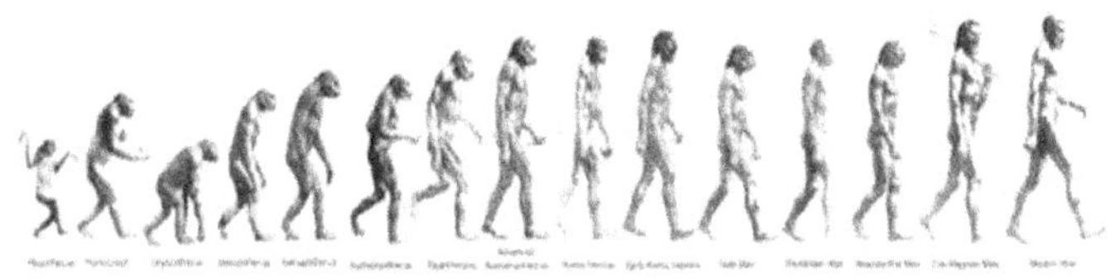

dark brown, leaning toward auburn. Washing and combing the hair dry was nearly an all-day event.

Adam arrived at the hut early the second day of the hunt. Adam stumbled in and sank to the mat by the fire, his shoulders were shaking and his large hands covered his face. Eve sat next to him and put her arms around him.

"What has happened?" Eve asked, gently.

"Abel is dead," he choked out.

"Oh no, how did it happen?" Eve asked, in tears herself now.

Adam rubbed his eyes and cleared his throat, taking a minute to compose himself. He asked the children to come and sit with them.

"I have some sad, sad news. Abel is dead." The children gasped.

"Yes, it is true. It was a hunting accident."

"How could it have happened?" Iyanna begged.

""He was hit by a stone from Cain's sling."

"Where is Cain now?" Yesima asked.

"Labbo is trying to console him," Adam said in a distant, sad voice.

Seth had crawled into Eve's lap. She hugged him as she wept. "Ma'a don't cry," he said. He didn't exactly understand what all the crying was about. It had come on quickly when Da'a got home. His mother and sisters were laughing one minute and crying the next. *What's happening?* He wiggled out

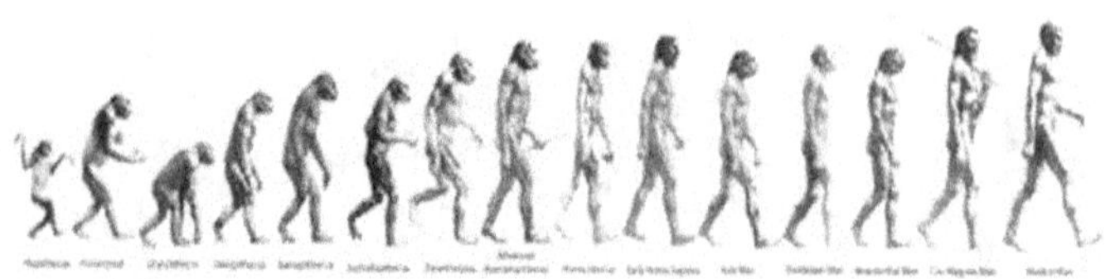

of Eve's arms and went to Da'a's lap. "Da'a, why are you crying?"

"Come for a walk with me and I'll try to tell you," Adam said.

He stood, took Seth's hand and walked slowly outside. At the same time, the girls got up and moved close to Eve to share their grief with her. As Adam walked, he began to talk to Seth.

"You are wondering what's going on, aren't you, Seth?"

"Yes Da'a, what happened? Why is everybody crying as soon as you got home?"

"I brought home some very bad news. Your brother, Abel, is dead."

"What is dead mean?"

"He has no more life. He doesn't move, talk or live. He is not coming home."

"Where is he?"

"He is gone forever. He'll not be with us anymore."

"Where did he go? And why did he leave us?" Seth started to cry.

"A stone from Cain's sling hit him. The stone hit him so hard it killed him."

"Like a deer?"

"Yes, but we'll bury him in the ground and mark the spot so we'll always remember him."

"We're not going to skin him and cut him up like a deer?"

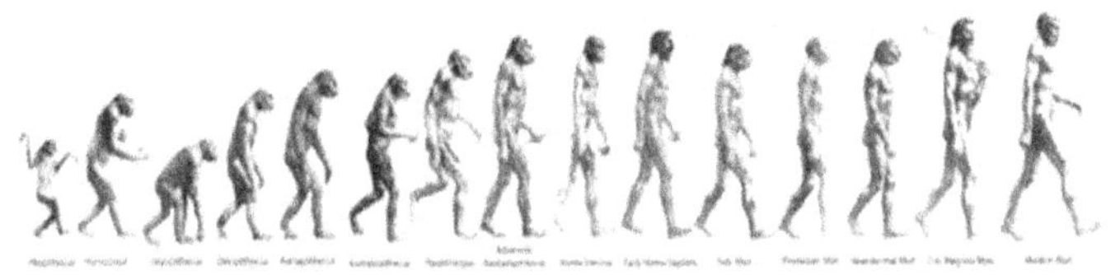

"Oh, gracious no, Seth. We treat people different from deer. Please don't say anything like that to your ma'a and sisters."

"All right. When will we bury Abel?"

"Tomorrow at sunrise. Do you want to come with us?"

"Yes, I want to see Abel again."

"He doesn't look the same. The stone made a mess of his head."

"Where is Cain?"

"He's feeling really bad. He's with Labbo. Let's get back to your sisters and ma'a. We need to be together at this time."

As time moved on, they partially recovered from their grief—life must go on. Several summers later, Cain chose a mate, Cobia, from the clan. They settled on the far side of the mountain, mostly by choice. Cain needed and wanted to start afresh. Seth was now taking on most of the activities his older brothers had done. He enjoyed watching over the animals. He did not work on the garden, leaving that to Eve and his sisters. Hatra gave as much advice as they needed. Adam continued to hunt and provide food for the family. When Seth was twelve summers, Adam took Seth on his first hunt. Seth had learned the principals of the sling, though he didn't like to use it because of "Cain's accident", as the family referred to it.

Chapter 17
Iyanna Disappears

It was late summer when the clan had an Autumn Gathering. Everyone went except Iyanna. Iyanna volunteered to stay behind to watch over the hut and animals. Seth had done it last year and Eve and Adam thought Iyanna should take her turn and Yesima would do it next year. Iyanna was in her sixteenth summer and quite capable of looking after the hut, animals and garden. She settled by the fire and began stitching hides into coverings, clothes as Hatra called them. Hours passed as she stitched and tended the fire in the fire pit. Iyanna had just put more sticks on the fire when she heard a rattling outside. *Certainly they wouldn't be coming back this soon,* she thought, as she neared the opening. No,

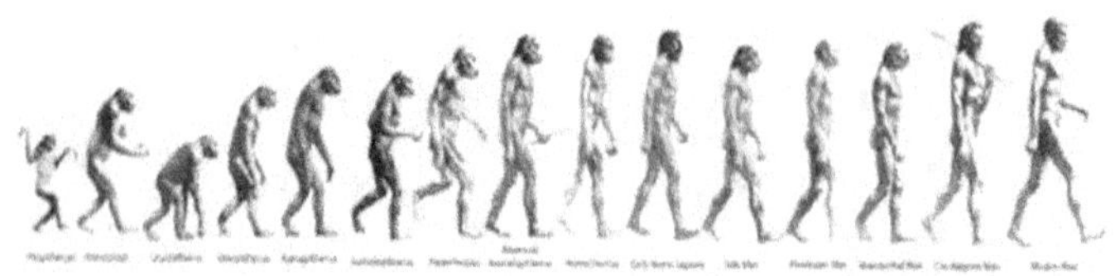

indeed the family had not. Instead, a large, dark complexioned man with a full black beard strode up to the hut. When he saw Iyanna, taller than most women with long, black hair and ebony skin, he was on full alert.

"Is this your hut?" he asked.

"Yes, I live here with my parents, sister and brother," Iyanna said.

"Is your father here?"

"No, they're all gone to the Autumn Gathering."

"I'm looking for a mate for my son. I've been watching you from afar for several suns. I think you would make a good mate for my son."

"I'm not interested in being anyone's mate. I don't know you."

"You don't need to know me. You'd mate with my son. He will be the leader of our clan when I die."

"What is your clan?"

"We don't have a name you'd recognize. We come from the northeast. We travel; we have no set place to settle."

"That actually sounds exciting; no settling, no living in a hut, just roving?"

"That's right, nothing like that for us. We go where we find places to raid to get the things we need."

"It is tempting. I'm tired of this hut and everything to do with my family. I'd like to see the world."

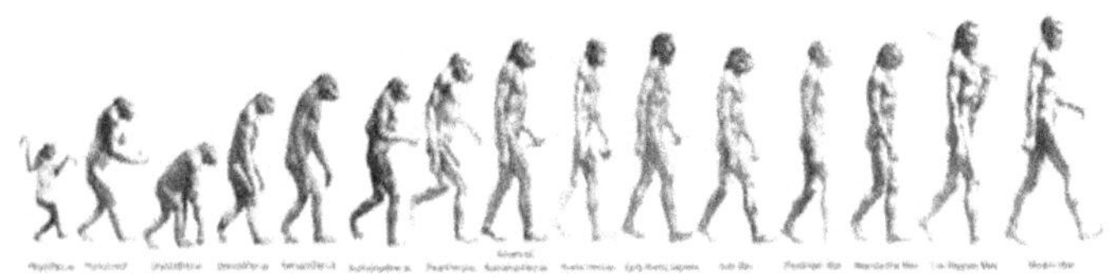

"We're going to head south from here, across the desert and beyond."

"I am sixteen summers and fully able to make my own decisions. I will join you and maybe be your son's mate."

"Come with me. It's only a short walk into the woods. My name is Hexar and my son's name is Hexar II."

"My name is Iyanna. I will collect a few of my things and I'll join you." She hurried into the hut, grabbed her amulet, a hide, put on her foot coverings and doused the fire with water from a nearby jug. She could think of nothing more she needed. She was ready to go, to see the world. *I can't believe I'm getting this chance to leave. To explore just like mother used to talk of, only I'm not coming back.*

Eve and Adam arrived home to the hut two suns later. It was unbelievably quiet. No one came rushing out to say she was glad they were home or asking of news from the Gathering.

"Where is Iyanna?" Eve asked, as she stepped into the hut to look around.

"Iyanna, are you here?" Adam called from outside the hut.

No answer.

"Where could she have gone?" Eve asked, as she exited the hut.

"I don't know. There are some tracks here. They're old. The wind has worked them over but I'll try to follow them," Adam said.

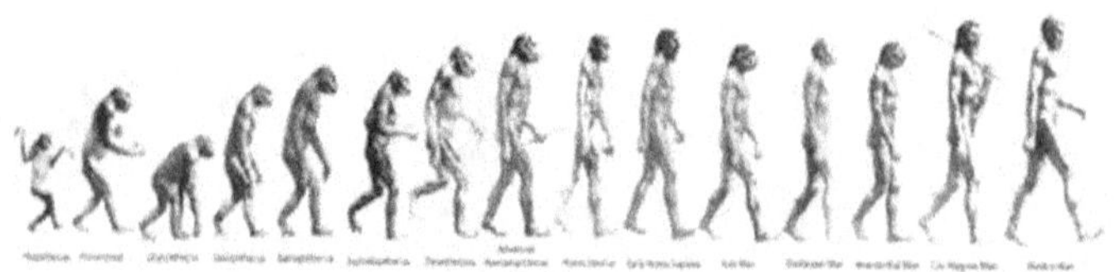

Seth looked the animal pens over and Yesima poked through the hut. Neither found any sign of Iyanna. Yesima said the fire pit was cold when she poked the ashes. The fire had been out for some time. No member of the family could come up with an explanation for Iyanna's disappearance. They waited for Adam's return from following the tracks. Perhaps he would find her or someone who knew the answer.

Adam returned before sundown. They met him at the hut opening with questioning faces.

"She must be gone," Adam said, "the tracks led a ways into the woods where many people had camped and walked around. I found five fire pits. It may have been a small clan. We've heard of roving clans. I think they took her."

"Or she joined them," Eve said, wistfully, remembering there'd been a time when she might have done the same.

"There is no sign of trouble in the hut," offered Yesima.

"None in the yard or animal pens," chimed in Seth.

"It looks, from the tracks, as if one person came to the hut and two people walked to the woods. No sign of dragging or blood. I think it's safe to say she left on her own will," Adam said, looking at Eve.

"Are you accusing me, Adam?" Eve asked.

"No, of course not, Eve. If you had known, you would have mentioned it," Adam said, though he raised his voice slightly at the end, making it a slight questioning, only Eve could discern.

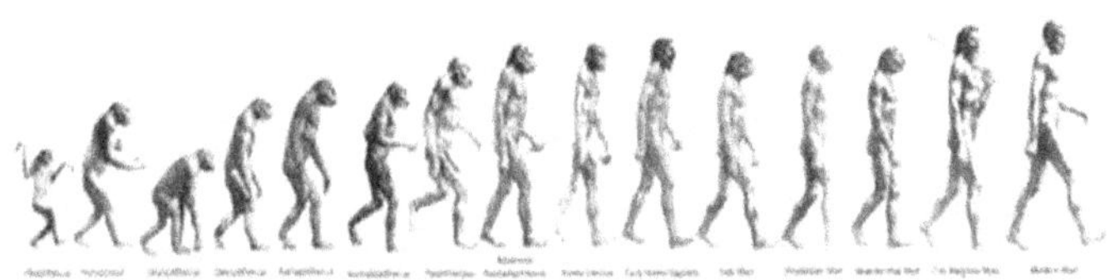

"I sure would have. I had no idea she had such a longing to be gone from the only home she's ever known," Eve said, knowing full-well Iyanna was doing exactly what she did at Iyanna's age.

"There is no use trying to follow the tracks. They've been gone for days now. If she changes her mind, she'll find a way back," Adam said.

"Are you sure, Da'a?" Seth asked, "We could go together and follow the tracks and call for her."

"It wouldn't do any good, Seth. When a girl of sixteen summers makes up her mind to leave, she will not want to listen to reason, even if we found her and talked sense to her. We have to let her go," Adam said, though he noticed Eve said nothing.

Yesima, at fourteen summers, piped up, saying, "I'll never do that. I'm never leaving my ma'a and da'a." Eve and Adam smiled, knowingly; spoken as the younger, innocent sister. The family left it at that. The family had shrunk again—down to four, now.

Eve woke early, sleep had eluded her most of the night. She checked on Yesima; she was still sleeping soundly. Seth's mat was empty, he was gone. Eve guessed in a minute where he had gone. She moved to wake Adam.

"Adam," she said softly, shaking his shoulder, "wake up. Shhh. Seth is gone. I think he went after Iyanna."

"All right," Adam said, "I'll look for him. Maybe he hasn't left yet."

Adam called for Seth and searched the animal pens. Seth was gone. *I'll try to figure out if he left some tracks.* He saw fresh footprints heading back to the forest. Adam followed the footprints to the forest. The footprints followed the clan prints left days ago. He followed the track out of the forest and onto the grass. From here, the clan and Seth's footprints headed directly south. *They are going to the desert. I have to reach him before he gets to the desert.* Adam increased his speed. He didn't know how far ahead Seth was or when he had left. Adam began to run, calling Seth every few minutes.

Seth had been walking for several hours; he could see the path of the clan entering the desert. He decided to sit on the grass and enjoy a biscuit and water before entering the desert. It was hotter here as the grass was about to be replaced by sand in the distance. Then he heard a distant sound. It sounded like a man calling his name. He realized it must be his da'a. *Should I answer and wait for him or keep moving? I'll wait for him. Two will be better than one on this trip. I know he'll want to join me. I could tell he wanted to look for Iyanna but Ma'a didn't want him to—that was odd, I think.* Seth started to eat.

Adam appeared before Seth finished eating.

"Seth, why did you leave without telling anybody?"

"I want my sister back and nobody seemed to want to look for her. So I'm following the tracks of the clan."

"I understand, Seth, but first, we don't know she went with the clan. It is likely, though. Also, I don't want you to go onto the desert by yourself. We don't know how far ahead they are and they are better prepared for the desert than we are."

"But Da'a, it seems like neither you nor Ma'a wants to look for her."

"Your ma'a and I think she left willingly. There was no sign of a struggle. Iyanna could take care of herself. If there had been an attempt to force her to leave, there would have been evidence of a struggle and someone would have been hurt. She had a stone knife and knew how to defend herself."

"I'm not so sure. What if someone just talked her into leaving with false promises?"

"That could happen, I suppose, but Iyanna is smart and she would know a false promise when she heard one. I think it's best if we go home and take care of the ones we have."

"Oh, Da'a, I don't want to lose her." Seth was sounding near to tears.

"I know, Seth, I don't want to lose her either. She'll remember us. That was a roving clan. Who knows, they may come this way again then we can see and talk to her and know the real truth." Adam knew such a scene was probably not going to happen but he was trying to convince Seth to give up the search.

"Da'a, do you really think that's possible?"

"Of course, it's possible but it won't happen any time soon."

"All right, Da'a, I'll give it up and hope she comes back sometime."

"Now you're thinking clearly. Let's get back to Yesima and Ma'a; they need us now."

Chapter 18
Adam Ages

Life moved on for the couple who had been forced to leave the Valley of Eden. Children grew to maturity; they took mates and settled in their chosen places. Cain on the far side of the mountain, Iyanna somewhere in the south, Yesima mated with Lobert and moved to the family hut on the mountain side, Seth took Letta as a mate and brought her to live in Adam's hut. *The children are raised and gone. I see Cain only at the Gatherings. I wonder about Iyanna; is she happy, does she have children? Yesima and Seth seem to be happy with their chosen mates. I'll have to talk to Eve but I want to leave our place to Seth. He has brought Letta here so I think he's hoping for this to be his home for life. We've never*

got around to discussing it but he seems totally concerned with the upkeep of this place. Lobert took Yesima to his place because he will, eventually, take Labbo's home. So much time has passed since Eve and I were driven out of the Valley and we arrived here. I don't know how I would have made it without Labbo and Hatra. All these thoughts make me want to talk to Eve, Adam thought.

Adam rose slowly from the log bench he'd made and placed on the north, shady, side of the hut. Seth and Letta had gone to Labbo's hut to get her 'things'. *Now's as good a time as any to talk to Eve.* As he entered the hut, he called out, "Eve, I have thought of something I'd like to talk to you about."

"All right, Adam, sit down. I've made some tea."

"Good, do you have any of those nut cakes Letta made?"

"Yes, we do, just a few are left. Seth ate most of them before he left. Yes, the nut cakes are very good. She shared them at the Gathering last year and people ate them all. Seth was so proud of her."

"That's the first Gathering we missed. I just didn't feel up to going."

"That's all right, Adam. Maybe we'll go this year."

"Maybe," Adam replied, with a non-committal sigh. He didn't know what would move him to go this year either. *I'm just too tired,* he thought.

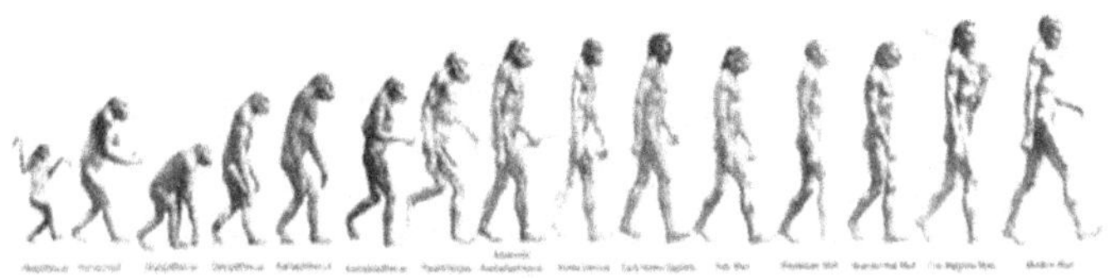

"What brought you inside on such a beautiful day, Adam?"

"I've been thinking," Adam began.

"Uh, oh," Eve teased.

"No, seriously, Eve. I've been thinking about the children. They all have mates and have chosen where they will live to raise their families. Labbo seems to have decided to leave their place to Lobert and Yesima."

"Yes, Lobert is the only male with a mate living there," Eve interrupted.

"I know. That's what brings me to the idea we should make a statement to Seth and Letta that they will have this place as their home, and their children beyond that."

"That's exactly what I was thinking."

"You agree then?" Adam asked, wonder slipping into his voice. *This may be the first time she agreed with me without countering.*

"Should we talk to Cain about it?"

Here it comes. I thought she'd question the idea. "No, I don't think that's necessary. We only see him at the Gatherings. He's never been here even to visit Abel's grave. I really don't think he cares about us."

"I think you're being rash, Adam. I think the reminder of Abel is too much for him to bear. That's why he's never visited. I think he cares about us. We've never visited him, either."

"True, but I don't have the energy to traipse all the way around the mountain to see him, either."

"All right, let's talk to Seth when he gets back. He may have some ideas of his own."

They sat in silence for a while, each lost in thought.

"It's been a good life, Adam," Eve said suddenly, as she finished her tea.

"Yes, I find myself looking back more now, all the way back to the Valley. I think I'm getting old, Eve. I don't have the energy I used to have. I'll let Seth and Lobert do the hunting this year. I doubt Labbo will join the hunt. He didn't go last year, either. Trudging through the woods is for younger men than me."

"Oh, Adam, are we getting old? I'm willing to let Letta do most of the cooking and care of the garden. I just don't have the energy. I make tea and do some weaving and that's about all I'm up to. I think Labbo and Hatra are at the same stage, maybe more. Somehow, I never thought it could happen to us."

"I know, Eve," as he put his arm around her. "We have had a good life. Some ups and downs but, on the whole, the children are adults now with their mates and we have to give everything over to them. Life goes on."

"And so it does, Adam, and so it does."

"Eve, come outside to the bench with me and enjoy this beautiful day," Adam said, as he rose a bit stiffly from the mat. Eve rose slowly to join Adam on the bench.

Seth and Letta arrived at the hut later that day. Adam was puttering around, making small repairs to the gate. Eve had returned to the hut to weave new sitting mats that really weren't needed. Letta proceeded to find places to store the things she'd brought from her home. Seth joined his da'a at the animal pen. The evening meal was a little later than usual. It was so warm Letta and Eve decided to cook outside, using the outdoor fire pit reserved for summer nights when the indoor fire would have made the hut too warm for sleeping comfortably. Finally, Eve went to get Seth and Adam for the meal. Eve and Adam sat on the log bench to eat their food, while Seth and Letta sat cross-legged on the grass in front of the bench to consume their meal. No one spoke until they finished eating.

"Seth and Letta," Eve began, "your da'a and I have been thinking." *Now what?* Seth and Letta thought. "We're well past the zenith of our years. We still have to look at the future, not ours, yours."

"Please, Ma'a, what are you trying to tell us? We'd like to stay here to raise our family. This is home to us."

"That's what we want to tell you, Seth. We want this to be your home for the rest of your lives. This home is now yours. We won't be here too long."

"Oh, Ma'a and Da'a, you aren't going anywhere for a long time yet. Please stay here with us. That's the way it should be," Seth said.

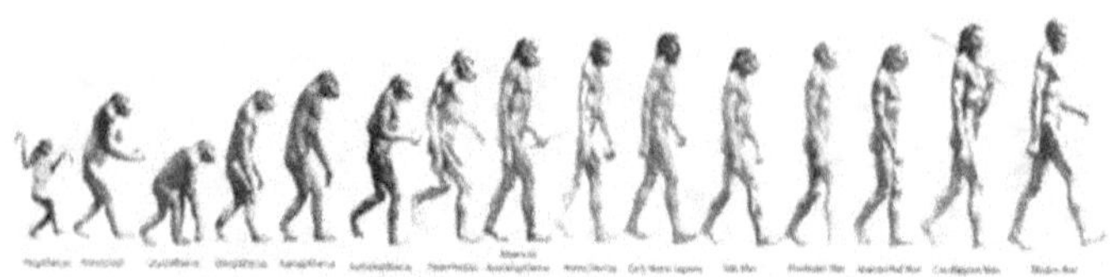

"Thank you, Seth. We hoped you would feel that way. We certainly won't stand in your way, if you want to make changes," Adam said.

"We haven't thought about any changes, Da'a. We like it the way it is," Seth said. Letta nodded in agreement.

They stood when the conversation ended. The biting insects were out now, after sunset. Seth and Letta lit torches to take inside while Adam covered the fire with dirt from a nearby pile for that purpose. Shortly after everyone was inside and Letta and Eve had cleaned the stone bowls with sand and leaves, they retired for the night after Seth extinguished the torches.

Adam continued to do menial tasks outside around the hut and animal pens. Eve helped Letta process the vegetables from the garden. They sliced and dried the carrots and left the parsnips in the ground to freeze over winter; that way, they would be sweeter come spring-thaw. Leaves used for tea were dried. Then Letta and Eve gathered nuts and berries from the mountainside. They dried the berries and nuts for winter meals.

Seth arranged to hunt with Lobert. Adam wanted to go but, again, Eve helped him see the reality of the situation, "You know you can't keep up with the young men. You tire quickly here. What would you do in the forest and on a mountainside, at that. It would mean you'd have to climb and you know you'd be in pain. Better to let them hunt and

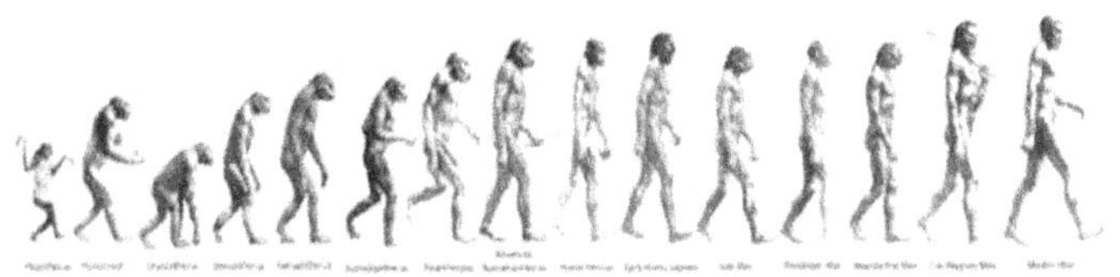

carry the deer out. Then you'd be rested and could help with the skins and the meat."

"As always, Eve, you make sense. I just wish I could hunt one more time," Adam said.

"Maybe Seth and Lobert could take you and Labbo out to the woods for a special hunt after they're done hunting. Ask him after the hunt, see what he thinks."

"Good idea. I'll do just that."

Seth and Lobert had a successful hunt. Each man brought two deer and a bear to their huts. The women launched into final preparations for the hides. As soon as the men finished skinning the animals, the women took the hides from the men and laid them out on the ground in front of the hut. They scraped as much of the connective tissue as possible from the hide then they treated the scraped side of the hide with a preparation of crushed acidic berries, urine and water. After the solution had soaked the hide for several days, they scraped, brushed and beat each hide with flat stones to smooth the inner surface of the hide. These hides were dried and cut for clothing or hung in doorways and window openings in the huts for protection from winter cold.

In the meantime, the men set to cutting the meat. Of course, the animals had been field dressed to preserve the meat and lighten the load for carrying. Using large, sharpened stone knives, Seth and Adam cut the meat in strips for drying and smoking, the only forms of preservation they knew because there

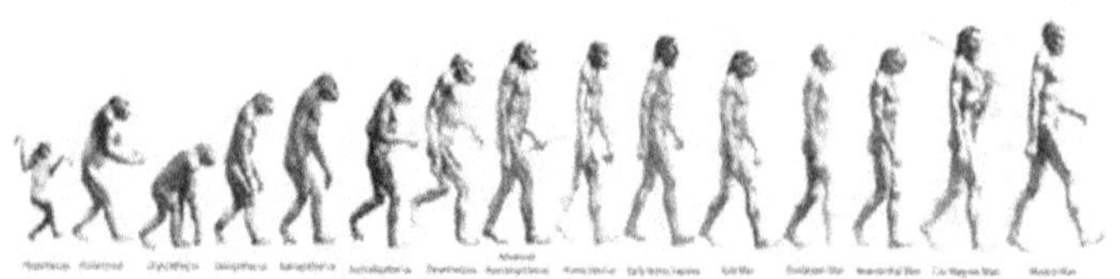

were no trees close by where pieces could hang in bags to freeze, as Labbo did. After all the meat was cut into strips, the men laid the strips on stick forms they'd built and placed near the fire pit. Wood in the fire pit was lit. The wood was green, making it burn slow and produce copious amounts of smoke. This preservation process took at least four to six suns. The fire must be fueled carefully day and night so it produced large amounts of smoke. The smoking and drying meat had to be watched. The meat was turned so both sides of the strip dried evenly. Eve, Letta, Seth and Adam took turns watching the fire and turning the meat. When the smoking and drying process was completed, the strips were wrapped in leaves and stacked on a flat stone in the hut.

Everyone rested after the meat had been processed. Eve and Adam were especially in need of rest. Eve considered asking Adam if he wanted to arrange for a special hunt *I wonder if Adam really can go on a special hunt this year. He seems to be moving slower and is in some pain nearly all the time. I should ask Hatra if Labbo is feeling up to it. Both men seem to be aging before our eyes. The coming cold weather will be hard on both of them. I'll not ask him about it. I don't think he's talked to Seth about it either. I'll ask Seth.*

Eve walked to the animal pens where Seth was working two suns later, while Adam slept.

"Seth, I have a question I've been thinking about for a few suns."

"What is it, Ma'a? It sounds important; you sound worried."

"It is important and I am worried, I guess."

"Well, Ma'a, walk with me over to the log bench and let's sit and talk"

"I don't want to sit on the bench. It's too close to the hut; your da'a will wake at any time and might overhear us."

"So it's about Da'a? All right, let's go to the far side of the pens."

Seth pointed at the flat stone for Eve to sit on and he arranged himself on the rungs of the pen fence rails.

"Now we can talk," Seth said.

"All right, Seth, have you noticed your da'a's failing health?"

"Well, yes, Ma'a, he seems to be moving slower and in a lot of pain."

"I don't know what to do for him. Could you take some time to go to Hatra and ask her if she knows how to treat pain?"

"Sure, Ma'a, I can do that. She may want to come to see him first."

"Be sure to talk to Yesima alone to make sure Hatra can make the trip."

"I will do that."

"I have another question," Eve said, as Seth started to move.

"What is it, Ma'a?"

"Did Da'a mention the special hunt you suggested to him before this year's hunt?"

"No, Ma'a, he didn't. He hasn't mentioned a word about it. I think he's forgotten about it. At least I hope so; I don't think he could get to the mountainside and walk on that slope."

"You are right. That's exactly what I wanted to tell you. I don't know how you could tell him that without hurting him and making things worse."

"I'm not sure either, Ma'a. I'll think about it and get prepared in case he suddenly remembers and asks."

"Please do. It worries me so. He seems to be declining fast and winter is coming. He's always in more pain in the winter."

"I'm going to build a platform bed for him to sleep on so he's not sleeping on the packed earthen floor."

"That's a great idea. I'll place a hide on the mat and a hide over him so he'll be warmer, too."

"All right, Ma'a, I'll go to see Yesima and Hatra when I'm finished here."

"Thank you, Seth. I'm so worried for Adam."

"I know you are, Ma'a. Please go inside, have a cup of tea with Letta and I'll let you know as soon as I return."

Later in the day, Seth returned.

"Hatra can't come now. Labbo is suffering a bad chill. He's feverish," said Seth.

"Oh my, I hope he'll get better. Did she have any suggestions for Adam?"

"Yes, she suggested willow bark for pain. Do you want me to go to the forest and get some? She says Letta will know how to prepare it."

"I'm surprised Letta didn't suggest it."

"Letta is not competent as a healer. She doesn't always remember remedies off-hand."

"I understand, I'm not being critical of Letta. I'm just so worried."

"I know, Ma'a. We'll get some help for Da'a."

Seth left for the forest in mid-afternoon. He knew where the willows were and collecting the bark was a simple task, using his sharpened stone knife. *I hope Letta remembers how to extract the medicine parts. Hatra seemed to say it was simple. I don't really want to go back to Hatra again. She is so distraught. I hope she can help Labbo; he looked terrible and sounded as if he were drowning. Yesima was just as worried.* Seth returned with the willow bark and, yes, she remembered how to process the bark. She apologized to Eve and Seth for not remembering willow bark for pain.

"I'll never be a natural healer but I remember some things my mother used. I just didn't remember willow bark for pain. I'm so sorry."

"Oh, Letta, it's not your fault. At least you remember how to use it," Eve said.

"I think we should start him with some tea. We can rub some bark on his knees and back but the skin will sometimes turn red and be sore."

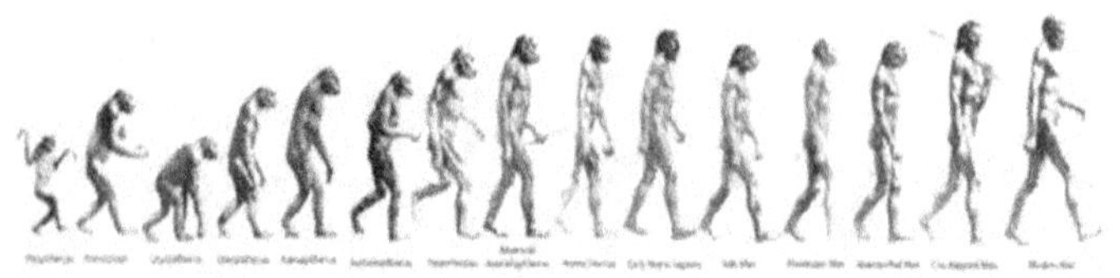

"All right, let's start with the tea and see how he accepts it," Eve said.

Letta prepared the tea and Eve took it to Adam. He drank the hot liquid gratefully.

"That tastes really good. Thank Letta for me. I'll take a nap now and see if I feel any better," Adam said.

"That sounds right, Adam. Does your new platform bed help?"

"Yes, it's quite comfortable; made for sleeping," Adam said, with a laugh.

Eve left his bedside and returned to Letta.

"Adam appreciates the tea. He liked it and is now taking a nap, so we'll try to be quiet," said Eve.

"Let's go out to the garden and make sure all the vegetables are in. I think there may be some onions out there yet," Letta said.

Letta and Eve went to the garden. Going to the garden was difficult for Eve, though she never expressed it. *Every time I come out here to the garden I think of Cain. I can see him cleverly transplanting wild vegetables to provide food for us. He loved this garden and was so proud of it. I still miss him after so long.* She turned away quickly before Letta could notice the tears starting to run down her cheeks. *Why does being in this garden always make me want to cry? I don't want anyone to see me crying here. I don't want to have to explain the pain of losing Abel and the guilt Cain took on.* Letta noticed Eve had stopped at the entrance to the garden.

"Are you all right, Eve?" Letta asked.

"Yes, dear, I'm coming," Eve said, as she hurried to Letta's side.

They picked the garden clean and took the rest of the vegetables into the hut for immediate use.

"I'll make a stew with the bear meat and these vegetables. I think that would be good for Adam, too," Letta said.

"Excellent idea. It will be good for all of us," Eve said and they set to work.

Winter winds blew a few suns later and the fire in the fire pit was built stronger and larger. It now had to heat the entire hut and counter the falling outdoor temperatures. Adam spent most of his time wrapped in hides, sitting or lying on the platform bed. Eve and Letta rubbed willow bark on his back and knees several times during the day. His stomach no longer tolerated the tea. The bed was moved as close to the fire pit as possible. Warmth seemed to help Adam, so Eve and Letta used warmed thin, flat stones for Adam's back and under his knees. All of these natural methods helped Adam enough so he could walk around the hut and participate more actively in family activities.

Spring came; the birds sang and the animals were ready to munch the new green grass. Seth took the animals out for grazing; Adam watched from the log bench on which he sat. Letta worked in the garden to plant onions, carrots, turnips and other root

vegetables Yesima had shared with her. Eve helped where she could but she, too, was hindered by back and leg pain. Eve opted to work inside the hut while Letta and Seth took up the more strenuous outdoor chores. Most days, Eve joined Adam on the log bench. Tea in stone bowls in hand, they sat enjoying the warm, relaxing time, reminiscing about their lives.

As spring advanced into summer, the temperatures rose higher and Adam became even more comfortable. He actually was able to join Seth on some of Seth's trips to the grazing pastures farther from the hut. Eve was able to spend some time in the garden hoeing with the stone hoe Seth had fashioned based on Cain's initial invention, which was inspired by Labbo.

It was on one of these bright, cloudless days Eve heard distant voices to the south. With her hand on her forehead, shading her eyes, she looked long in the direction of the sound. Unable to see from where the sounds were coming, she returned to her hoeing job. The sun reached its zenith and Eve was too warm to continue hoeing. The sounds had grown louder now and, when she looked again, she could see a throng of people advancing slowly, in the shimmering desert heat, toward them. She entered the hut and told Letta it looked as if an entire clan were coming. Letta went outside with Eve to assess the coming people. They were moving slowly, so Letta believed it was a roving clan, which might or might

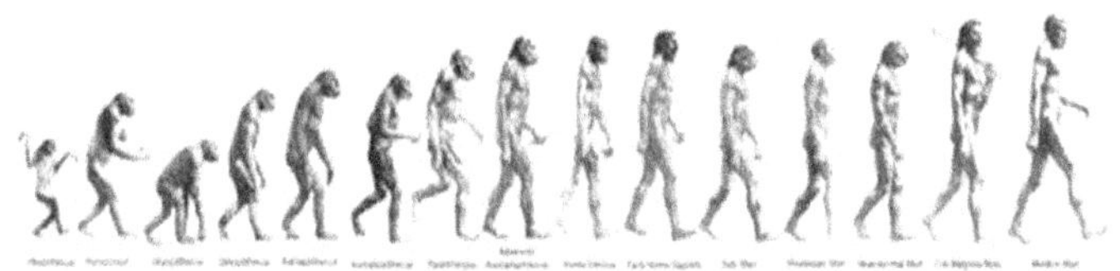

not pose a danger. Eve thought it best to alert Seth and Adam to bring in the animals. Letta said she'd hurry out to get them.

By the time Letta reached Seth and Adam and they brought the animals back to the pen, the clan had nearly reached the hut. Adam sat on the log bench, welcoming the seat after the hurried walk home in the heat. Before long, the clan was upon them, with everyone talking at once, it seemed. Eve came bursting out of the hut, "Adam, Iyanna is here."

Adam was speechless.

"Did you hear what I said, Adam?" Eve said, still yelling.

"Yes, Eve, probably Yesima has heard you, too," Adam answered.

"Where are they? Bring them around to this side."

Letta led a man and woman with a baby in her arms around the hut to see Adam.

"Da'a, oh Da'a, it's so good to see you," the woman holding the baby cried. She handed the baby to Eve and ran to sit by Adam to hug him.

"Iyanna, you've come back. I always knew you would," Adam said, into her neck and long, black hair.

"Yes, we are a wandering clan. We won't do any marauding here, though. I want you to see my baby boy. We named him Hexar III. Ma'a, bring him closer to Da'a. Also, my mate, Hexar II is now Clan Leader. His father, Hexar, died this past autumn."

Hexar II came forward to meet and honor Iyanna's father in a traditional clan greeting. Iyanna took the baby from Eve and walked a little way from Adam, while Letta and Seth said their greetings to Hexar II.

"Ma'a," Iyanna began, "Da'a has aged more quickly than I expected. I know I've been gone for several seasons but he's looking old. His hair is nearly white. I didn't expect that. Has he been sick?"

"Oh, Iyanna, he has been in great pain for nearly six seasons. We have missed two Gatherings and he missed the hunt this last year. Last winter was the hardest on him. He had so much pain, we used willow bark, which helped, but I dread to think of another winter for him."

"Ma'a you seem to be holding up well, though."

"Not too bad yet. My legs and back bother me a bit but I do what I can."

"Your hair is not nearly as white as Da'a's; just a bit of gray."

"He is older than me by about ten or twelve seasons."

"What is Da'a's problem? Where is the pain?"

"Mostly in his lower back and knees. He's just wearing out, Iyanna. Life has not been easy and he's done much heavy lifting."

"I know, Ma'a. Let's go back to the others and talk to Hexar II."

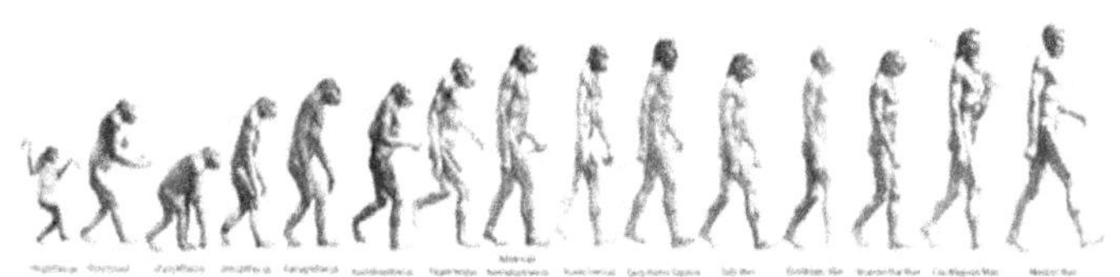

They went back to the bench to join the family. Letta piped up with an offer of tea. Seth readied the outdoor fire pit to heat the water for the tea. Hexar II rose from the bench and motioned for Eve to take the seat. He joined Iyanna and Hexar III on the ground, sitting cross-legged. Much small talk ensued, as they discussed the clan, Iyanna's life in the clan and where they were heading. Eve filled them in on Labbo and Hatra. Seth talked about the last two Gatherings he and Letta had attended. He talked of seeing Cain at the meetings and that Cain had never visited them here. He stopped short at that point. *I don't want to bring up conjectures as to why. That would probably open old wounds for all of us, especially Da'a; besides, I don't know how much Iyanna has told Hexar II about Cain and Abel. Better left untold,* he decided.

"How long will you be in the north?" Adam asked.

"I'm not sure," Hexar II answered. "It depends. If we find sufficient shelter, food and hides; we may be there for six or eight seasons, maybe more. We're carrying a large amount of bounty to trade. If we can trade to our advantage, we'll stay on as long as our supplies last."

Adam nodded. He understood the lifestyle of the roving clans, though he'd never lived in one. He was disappointed in that he recognized the unsettling probability he'd not see them again. *A premonition,* he wondered.

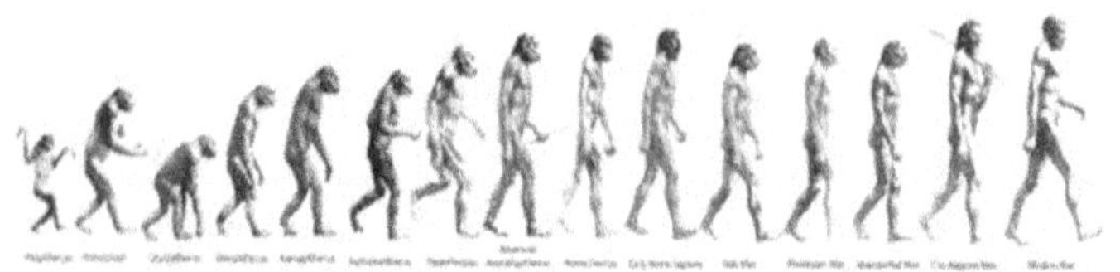

Letta served the tea with help from Seth. The shade and a soft, cool breeze from the mountains made the day near perfect. The only noise was the background bleating from the animals, displeased because they'd been hurried back to the pens at mid-day.

As sundown approached, Letta, Eve and Iyanna went into the hut to prepare the evening meal. Iyanna called a young slave woman to hold Hexar III while she helped Eve and Letta. Eve and Adam were disquieted about the idea of slaves in their midst, but said nothing. After the meal, as it was growing dark, Adam stood and offered Hexar II a place in the field between the hut and the mountain where the clan could settle for the night. Hexar II thanked Adam and walked to join his clan and move them to where they could settle for tonight. Hugging Eve, Adam, Seth and Letta, Iyanna bid them goodnight and promised to see them briefly in the morning.

"They're not staying long," Adam said, wistfully.

"No, Adam, they're not," Eve said. "I guess roving clans have to keep roving," Eve said, with a smile, attempting to lighten Adam's mood, as well as her own.

"Yes, roving is a characteristic of roving clans," Adam said, returning the attempt to place humor in a non-humorous situation.

As Eve and Adam slowly tread into the hut, Seth poured dirt on the fire pit that had reduced to ash with some coals beneath. They noticed the clan had

settled and most of the noise was gone. Nightfall had decreased the noise from the animal pens, also.

Morning came. Noise from the waking clan increased rapidly as did the bleating from the animal pens. Seth rose to take the animals out to pasture but, first, he started the fire in the outdoor fire pit so Letta and Eve could heat water for the morning tea. Seth decided to keep the animal flock and herd close, until the clan left. He knew the animals were hungry so would graze immediately, not prone to wandering until later.

Iyanna was the first to come to the hut. "I want to spend as much time with you as possible," she said.

"Come outside with me, Iyanna," Adam said, as Iyanna followed him to the log bench.

"Where are you heading 'up north'?" asked Adam.

"We'll go over the mountains, across a broad plain and a large river. The river will be the most dangerous part. Hexar II says the water level will be lower by the time we get there, mid to late summer," Iyanna explained.

"Have you been there?"

"No, I've not been north. I only know what my mate and some of the older clan women have told me."

"Well, take care of yourself."

"I will, Da'a. I always do."

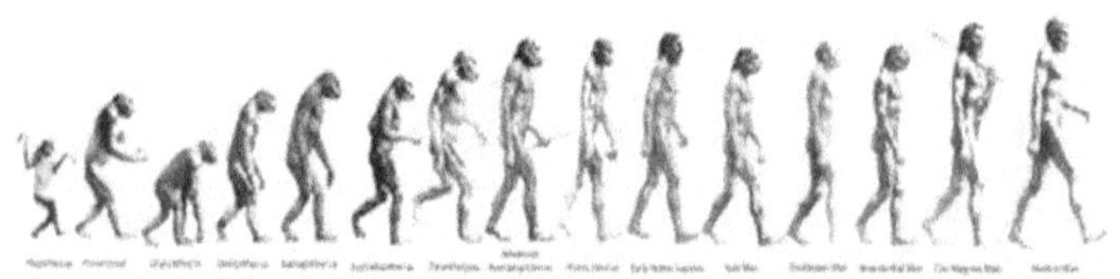

"Yes you do, to the consternation of us left behind."

"I told you, Da'a, I am sorry. I wanted so much to see what was out there and an opportunity came along, you weren't here; I made the best decision of my life."

"I understand, Iyanna, I guess. Those are almost the same words your ma'a used when she went off to explore, often without my knowing she was leaving or where she was going."

"Ma'a and I often talked of her explorations; that's mostly why I wanted to see the outside world. It sounded so very interesting to see new plants and animals and what challenges they brought. She told me about riding a stone in the swamp that turned out to be a crocodile. And the apple tree with the voice. Those stories were the best."

"It would have been best if she hadn't told you those things. I'm not sure what her intentions were but I think they did not have the intended result."

"What could her intention have been but to tell me about her explorations?"

"It's nearly impossible for me to decipher her intentions. They are known only to her. On the other hand, maybe she always wanted you girls to be like her and enjoy the quest. Your ma'a was less disturbed when we arrived back home to find you gone than Seth and I were. It was as if she saw herself in your disappearance and she was not worried, maybe even pleased."

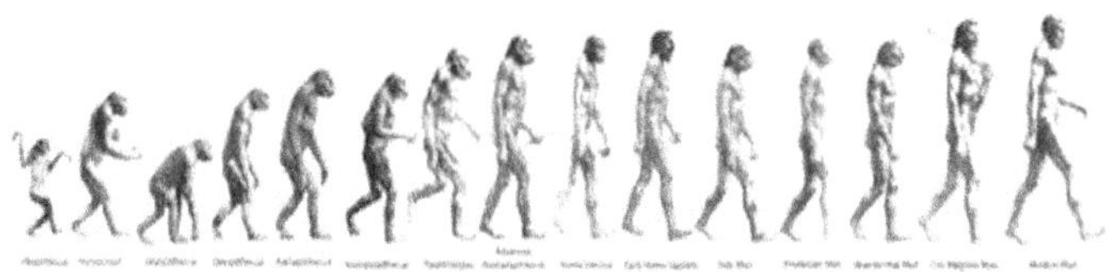

"That might be going too far, Da'a. I doubt she was pleased."

"Maybe not but I couldn't tell. She quickly decided you'd left on your own because nothing was disturbed, no blood or sign of a struggle."

"Ma'a is perceptive. She knows what to look for—what is there and not there."

"You are right on that. Seth was most upset. He took off in the moonlight that night, intent on following the tracks. He was near to entering the desert when I found him. I had a hard time convincing him to give up the chase."

"Why did he want to follow us? The desert would have killed him. He would not have been able to carry enough food and water. The oases are far apart and, though they have water, some of it is not very good and figs, olives and dates are not plentiful at every one, either."

"I know. I was finally able to get Seth to see the reality of the situation by explaining that to him. I told him again how your ma'a and I crossed the desert in a little more than twelve seasons."

"We had some difficulties at a couple of oases but Hexar was able to straighten things out. I never learned the whole story and that was just as well."

At this point in their discussion, Eve came to the doorway, "We have a morning meal ready for you. Letta is calling Seth. He's coming now," she said, as she peered in the direction of the animals.

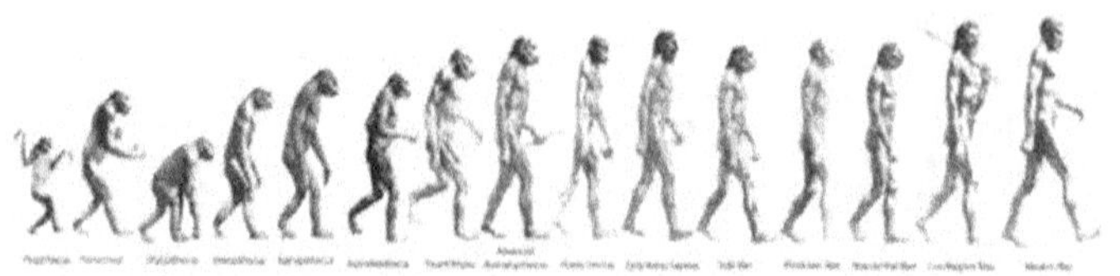

When the morning meal was finished, they gathered round Iyanna, for they knew she was taking her leave. "Oh, Iyanna, I so hate to see you leave but I know you must," Eve said, with tears in her eyes.

"Yes, Ma'a, I must. Hexar II is a good mate and I am looking forward to the trip north."

I almost wish I was going along. In my younger days, I would have ... followed, at least, thought Eve.

Next, Iyanna bid Letta and Seth farewell. "Please don't try to follow us this time," she jibed Seth. He pulled away abruptly. *Da'a must have told her about me,* Seth thought. He could feel the blush rising from his chest up the neck to his face.

Adam waited for Iyanna to finish with the rest. Eve and Letta were crying softly, holding each other. Seth suddenly remembered the animals and left quickly, mentioning the animals as he passed Adam. *He's a good shepherd and he wants to get away from the crying,* Adam thought. *Perhaps, he wants to cry in private.* Adam put his arms around Iyanna when she came to him.

"Oh, Da'a, I will miss you so much. I wish you were able to come north with us. I know that won't happen. Please rest and stay as warm as you can this winter. I want to see you on our way south several seasons from now."

"I doubt I'll be here when you come through again. Continue to be a good mate and help Hexar III to grow to be the man his father is." Now it was

Iyanna's turn to dissolve into a crying mode as Adam held her close and patted her head.

"Oh, Da'a' please don't leave us."

"I know, Iyanna, but I'm old and have had a good, full life; I need the rest. Now it's your turn to keep the family growing."

"I know, Da'a, and I will. I might have another child up north, hopefully a girl." One more kiss on her Da'a's check and she hurried out the hut door.

As every autumn, the leaves began to turn, the animals were healthy and in fine shape, thoughts and plans turned to the Autumn Gathering. Seth and Letta would drive the herd and flock to the Gathering where they'd be sold or traded for tools and household items they could not make. Eve and Adam stayed in the hut, often after mid-day, they could be found on the log bench with bowls of tea and a small fire in the outdoor fire pit.

Not long after Letta and Seth returned from the Gathering, the winter wind came down from the mountain and snowflakes danced in the air. Seth gathered wood for the winter fires for several suns, until he and Adam agreed they had enough wood for the winter season. Seth joined Lobert and two other clan members for the hunt. Seth hurried back to everyone's surprise. "Labbo has died," Seth cried, as he rushed into the hut. Letta let out a muffled groan

then started to keen. The most agonizing sound any of them had ever heard.

Eve cried and began to howl, her interpretation of Letta's keen.

Adam and Seth left the hut so they didn't hear the women so loud.

"How is Hatra?" Adam asked.

"Hatra and Yesima are in deep mourning. They sound like Letta," Seth said.

"Will you and Lobert still hunt?"

"Yes, we have to, though we don't want to."

"Yes, I understand. Be careful."

"I will, Da'a. I must go now."

Two suns later, Seth and Lobert arrived, carrying a deer and a bear. Now the women had work to do so the keening and tears stopped and the animal processing began. Lobert hurried back to his hut to help with their processing. Adam helped as much as he could but the cold weather was beginning to take its toll on his joints again. "I can't work out here. Too much pain," Adam told Seth. He hobbled into the hut to seek the warmth of the fire.

Eve bundled him in hides and told him to sit by the fire. A short time later, he threw off the hides saying he was too warm.

"Adam, you have a fever. I'll make you some tea," Eve said.

Adam drank the tea. He complained of being weak so she helped him to the bed and placed several hides over him. He lay down and dozed off. He did

not wake for the evening meal but no one was worried because they thought he needed the sleep. Eve felt his head and realized the fever had not abated. Eve, Letta and Seth slept an uneasy night, often waking to listen for Adam's breathing. He started to cough during the night. By morning, his cough was longer and deeper. He had trouble breathing and was still feverish. Two suns later, Adam was in a coma. He did not wake or communicate. His breathing was shallow and labored. Adam had been losing weight all summer, now Eve held him with his shoulders and head in her lap, slowly rocking him. "Don't leave us, Adam," she said, while trying to hum.

Seth put his arm around Eve's shoulders. "Da'a is ready to go. He's lived a full life and needs the rest. I overheard him tell Iyanna that before she left."

"I wonder if Labbo's death hastened Adam's," mused Eve.

"I doubt it Ma'a. Da'a's been getting thinner each moon. We've all seen it but just didn't want to mention it."

Letta approached the bed and motioned silently to Seth to come away. They put on animal hide capes and stepped out the door of the hut. Letta wanted to be sure they were out of earshot of Eve. "Your Da'a will be dead before nightfall. He's almost there now. It won't be long now."

"I know, Letta. Is there anything we can do for Ma'a?"

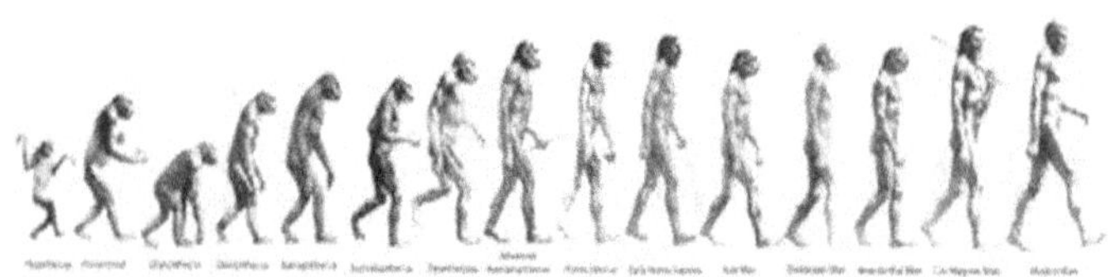

"I don't think so. Your ma'a is a strong woman. It's best if we let her do what she's doing now, it's a form of mourning. She knows what's happening. I'll help you feed the animals. We'll let her have some time alone with Da'a."

They'd finished feeding the animals and were approaching the door of the hut when they heard a scream. Seth and Letta ran into the hut and over to Eve. Eve was crying and rocking Adam's body. Seth moved his da'a's body off Eve. Letta reached to help the sobbing Eve off the bed and to a mat by the fire pit. She gently placed a hide cape over Eve's shoulders and put some water in a stone carafe on the fire to heat for tea. Seth motioned to Letta to go outside with him.

When they arrived outside, he told Letta in a low voice, "I'll dig Da'a's grave then I'll go to tell Yesima and Lobert. Lobert will know how to reach Cain. Let Ma'a know if she asks."

Letta nodded, wiping tears from her eyes and reached up to wipe a tear from Seth's eyes, too. "Bring Yesima back if she can come."

"I'm sure she will want to come to be with Ma'a." They hugged and Seth was gone.

Seth arrived with Yesima. She hugged Eve and saw Adam's body on the bed and the keening started. The sound was more than Seth could bear. He donned a heavy hide cape and went outside to work in the animal pens. Though he dreaded it, he went back to the hut at sunset. The women had quieted and

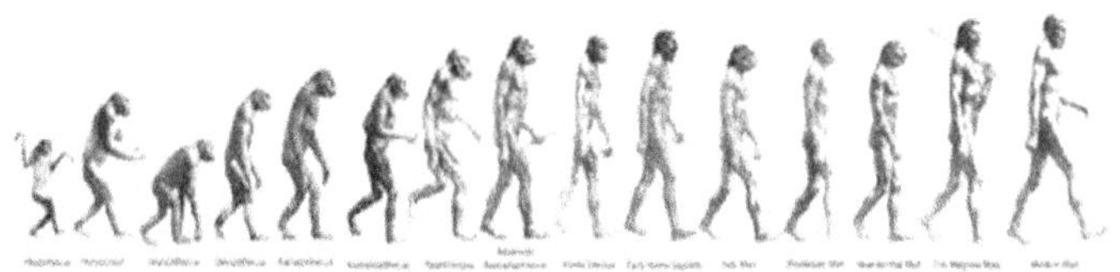

Letta and Yesima had a warm meal of stew with bear meat ready. It was hearty and warming. They tried to encourage Eve to eat a small amount of stew. She declined but finally finished the small amount they had served her.

The next day, late morning, Lobert and Cain arrived. Cain was solemn and said little after wrapping his arms around Eve. He looked long at Adam's body then asked Seth if he could help with the burial. Seth agreed and Cain, Seth and Lobert carried the body to the grave Seth had dug. The women covered themselves in heavy hide cloaks and followed the men to the grave site. For a few moments nothing was said; no sound could be heard but the wind in the naked trees and the gentle crying of the women. The clan had no tradition but to bury the dead as soon after death as possible. The grave was covered and marked by a large stone, bigger than the one that marked Abel's grave. The women turned and walked to the hut. The men stood outside for some time before returning to the hut.

Though invited for tea, Lobert and Yesima declined, saying they needed to get back to their hut and Cain decided to join them because he had further yet to go to get to his home. Letta, Seth and Eve settled to an evening of warmth and silent mourning, each in his or her own thoughts.

Chapter 19
Eve Finds a New Home

Eve mourned the loss of Adam longer than anyone expected. Though Eve prided herself in self-sufficiency, she and Adam became co-dependent after they were expelled from the Valley of Eden. Not immediately, mind you. Each became more dependent on the other as they grew older, perhaps, as a result of raising their children. Aging alone may have been a major factor. When one can no longer enjoy the activities and way of life that being self-sufficient requires and one finds necessary for one's well-being, depression results. Eve thought about these concepts, perhaps not in these specific words, but they tumbled through her mind, just the same. *Oh, Adam, how I miss you. I never realized how*

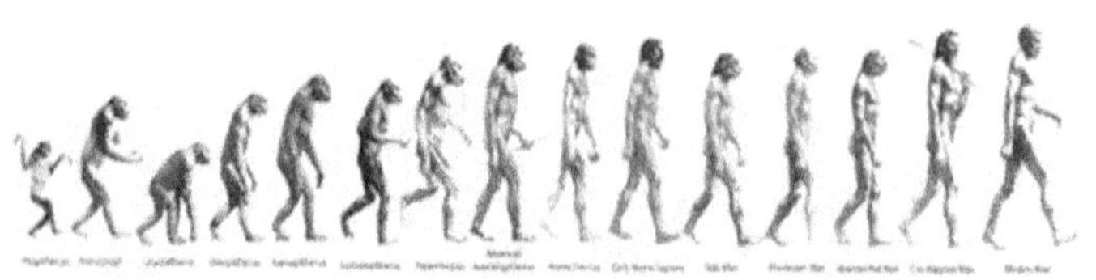

much I'd miss you in times past. I never thought about you dying, being gone forever. When I was young, I never thought that far in the future. When I ran from my mother and found the Valley, I thought my problems were over. Meeting you, Adam, was great, so long as you let me have my time to explore. Then, when we left the desert and we settled here, time seemed to speed up, the children came, grew up, Abel died and Iyanna ran away and Cain and Yesima found new mates and homes. Now, Adam, I'm on my own again but it's different this time. I can't explore this time. I'm too old and I lack the energy to go out there by myself. Maybe I'm just feeling sorry for myself.

I wonder how Hatra is bearing up, losing Labbo. I'd like to talk to her again. I haven't seen her in many seasons. Maybe I'll go to see her; I'd see Yesima at the same time. I need that. I need to get away from here. Not strike out on my own though but why not, I don't need to tell anyone where I'm going or when I'm going. That wouldn't be fair, though; Seth and Letta would worry. I never used to worry about Adam, what he thought or if he worried about me. It's different now. Having children shows you how much you worry about someone else. I guess I assumed too much when I pledged to mate with Adam for life. How he must have worried about me. I didn't worry about him. I thought he could take care of himself. I wouldn't change anything, though. I wouldn't do anything different. I just wish I was the same as when I was younger. Oh, well, I'll tell them

I'm going to Hatra and I won't let them talk me out of it.

The next morning, Eve dressed in her better hide and, after the morning meal, announced to Letta and Seth, in her indomitable way, she was going to visit Hatra and Yesima. Letta wanted to object but she glanced at Seth in time to see the nearly imperceptible shake of his head. Seth rose, saying he was going to the animal pen. Letta followed him. *They're going to try to figure out how to stop me. I can feel it. It doesn't matter, I'm going.*

When they arrived at the animal pens, Seth turned to Letta. "So Ma'a is going to visit Hatra and Yesima. Don't try to talk her out of it. She won't be dissuaded, besides it will be good for her."

"I'm not so sure, Seth. It's a long hike. Do you think she can make it? What if she falls and can't get help? I think one of us should accompany her."

"She'd never agree to that, Letta. You know how independent she is. She used to go away from Da'a for suns at a time. He worried so much but she told him she could take care of herself."

"Yes, Seth, but that was when she was younger. She isn't as strong as she used to be."

"She's as strong willed as ever. She won't listen."

"Maybe you could follow her without her knowing it then we'd feel better."

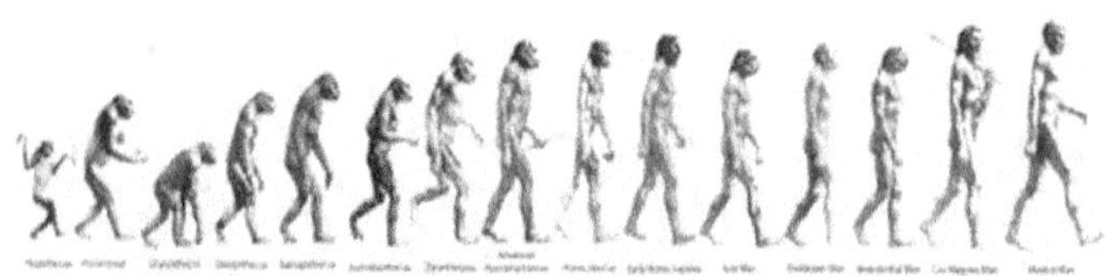

"Then you'd feel better. She'd think I might follow her. She has ways of figuring things like that out. Just let her go."

"Oh, Seth, sometimes I don't think you understand. What if I go to see my ma'a a few days from now and take her some food then I'd know Eve made it safely."

"Nah, Ma'a would figure you were checking on her. She might make a scene. She's capable of that."

"All right, I'll just have to worry about her then."

"We've all had to do that from time to time. It's always turned out all right. It will this time too. You'll see."

"I wish I had your gift of optimism but I'll let it go."

"Thanks, Letta. Ma'a will be fine. Please don't worry," Seth said, as he put his arms around Letta and held her close for a few moments.

"I better get back," Letta said, as she turned to retrace her steps back to the hut.

Predictably, Eve was gone when Letta arrived back to the hut. *Seth isn't worried or at least he wants me to believe he isn't worried. I think it's a long trip for an old woman to make by herself. Maybe I should follow her. Then Seth would be mad, I don't want him to be mad at me, either. Oh, what to do ...*

Eve left on that bright spring day. The sky was blue and birds sang. The nearer she got to the

mountain, the louder the birds sounded. Eve started up the mountainside when she stepped into a hole and twisted her ankle. It hurt so badly, at first, she thought it was broken. She sat on the ground on a bed of leaves and rubbed her ankle. It was starting to swell and it was flame red. She tried to stand but that was impossible. Crawling to a fallen log, she worked, using her arms and good leg to achieve a sitting position. *Maybe I can stand from this sitting position and walk again. I'm not that far from Hatra's, though it is uphill from here. I wish I had lion with me, he could help. I haven't thought about him in a long time. I wonder if he's still alive. I had better try to stand on this ankle again.* She stood and quickly plopped down on the log again. The pain felt like a hot metal rod in her leg going up from her ankle and no strength was there. *It must be broken; I can't put any weight on it. The sun is behind the mountains. It will set soon. I'll have to crawl the rest of the way. That will be slow and take much effort but I have no choice.*

Eve started to crawl up the mountainside. She knew no one would help, that's the way she wanted it, right? She'd crawled about halfway to Hatra's hut when she came eye to eye with a snake. It was a large, golden-eyed snake, about five paces away. Eve stopped on her hands and knees, which put her about eye level with the snake. The snake peered at her, flicking its forked tongue in and out of its mouth. She mocked the snake, doing the same with her tongue. After a little while, the snake collected all the

information it wanted and slithered away. It had probably not met a human eye to eye before. *It doesn't know what to make of me but I don't seem to be a threat so it wandered off or is it the work of the sorceress?* Eve had not thought of Lilith in many seasons and decided not to think any more about her now. She gave the snake no more thought.

It was growing dark when she finally neared Hatra's hut. "Hallo, Hatra," Eve called out as loud as she could. There was no answer, although the hut was lit by torchlight. Eve crawled on further, now almost to the hut door. "Hallo, Hatra, Yesima," Eve called again.

The hide was pulled away from the door and Yesima peered out. "Is someone out here?" Yesima asked, tentatively.

"Yes, it's your ma'a. Look down. I'm on the ground. I fell and hurt my ankle. I need help."

"Oh, Ma'a, are you alone?" Yesima said, as she finally saw her ma'a as her eyes adjusted to the ensuing darkness. "Lobert, come here to help me with Ma'a," Yesima called.

Lobert came out on the run. What's wrong? What happened?" he asked.

"Let's just get her inside then she can tell us," Yesima said.

Lifting Eve up to stand on one leg with her arms around each adult's shoulders, she was able to hobble into the hut. They sat her on a log bench. Hatra brought her a bowl of tea. "Eve, you look like you've had a hard journey. Please tell us what

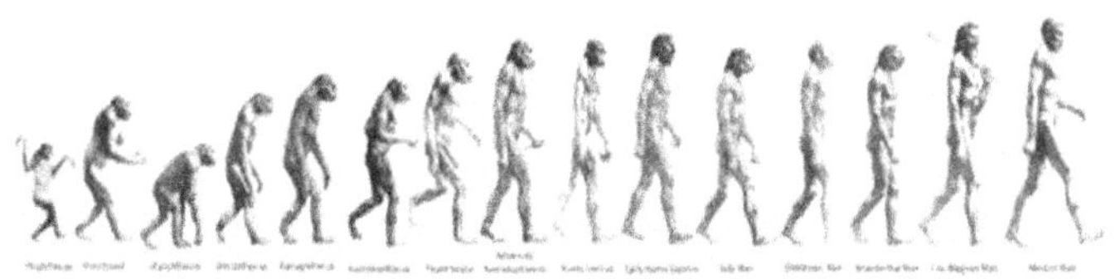

happened if you feel up to it," Hatra said in a kind, calming voice.

Eve described her decision to make the trek alone. She described the beauty of the day then the accident and the snake. Everyone sat in rapt attention. Lobert was aghast that the snake didn't strike. Yesima and Hatra said "Let's look at that ankle."

They set to work cleaning and studying the ankle, prodding and moving it back and forth and around. Eve yowled during most of that exam. "It's broken, Eve" Hatra said.

"I feared so, when I couldn't stand on it," Eve said.

You crawled all the way up the mountainside?" Lobert asked, unbelievingly.

"Yes, it took most of the later part of the day," Eve said.

"That's my ma'a," Yesima chimed in, proudly.

"Now, I'll set your ankle. It will be painful. I've made some quite strong willow bark tea for you to drink while I assemble all the material." Hatra turned to Lobert.

"Lobert," she said, "I need two strong sticks and two flat pieces of thick bark to make a cast. The ankle has to be held straight and can't be moved."

"You won't be walking for a while. Then Lobert will fashion a stick for you to use as a crutch," Hatra told Eve.

It was late and everyone was visibly exhausted by the time the 'cast' was finished. Hatra

had placed a mat on the hard-packed dirt floor, covered it with a hide and set a hide for covering down next to the mat. Yesima and Hatra carefully helped Eve to lie down on the mat. Yesima and Hatra lifted the hide and placed it over Eve. "Rest now, Eve and let us know if you need anything," Hatra said.

"Thank you," Eve said, with sleep in her voice.

Two moons had past and Eve's ankle was healing. She used the stick crutch to move within the hut and to only go outside to relieve herself where Lobert had fashioned sticks and a log for the purpose. Any weight on her ankle was still met with some pain. *How much longer will I have to have this 'cast' and crutch? I wonder if I'll ever see my hut again.* Lobert had made the trip to Letta and Seth to tell them of Eve's accident. They'd promised to make the trek to visit Eve one day.

Spring advanced to early summer when Hatra told Eve she thought it was time to try to walk with the help of the crutch but without the 'cast'. This was a welcome suggestion to Eve, she readily agreed.

"Hatra, I've dreamed of this day for moons," Eve said,

"Let's try and see how you feel," Hatra said, with Yesima looking on.

After the sticks, bark and wrappings were removed and with her crutch under her arm, Eve stood, with equal weight on both legs and feet.

"I can stand and it doesn't hurt. It just feels a little weak," Eve said.

"That's normal," Hatra said. "You haven't put any weight on it for so long; the bones and muscles need to be used. Just for a short time at first then longer times. You will feel them getting stronger. Don't do too much right now—just a little walking around in the hut. When you have to go outside where the ground is not as flat, be sure to get one of us to help as you did before," Hatra instructed.

"Thank you so much, Hatra. I wonder if I'll ever be able to go back to my hut."

"Not for a long time, Eve. That's a long walk."

"Ma'a, Hatra and I have been discussing this. We think you should just stay here. We'd like to have you here. As you can see, there is plenty of room and we can spend time talking as we work. Three people to do the work will give us more time to make hide clothing, weaving and gathering of fruit and nuts. What do you think?" Yesima asked.

"That is a most generous offer. If I'm not going to be able to walk back to my hut, I don't have a choice, do I?" Eve asked.

"Oh, Ma'a, we're not holding you prisoner. You need to be here where there is always help if you need it. Letta will do just fine without you. Seth has enough to do with the flock and herd," Yesima said.

"I want to see Seth and Letta again. I hope they can come here this summer," Eve said, wistfully.

"They told Lobert they would try to come but if they can't, they're sure to come on their way to the Autumn Gathering," Hatra said.

"I want to talk to them before I make a final decision," said Eve.

"That is fine with us. We'll all be together and you can judge the reactions of everybody at that time," Yesima said.

It was decided to wait for Seth and Letta to arrive before Eve made a final decision. Summer was well advanced and Letta and Seth had not yet made the trek to visit Eve.

"Letta, we should have visited Ma'a before now," Seth said one late summer morning.

"You're right, Seth, we've let too much time pass. She must think we don't care."

"Oh, I don't think she misses us that much. She has Yesima and Hatra. She'll probably want to stay there."

"I don't know, Seth. You're being quite casual about Eve."

"No, I'm not. I just think it's better for her to be with Hatra and Yesima. Yesima must be about as good a natural healer as Hatra by now."

"You are probably right. She tried to teach me but I wasn't that interested. I learned a few things but I wasn't that good at it nor was I interested."

"We'll go by there on our way to the Gathering. We'll see them all at that time."

"All right, that makes sense."

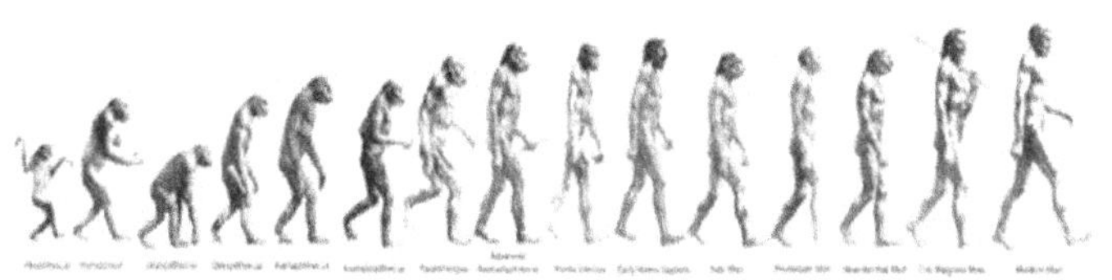

I wonder what Seth and Letta are thinking ... probably enjoying the time together without their parent. I think I'll decide to stay here with Hatra and Yesima. Hatra is aging fast. Yesima does most of the work now. Hatra spends most of her time sitting on the log bench outside the hut. She seems out of breath when she walks more than a few steps and she drinks more willow tea for the pain in her left arm. I wonder what's causing that. Neither Hatra nor Yesima seem to know, either.

One morning, Hatra didn't rise from her mat. Yesima tried to awaken her but got no response. She put her hand on Hatra's forehead and she recoiled. It was cold. A scream and Lobert came running into the hut.

"She's dead. My ma'a is dead?" Lobert said in disbelief. He walked over to the body and felt her skin. He folded Yesima and Eve into his arms and they sobbed together for several minutes. Yesima and Eve looked to Lobert and he said, softly, "I'll dig her grave next to Da'a." He slowly retreated to the outdoors as Yesima and Eve began the ritual keening.

Lobert finished digging the grave and went back into the hut. The women stopped keening long enough to make tea.

"You are finished digging? Everything is finished and ready here," Yesima said, as she finished her tea.

"Yes, we should get on with the task," Lobert said.

Lobert picked up the body wrapped in a fur and the mat and carried the load to the gravesite. The load was lighter than he'd expected. *I know Ma'a had lost weight in her final years. She must have been unwell for longer than we thought. She never complained or let us know she didn't feel well.* Lobert covered the grave and placed a stone as a marker. The women grieved silently for Lobert's sake or maybe it didn't seem necessary for keening in the outdoors. The women returned to the hut and the keening started anew. Lobert stayed outside, sat on the log bench for a while then rose and set to work gathering firewood for the winter.

The time for the Autumn Gathering was fast approaching. Lobert, Yesima and Eve were sure Letta and Seth would be arriving soon, on their way to the Gathering. Yesima and Eve gathered quantities of berries, nuts and leaves for food and tea. Smoked deer meat strips had been held aside in anticipation of the visit. Lobert had killed an extra deer early in the summer to supplement their food supply with Eve's arrival. The braying of the animals and the vocal sounds of Letta and Seth shepherding the flock and herd came first to Lobert, working outside. He dropped his stone tools and rushed into the hut.

"I think I hear them coming. Seth and Letta are bringing the animals. Come outside and listen," Lobert said, excitedly.

"Oh, how wonderful," Eve and Yesima said together, as they stopped what they were doing and rushed outside.

"Now listen," Lobert said.

There were the sounds again, closer this time.

"I've refurbished the extra pens. I hope Seth hasn't enlarged the flock and herd too much," Lobert said.

They waited longer, listening to the sounds growing nearer until Yesima spotted Seth herding a few stray goats back to the drive. Though she wanted to run to them, she knew that would not be an acceptable action. Her coming to them would spook the herd and scatter them, making bringing the herd back together a difficult task to complete before sundown.

Seth, Letta and Lobert completed the job of confining the herd and flock into the pens then it was time for hugs all around and such a joyous reunion it was, until Letta asked, "Where's Ma'a?"

The question brought the reunion to solemnity.

"She's gone," Lobert said in a soft voice, looking away.

"What do you mean?" Letta asked, still not understanding the gravity of the situation. Instead, she started to enter the hut.

"Letta, come here. Ma'a died over a moon ago," Lobert said, as he held Letta close and she burst into tears.

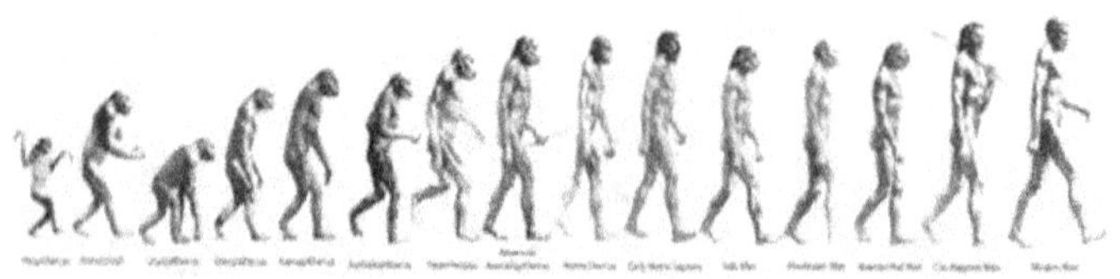

Seth held Yesima as she began to cry again, too. Eve stood alone, her jaw set. She had grieved aplenty; now it was time to take control and let the children grieve. *Everyone passes. It's painful at the time but it is the way of things. We older ones must pass to leave the world to the new, the younger ones. If we stayed on forever, the young ones would be hindered by our old ways. They'd never advance; never try new things, always asking us for advice and help. They have to do it the best way they can, maybe invent new solutions along the way. I better go inside and prepare some tea then start the evening meal.*

Saying nothing to the mourners, Eve went into the hut, built a larger cooking fire in the fire pit to heat tea water. While the water heated she began to place the vegetables and meat with water in the large pot to cook the stew. She called the young ones into the hut for tea.

"It feels good in here, "Yesima said, as she rubbed her arms.

"It was getting uncomfortably chilly out there. The sun is down," Letta said.

Seth and Lobert said they didn't notice it was so chilly. Yesima and Letta looked at each other, eyes rolling. Eve served the tea and assured them the stew was cooking on the fire.

Seth noticed Eve walked with a slight limp. "Ma'a, you seem to walk with a slight limp, did you hurt your foot?"

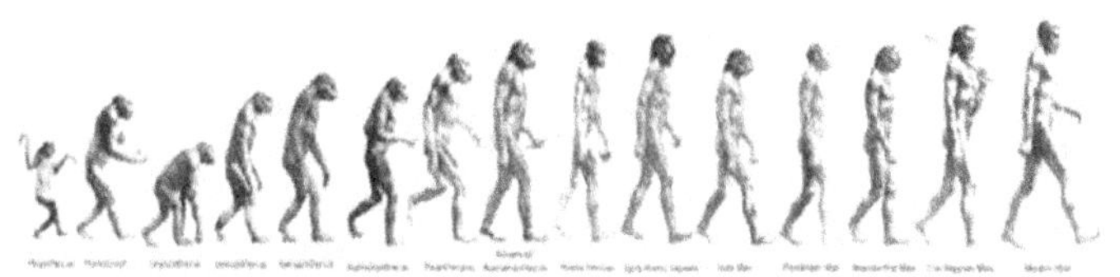

"It's a long story. Are you ready for it?" Eve asked.

"Yes, we want to know," Seth said.

"All right, I'll tell you all when we have the stew," Eve said.

Yesima and Eve served the stew. As Eve finally sat to eat, she said, "Now, I'll tell you my story." She told the entire story of her walk to Hatra and Yesima that day, so long ago it seemed, though only five moons.

"The snake was interesting. They are dangerous, Ma'a. Surprised it didn't strike," Seth said, in wonder.

"It was as if it were under a spell," Eve said. *I want to tell them who I really think controlled that snake but I can't. I've never told anyone about Lilith except Adam. I won't tell them now, either.*

"Oh, Eve, you must have been in great pain to have crawled up the mountain to the hut," Letta said.

"Yes, but I didn't have a choice. I had to get help," answered Eve.

"Ma'a, Da'a always said you were going to have a problem someday when you went off by yourself. He always worried, terribly," Seth said.

"Your da'a always had problems when I went on an exploration. I never got hurt," Eve said.

"Ma'a, you should not go on any more explorations. For us, please?" Yesima begged.

"No, my exploration days are over. I can't walk far, now. I want to go to the Gathering one last time but I know that's impossible," Eve answered.

"Yes, it is Ma'a. We'll see Cain there and we'll tell him you're here. Maybe he'll come to see you after the Gathering or during the hunt," Seth said.

"That would be great. I'd like to see him. I wish I could see his family. I've never met his mate or any of his children," Eve said.

"His mate, Cobia, and the children don't come to the Gathering often," said Seth.

"That's right," added Lobert, "I met his mate several Gatherings ago."

"He does seem to keep to himself on the far side of the mountain. I wonder if there is a problem," Letta said.

"It goes back to Cain's accident. He didn't mean to hit Abel with that rock from the sling but he still feels some guilt. I guess he feels better to distance himself from us," Eve said.

"That's too bad. He seemed friendly but quiet at Adam's burial," Letta said.

Everyone sat lost in their own thoughts for several minutes until Yesima stood to carry the bowls to the work bench and Lobert rose to encourage everyone to seek their sleeping mats.

"Well, let's get some sleep. We'll leave for the Gathering at sunup tomorrow morning," Lobert said.

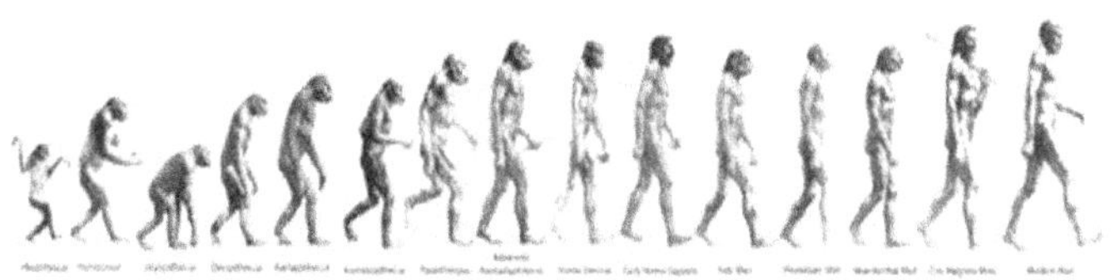

Eve's limp got worse over the next several seasons, to the point where Lobert made a log bench for her to sit on most of the day. She tried to walk about the hut but it became increasingly painful for her. She fell a few times after which Yesima and Lobert insisted she stay on the bench and ask for help when she needed to walk. Asking for help made Eve feel dependent, which sent her into a downward spiral of depression. Eve cried often and sat bundled in a hide, seemingly in a dream or faraway place. Her pain and depression sapped her energy to where she could no longer leave her mat.

One bright spring morning, Yesima could not rouse her ma'a. "Ma'a, wake up." Yesima tried to awaken Eve. Lobert heard Yesima scream and came running into the hut.

"Wwwhat?" shouted Lobert.

"It's Ma'a, I can't wake her," Yesima cried.

Lobert, too, tried to waken Eve then, turning to Yesima, he said, "She's dead, Yesima," and he held the sobbing Yesima close.

Yesima recovered to a point and Lobert and Yesima began to plan what to do next. Yesima wanted to get word to Seth and Cain as soon as possible but Eve's body would need to be buried before anyone could get word of her death to either of them.

"I'll dig the grave, we'll bury the body then I'll make the trips to tell Cain and Seth," Lobert said.

"All right, I wish they could be here before we bury her but that doesn't seem possible," Yesima said, as she dissolved into tears again.

"No, it isn't possible. It is the best we can do. Do what you must for the body and I'll be back when the grave is ready," Lobert said.

They buried the body as the sun made its way to the western horizon. Yesima cried as Lobert covered the grave and placed a stone atop it as a marker. They buried Eve next to Hatra's grave. Somehow, it seemed right for Eve to be as close to Hatra in death as she was in life.

Lobert returned with Seth and Letta two suns later. Lobert left to get Cain the next day. While Lobert was gone, the brother and sister commiserated about their mother, their time growing up and their father, too. Conversations often led to periods of tears and long intervals of silent mourning. Finally, nearly six suns later, Lobert and Cain arrived. Now, the mourning began again with discussions and recollections of their mother. Cain could supply information about her they did not know because Cain was older and had left the household when Seth and Yesima were much younger. They wept when alone while Lobert and Cain were out tending the flock. When Lobert and Cain came in, Yesima and Letta began to recover and talk.

"I wish Iyanna could be here then we could all be together," Yesima said. "I haven't seen her in

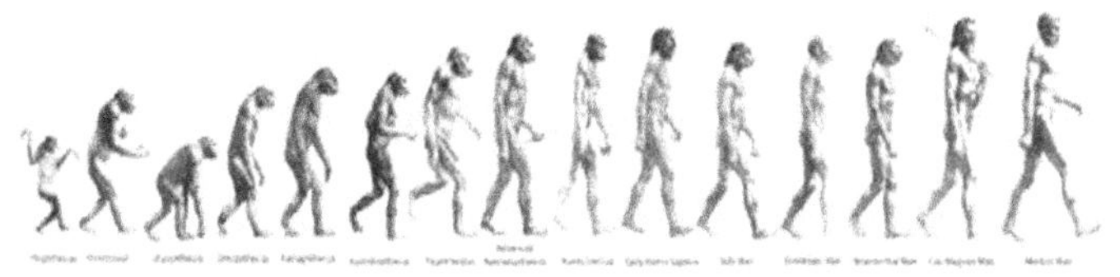

so many seasons. I wonder how she is and where she is."

"She was well when she stopped by here last, moving north with the clan. They must have found a good place to stay. They haven't passed through going south, yet," said Seth. "Of course, they may have taken a different path," he added.

"I haven't seen her for many suns," Cain said, as he remembered the last time he'd seen Iyanna, so long ago.

Silence overtook them at that comment. Iyanna was the missing piece in their reunion, as it had always been since she had joined the roving clan and left without a word those many seasons ago. Breaking the silence, Yesima rose to rekindle the fire in the fire pit to make tea and begin to prepare the evening meal of meat and vegetable stew. At that, the brothers began to talk again, catching up on family information but in reduced intonation. Yesima could not understand their words nor did she try. The brothers rose and walked outside, saying they'd be back to eat. She assumed they were going to alert Lobert the evening meal was to be ready soon.

Yesima called them in for the meal was now ready. Conversation revolved around Eve and her final seasons, her broken ankle and how it had only partially healed.

"She was old when it happened," Yesima said. "Bones don't heal quickly or completely when you are old."

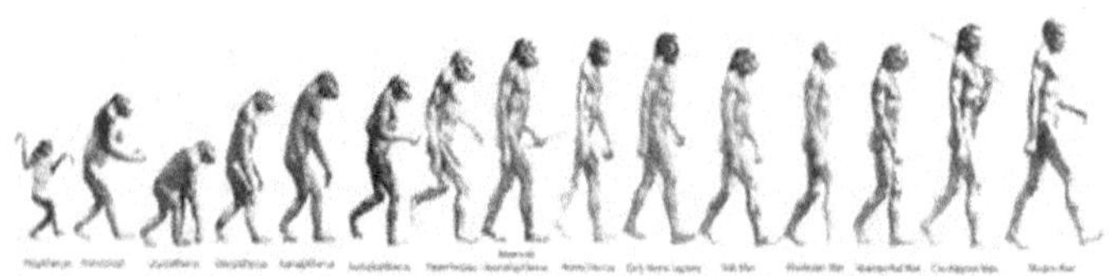

"Yes, and we couldn't get her to stay sitting and ask for help," Lobert said, almost defensively.

"Not a surprise, that's the way Ma'a was," Seth said, with a wan smile.

"I don't remember her ever asking anybody for help. She only sat still when she was weaving," said Cain, with a lame smile.

Conversation stilled at that point and they continued with the meal until finished.

"I'll be leaving at first light tomorrow. Let's all go to the grave tonight to say our final farewells to Ma'a," Cain said.

The summer sun had not set yet when they gathered at Eve's gravesite. Lobert and Yesima joined arms with Seth, Letta and Cain as they stood to pay their final respects. No one said anything, quiet sobs from Yesima and Letta was the only sound. Dusk lay over the land when the solemn family made their way inside the hut and to their sleeping mats.

The next morning Cain rose and left before the others awakened. The day seemed as all the other days. Seth and Letta said their goodbyes and Lobert and Yesima settled into their lives.

The lives of this generation would move on through the following generations to today.

Author's Notes

[1] The Valley of Eden, often referred to now as the Fertile Crescent.

[2] *Homo habilis*

[3] Now called the Nile River.

[4] Probably southern Egypt or northern Nubia

[5] In the Tigris-Euphrates river system, the marshlands are located at the confluence of these two rivers in southern Iraq, partially extending into Iran.

[6] Now known as Cyprus trees.

[7] A crocodile.

[8] Berean Study Bible Genesis 3:16-17

[9] Developed into axes

[10] Pronounced (Ya see' ma)

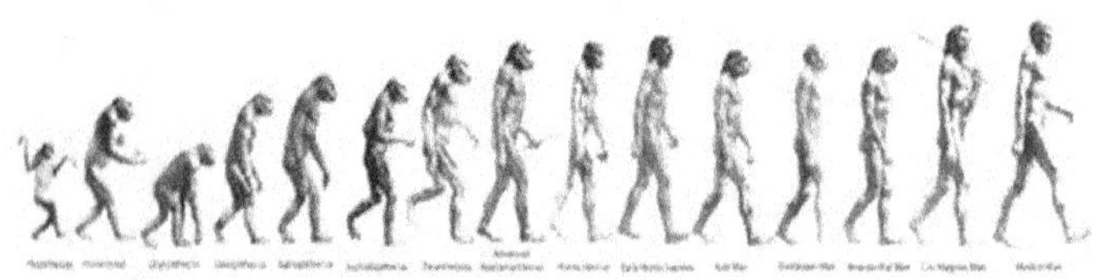

Also by Mary Jo Nickum

Mom's Story, A Child Learns about MS

Aquitaine Reluctant Reader Series
>#1 Looking at the Cat, an Eye on Evolution
>#2 The Coelacanth; the Greatest Fish Story
>>Ever Told
>#3 Who Was Macho B and What we know
>>about Jaguars
>#4 Fire in the Trees
>#5 The Making of the Grand Canyon
>#6 The California Condor, "The Big Ugly"

Strong Women series
>A Girl Named Mary Book 1
>Eve, the First (Liberated) Woman Book 2

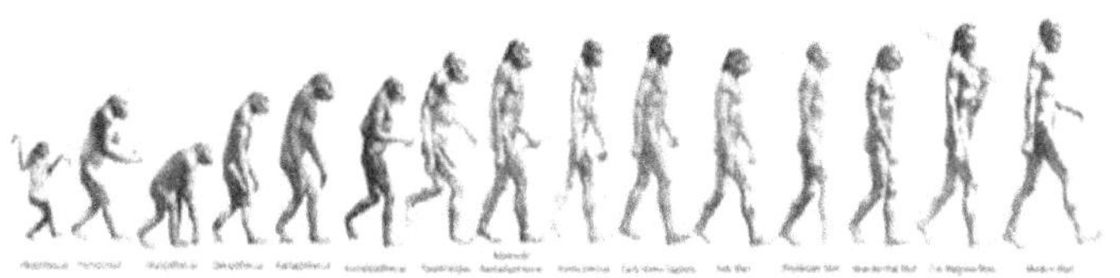

About the Author

Mary Jo Nickum is an award-winning author. She has published *Mom's Story, a Child Learns about MS* and *A Girl Named Mary, a Story about the Girl Who Would Become the Mother of Jesus*. She is a retired librarian and an English teacher. Mary lives with her husband, John, in Fountain Hills, Arizona.